Hatteras Girl

Books by Alice J. Wisler

Rain Song
How Sweet It Is
Hatteras Girl

Hatteras Girl

Alice J. Wisler

BETHANY HOUSE PUBLISHERS
Minneapolis, Minnesota

Hatteras Girl
Copyright © 2010
Alice J. Wisler

Cover design by Paul Higdon

Published by Bethany House Publishers
11400 Hampshire Avenue South
Bloomington, Minnesota 55438

Bethany House Publishers is a division of
Baker Publishing Group, Grand Rapids, Michigan.

Printed in the United States of America

Library of Congress Cataloging-in-Publication Data

Wisler, Alice J.
    Hatteras girl / Alice J. Wisler.
       p. cm.
    ISBN 978-0-7642-0732-7 (pbk.)
    1. Single women—Fiction. 2. Outer Banks (N.C.)—Fiction. 3. Bed and breakfast accommodations—Fiction. I. Title.
    PS3623.I846H38   2010
    813'.6—dc22

                                     2010016287

For Carl,

who convinced me to grow old with him

"To be satisfied with what one has;

that is wealth."

—MARK TWAIN

1

Seated at the mahogany counter on a wobbly barstool, I wait for Mr. Wealthy and Available. As I sip my Diet Pepsi, I run my index finger across the grooves in the wood, pretending that I'm admiring the surface and the way the overhead lights bring out the soft shine. Really, I'm eavesdropping. Other people's conversations are wonderfully fun—particularly those of Outer Banks tourists.

At a table near me, a father with a Boston accent tells his sons that tomorrow they're going fishing in Pamlico Sound and then to see the Cape Hatteras Lighthouse. One of his sons slurps his drink and then asks when they're going to see the alligators at the wildlife place. I imagine he must be talking about Alligator River National Wildlife Refuge.

"Dad, you promised," the boy says eagerly.

Dad agrees, but not without clarifying the rules: "You two need to eat all your chicken tonight. And no texting at the table."

James Taylor's melodic "Carolina in My Mind" fills the restaurant, but I tune my ears to other fragments of chatter.

"I know he's balding and a little round," I hear a woman confess to another at the right side of the bar. She sounds like she might be from New York. "But I love the way he treats me."

"He's a Red Sox fan," someone—I presume her friend—says with disdain.

"I know," comes the reply. "And my team will always be the Orioles." A sigh follows. "He told me I'm the glittery constellation in his sky. Isn't that romantic?"

"That is."

"With true love, baseball shouldn't matter."

A giggle forms in my throat, and to squelch it, I quickly lower my head, pick up my pen, and open my notebook. Flipping to a clean page, I draw clusters of miniature globes, add stems to their bases, and place leaves near the petals. After shading them with the tip of my pen, I'm pleased with the garden of geraniums I've created.

I'm not as pleased with my reason for being at the Sunnyside Grille tonight. My aunt Sheerly has set me up with yet another man. I hope this one will be all she claims he is. My relatives here in Hatteras have a goal this year—to see a diamond on my finger by December 31. They're a bunch of sweet folks, worth far more than Blackbeard's treasures to me, and as hardworking as the summer sun. But lately, I think they've gone into overtime trying to find Mr. Right for me. I don't want to appear finicky; I appreciate their efforts and that's probably why I've been on four blind dates just this spring. Also, I'll be thirty in August.

The unsuspecting staff of the restaurant thinks I'm here writing up an article for *Lighthouse Views*, the Nags Head magazine I work for. Betty Lynn, barely twenty-one and dressed in a pair of khakis and a yellow T-shirt—the uniform for the Sunnyside Grille employees—stops beside me on her way to a table of guests. She whispers, "Always busy writing. When are you going to interview me?"

Betty Lynn is the type of girl who thinks her good looks and ability to balance a quarter on her nose while sipping juice through a straw are worthy of a magazine article. Actually, my editor usually assigns me interviews with the owners of Outer Banks businesses for features in the magazine.

"I'll never get a break tonight," she tells me, fluffing her blond hair. "The hostess didn't show, so I have to seat guests *and* wait tables."

"Maybe you'll get twice as many tips," I offer hopefully.

Her blue eyes hold doubt.

I glance at my cell phone to check the time. He's late, this wealthy-and-available man. I wonder if he's doing a million-dollar business transaction with other successful people. Maybe he's tied up in a board meeting or taking his yacht for a cruise down to Beaufort.

When Betty Lynn leaves, my mind wanders to wondering why we label folks with money as successful. I think about how God must rate our success and decide it has to be on much different terms. Jesus chose twelve disciples to hang out with, and had they lived today, I don't think any of their names would appear in *Fortune 500* magazine.

Buck Griffins, one of the waiters, motions toward my empty mason jar. "Would you like more Pepsi?"

Closing my notebook, I give him a smile I've been practicing all afternoon. Each time I get ready for a date, I borrow a pair of my housemate and friend Minnie's gold hoop earrings and smile into my dresser mirror for a while.

"What time is he supposed to be here?" Buck asks as he refills my drink from the soda fountain.

I watch the bubbles float to the top of the glass. "What do you mean?"

Buck grins. "Your date. You are meeting someone, right?" He

nods toward the neon green fisherman's hat I've placed beside my notebook.

So much for incognito. Buck knows me too well. Of course, I have suggested the Grille for all of my recent blind dates, and Buck was working at least two of those nights when I entered the restaurant with the fisherman's hat. Carrying the hat is one way I make it easy for my dates to spot me. When they ask what I look like, I briefly describe my looks and then say I'll have a bright green fisherman's hat with me.

Tonight will be better than all those other dates, I tell myself when Buck heads to the end of the counter, where a customer orders a burger. *Please, God, let this Douglas Cannon be pleasant. Oh, more than that. Let him be interested in me, and me in him.* As I finish the silent prayer, my eyes roam around the restaurant.

There's an assortment of old-fashioned skillets and Pepsi glasses lining the shelves across the back wall behind the bar. Aunt Sheerly told me the owner picked up these pieces at an auction years ago. The Grille's décor also includes travel posters of New Orleans— masquerade masks, a jazz band, and patrons dining along a busy section of Bourbon Street. I want to be like one of the couples at a corner table on the poster near me. The woman has a contented look on her slender face, and the man is gazing into her eyes over a plate of what looks to be oysters on the half shell. I catch my reflection in a narrow mirror by the sign for the restrooms, smile, and smooth my straight black hair. Maybe tonight I'll get to dine with a contented look on my face.

Buck saunters back over to me and picks up my hat. He twirls it around with one finger as a whimsical look stretches across his face. This guy hasn't changed a bit. He's as silly as he was when he and my younger brother Ron were kids. The two of them once got away with putting jellyfish into a large pot in the high school cafeteria. I don't think Mrs. Straybutton ever forgave them for the scare she had when she took the lid off the pot to prepare spaghetti for lunch that day and was greeted by three slimy sea creatures. I overheard her in Principal Miller's office exclaiming, "Those nasty critters were swimming in filthy water in my kitchen! We must shut the school down and have it cleaned top to bottom! Call the janitor; alert the fire department! Does the mayor know?"

I glance up at Buck and tease, "I just hope you haven't put any jellyfish in my Pepsi."

He raises his hands, feigns innocence. "In the whole history of Manteo High, no one has ever proven Ron and I were guilty."

"You two were lucky."

Buck's eyes flicker, and I see that they still hold that childhood mischievousness. He's had shoulder-length blond hair ever since ninth grade when he and Ron decided to grow their hair out. Watching him place my hat on top of his head, I picture him as he looked at fifteen in swimming trunks—wiry and thin. Now the lines of a muscular chest fill out his yellow Grille T-shirt.

Taking off the hat, he asks, "Do you ever wear these, or just bring them along for show?"

I'm about to tell him how my fishermen's hat collection started when at my left shoulder I hear a man's voice. "Excuse me. Are you . . . Jackie Donovan?"

2

The first thing I notice is that his voice is deep. When I turn, he's there in full view. The wondering what he looks like is over. He's not Johnny Depp, George Clooney, or even my mother's all-time favorite, Humphrey Bogart, but he's breathing—and male. In reply to his question, I nod.

"I'm Douglas Cannon." When he stretches out his arm, it brushes against the woman seated on the stool beside me. He murmurs, "Oh, sorry."

He's nervous. It's not that he's stuttering, or that his hands are shaking; I just sense that he's nervous by the way his voice crackles like static in a sound system.

Stepping off the barstool, I steady it as it tilts toward the same woman, then grab my purse. I wait for Buck to hand me my hat. Turning to Douglas, I give him a smile that I hope is kind, happy, and able to set him at ease. "Nice to meet you. I'm Jackie."

His Adam's apple moves as he clears his throat. "Shall we get a table?"

As she approaches, Betty Lynn sizes this man up. She glances at the floor and then at his shoes, the ceiling, and then his face. I follow her and Douglas to a table by a window with a view that overlooks the quiet Albemarle Sound.

Seated across from each other, Douglas and I look at our plastic menus in silence. The menu is like the face of an old friend; I almost have it memorized, and usually I have the chicken salad sandwich with coleslaw on the side. Although my favorite item is the bacon cheeseburger, I think I will avoid that tonight. I enjoy this burger best with lots of mustard and mayo, and by the time I've added those condiments, it's too drippy to eat on a first date. The magazines always warn you to be careful about these kinds of things.

Douglas has brown eyes and a sincere look about him, the kind of man who probably believes in justice, truth, and helping old ladies across busy streets. He asks what I'd like to drink. Suddenly, I'm aware that I left my mason jar of Diet Pepsi at the counter and did not offer to pay Buck for it. I relax; I'll ask Buck to add it to my tab.

"I'll have Diet Pepsi."

"You drink that diet stuff?" When he makes a face similar to the one Minnie's son, Zane, displays when Minnie insists he try a bite of flounder, I feel my heart slip into my sandals.

"I like the taste." I try not to sound too defensive.

"I read how they make the diet stuff. Disgusting. I'd never touch it," he tells me. "That low-calorie soda isn't good for you, anyway."

Perhaps I should have asked his approval before ordering my beverage. When Betty Lynn comes by to take our order, I eye Douglas to see if he'll comment on my choice of the chicken salad sandwich.

He doesn't have anything to say to that. He orders a Reuben without any mayo and asks if he can have fries instead of coleslaw. He tells me he doesn't like mayonnaise. And that he doesn't eat broccoli. Or artichokes. And on pizza, he prefers just sausage and the best brand is actually made in Bari, Italy, and called Bari Sausage.

I feel like I'm supposed to be taking notes.

He then tells me he would like to be in Asia, and I wonder if he's saying this for my benefit since I'm half Korean. All my life, people have either tried the affirmative by saying something like, "I really like ramen noodles" or gone to the other extreme and made jokes about slanted eyes. No one has ever told me they would rather be in Asia.

Through the window, I watch a seagull swoop onto one of the thick posts by the pier. He poses as if waiting for a photographer to snap his portrait for a postcard.

Sometime after Betty Lynn brings our meals, commenting as she always does that "The fries are extremely hot, so be careful," and Neil Young's "Heart of Gold" has finished, Douglas tells me he recently spent five weeks in the Philippines. As I try to recall where that country is located on a map, and then am pretty sure it's south of Mom's homeland of South Korea, he says, "I fell off a jeepney once."

He looks at me expectantly. Swallowing a bite of chicken, I wipe my mouth with a napkin. The paper napkins here are large, but stiff. Buck's told me with a smile that they're starched at a nearby dry cleaner. "What's a jeepney?" I ask Douglas.

Leaning across the table, his elbows touching the edges of his plate, he explains. "Jeepneys are old American G. I. jeeps converted into public transportation. They're open in the back where you enter and exit. Passengers sit on parallel benches. The jeepney drivers are madmen as they skirt around Manila. It can be a harrowing experience."

I try to picture one of these vehicles as Douglas continues with his story.

"The driver let the six people in front of me off, and they managed to stay safe, but when it was my turn to step out, he just took off. He didn't even bother to check his rearview mirror, I guess. I had one foot on the road and one in the back of the jeepney."

I swallow a mouthful of Diet Pepsi and try to imagine the scene. I've spent all my life in North Carolina; I don't even own a passport.

"But I was only bruised a bit because I fell on my face. I didn't need stitches or anything."

"Oh, good," I say weakly. I stare at the rest of my sandwich and then twirl my fork around in the coleslaw. I know the cook in the kitchen who makes the coleslaw; they call him Dude of Slaw. I'm pretty sure Buck gave him that nickname.

Douglas's story is like the bunny on the Energizer commercials; it keeps going and going. Around a mouthful of bread and corned beef, he says, "That wasn't as bad as when I got stung in the South China Sea by something that looked like a baby shark."

"Really?"

He continues, the food in his mouth packed in each cheek. "We were scuba diving at a coral reef. I felt something tug at my leg and then felt this burning pain."

"How horrible," I say when he pauses to take another bite of his sandwich.

"Blood was gushing out, I mean it was gruesome. Then my whole leg began to swell." He moves his hands across his plate for emphasis. "I managed to get out of the water without too much difficulty. Then I couldn't move my leg. It was throbbing with this terrible pain."

"How horrible." I guess I won't eat any more of the chicken salad.

"The friends I was with wanted to get me out of the sun, so they found this cave down by some rocks. I could hardly walk but managed to go inside the cave. It was dark and filled with bats and snakes."

Again I say the only thing that comes to mind: "Horrible."

Suddenly I wish I was home playing my flute, or walking on the beach, or watching the sunset.

"The snakes weren't poisonous. At least that's what Sergie told us. However, the bats were swooping low and tugging at our hair."

I feel claustrophobic, and as he continues on, I try to refrain from saying again how horrible this all sounds. Suddenly, something inside me tells me that I don't have to stay any longer. My meal is finished—well, almost—and I don't want, or need, dessert. I recall a sitcom episode I watched with Minnie in which the main character was out with a drastically boring date and pretended she got a text from her mother. She claimed her mother was in jail and she had to go bail her out. Could I pull that off?

I reach into my purse, find my cell phone, and take a breath. I rub my thumb across the front of the phone as Douglas talks about his hospital visit to treat his infected bite. Through the window, the sky's light has faded, the seagull taken off from its perch on the pier.

Douglas doesn't seem to mind that I'm more interested in what's outside. His story is still going. "The doctor spoke with a heavy accent, so I only understood every third word. From what I could tell, he was saying things like *needle* and *injection* and I swore he said *surgery.*"

When he pauses to take a sip of his non-sugar-free beverage—sweet iced tea—I realize this is an opportunity I can't miss. Flipping my phone open, I pretend to read a message. I hope I sound truthful as I exclaim, "Minnie needs me!" I can't say my mother's in jail; she'd never forgive me if she found out.

Douglas says, "The leg healed and I was back scuba diving a month later in Florida. There's barely a visible scar now."

I gulp, hoping he isn't about to raise his pant leg and show it to me. Gathering courage I repeat, "Minnie needs me."

He has already started in on another saga about his friend

from Jamaica. Suddenly, something clicks; his mouth stops moving. "Minnie?"

Finally, I have his attention. "Yes, she needs me right now."

His face holds confusion.

Quickly, I add, "She has a five-year-old." If that doesn't work, I can tell him that her husband died and her mother, a stroke victim, sits all day in a wheelchair at Morning Glory Nursing Home. Those are the playing cards I keep in my hand to use when I decide we all need a little sympathy. Although the other night, Minnie didn't think I should have used them just because the pizza deliveryman brought pineapple pizza instead of extra-cheese. We got two free cheese pizzas and a profound apology; I was grateful, and hungry.

Douglas doesn't respond, so I say, "Zane is a lot to handle. I have to go now." I stuff my cell phone back into my purse.

His face looks like a fallen branch after a thunderstorm—twisted, dark, and bent out of shape.

"I'm sorry." I rise, my purse and the fisherman's hat in one hand.

Three women seated at a table near us are fixated on me. I think I recognize one; she likes her hair frosted and is always telling Aunt Sheerly that her son is going to be the next president of the United States. Sheerly replies, "Is he single? Because my niece is a lovely girl. She plays the flute, you know."

I lower my voice. "Really, I need to go."

As I leave, winding my way through the tables and booths, Buck gives me a quizzical look across the bar. I almost want to let him know why I'm leaving early, but something tells me it's best to head out the door and fill him in later.

3

I drive to the Bailey House. Just like the song about the horse knowing the way through the woods to Grandmother's house, my truck is familiar with the route to this bed and breakfast by the Albemarle Sound.

The air tingles with the softness of spring, permeated with the scent of sea salt. I roll down my window, and coolness flutters against my bare arms. My fisherman's hat mocks me as it bounces on the passenger's seat. I see Aunt Sheerly's face, her sly smile as she asks me how my date went. "Was he a nice man? He's wealthy and available, you know."

I already know that I will reply that yes, he seemed fine, but I don't think it will work out. That's what I said last month when she set me up with Cuddy Jones. His real name's Christopher Cudland Jones the third, but like many kids, he received a nickname from his elementary school peers. Cuddy had a massive beard, and I never knew where his eyes were focused. At least tonight's Douglas Cannon had warm eyes.

The next voice that comes to me belongs to my mother. "You

not tell truth. You break Ten Commandments." For someone so well schooled in the rights and wrongs laid out in the family Bible, I should be better at avoiding lies. "Minnie really *could* need me now," I say aloud in my defense. "I'm not a big, bad liar. Just a little one."

As I pull into the slender driveway of 3 Red Pelican Court, my headlights shine against the brick two-story Bailey House Bed and Breakfast. This home's large front windows have been boarded, dark shutters pulled over them like sleepy eyelids. The front door, a deep scarlet color during my childhood, looks worn and dull now—neglected over time. I inspect the roof, the eaves, the two dormer windows that protrude from the upstairs bedroom known as the Earl Grey Room, the tilted balcony off the English Breakfast Room, the two dirty white columns by the front stoop, and the winding stone walkway leading up to the main door that always opened so comfortably for us.

This house has been a respite for me since my middle school days when Minnie and I first went there with Irvy, Minnie's mom. After that initial visit, Minnie and I often stopped by the house after school. We'd follow the sidewalk down Juniper Lane, duck under the sloping branches of the mimosa tree, and then make a right onto Red Pelican Court, a short cul-de-sac. Once we were at the Bailey House, we'd hop up the seven brick steps to the front door. I knew to let Minnie be the first inside; even as a child she was opinionated, dramatic, a little bossy—and she liked to be first. But she was a loyal friend.

At a rectangular butcher-block table reserved for Minnie and me inside the Baileys' forest green sunroom, Mrs. Bailey would greet us with her crooked smile and British accent. "Girls! How delightful to see you. So glad you came round to pay me a visit. Put your book satchels down and have a seat."

Minnie and I smiled whenever she called our book bags *satchels*.

We'd slip them against a corner of the dining room, out of the way of the guests who were seated in the parlor reading the daily paper. I always felt Mrs. Bailey had been waiting all day for this moment when we would walk in; she was just so pleased to serve us her renowned lemon cookies on floral-scented paper napkins. Glass tumblers of raspberry cream soda were also brought to us by the home's loyal handyman, Ogden. I knew that if I said, "Thank you, this is very, very delicious," with an emphasis on *very*, Mrs. Bailey would grin and then give a slight nod toward Ogden. Ogden would make his way into the kitchen slowly—he did have a bad leg—and when he entered the sunroom again, new bottles of soda would be in his hands. As he took off their caps and filled my glass, and then Minnie's, Mrs. Bailey would place one more powdered-sugar-glazed cookie on my napkin. She wouldn't give Minnie another treat until Minnie agreed that "Um . . . oh yeah, this is all good. Very good."

Seated in my truck, I reminisce about the night Minnie and I were invited to sleep in the English Breakfast Room. That was the first night we decided that when the Baileys got too old to run the bed and breakfast, we'd take over. We made a pact to be like the Baileys and provide savory and healthy breakfasts, delicious desserts, and a listening ear for all weary travelers. Our plan was sealed when we heard a young tourist from Michigan tell us that she'd been spinning in circles for years, her heart and mind foggy with uncertainty. Thanks to five nights under the Baileys' hospitality, she now knew exactly what she wanted to do with her life. She would head back home to Ann Arbor, get her degree in oceanography, and wait to marry her boyfriend. She had taken care of her ailing mother for three years until her death, and now it was time to pursue her own dreams.

It's easy to remember how I felt that night when I realized how helpful Mr. and Mrs. Bailey had been to that young woman. They were older than my parents, yet they bridged the generations by reaching out to any tourist who came across their home's threshold. They made every guest feel like someone special. I was proud to know them.

"Minnie," I'd said later as we sat on the glider under the pergola, swaying lazily beside the Siamese cats, Buoy and Gull, "we can carry on this house's traditions." My heart was calm and full at the same time—a feeling you get when you recognize that what you're called to do is as clear as each star in the Big Dipper on a wintry night.

Suddenly, into my remembrances, lights flash twice.

4

The driver's-side window of the blue car lowers as the vehicle pulls up behind my truck. I hear a male voice call out, "Don't you know it's dangerous to be out here all alone?"

Relief washes over me like a foamy wave on a sweltering day. I'm glad that it's my uncle's voice that breaks the silence of my own private sanctuary and not the words of the convict from the eleven o'clock news that Minnie's been telling me about.

"Hi," I say. I roll down my window, stick my head out, and give Uncle Ropey a smile.

"You do know it's not safe for you to be out here by yourself?" Ever since Aunt Sheerly's salon was robbed, Uncle Ropey believes he needs to let us know that these parts aren't as safe as they once were. Sheerly feels the same way; I know because she wrote a song about it. Some of the lyrics are: "They're gonna get that bum. His time will come. The jail will hold him tight so that he will be out of sight." The tune is catchy, and after hearing her sing it one Saturday at The Rose Lattice in Buxton, I found myself humming it at my desk at work.

I get out of my truck. "This place is always safe to me." Then I look into his round, rosy face. "What are you doing here?" The Bailey House is on a cul-de-sac and not exactly a location you end up unless you're lost or want to be here.

He avoids my question and leans out of his window as his gaze roams over the large home. "Needs some fixing up, wouldn't you say?"

"Yeah," I breathe, looking at the dandelions congregating under a faded birdhouse, yet also noting that the lawn has been recently mowed. "It's just not what it used to be." Swiftly, like a torchbearer in the Olympics, I head up the steps toward the front door. "Here, there were two potted plants." With my hands, I motion to where they once stood. "On both sides of the door. In the spring and summer, they were flowering like geraniums or impatiens. In the winter, they were ivy topiaries."

"Ivy topiaries," he says with fingers cupping his chin. "Now that is something I know nothing about."

Laughing, I add, "And you probably don't care about them, either." Mrs. Bailey sure did, though. I remember how she scolded one of her visiting grandsons when he knocked over the right topiary while throwing a football.

A ticking noise stops me from saying any more. There's a click, and then the electric lantern hung on a black pole to the left of the stairs sprays out a beam of light.

"Must be on a timer," observes my uncle.

I glance around to see if any other lights have come on and then walk down the steps. "Have you ever been to the garden back here?"

He shakes his head.

"It's like being in a magical world," I say, catering to his adventuresome spirit.

He turns off his car and together, under flowering crepe myrtles the color of ripe peaches, we walk to the rear of the house. I unlatch the garden gate, give the handle a tug, and Ropey follows me inside. We make our way over the stone path to the patio, past deteriorating flowerbeds overgrown with fat weeds. A solitary burgundy rose dangles from a thorny stem. Honeysuckle bushes spread out over the backside of the house like octopus tentacles. At the wooden pergola, covered in twisted wisteria vines, Ropey bends down to study a section of cracked stones in the patio. I walk over to the pond.

The crevices in the low retaining wall around it are caked green with algae. A spider crawls along the mermaid-shaped fountain that sits in the middle of the pond. When the fountain is turned on, water bubbles from the mythical creature's navel, a sight Minnie and I grew to love. Now a feathery web stretches from the mermaid's left hand to her right.

Standing in the diminishing light, I recall the last time I ventured to the Bailey House, in late winter when a layer of ice coated the pond. The wind blew fall's leftover leaves around my shoes, and my nose and fingers grew numb from the cold. I asked God to let it happen. "I want this bed and breakfast," I said, zipping up my fleece jacket to my neck. I could hear the lapping of the Sound's water over the far fence. Lifting my face toward the stark branches of the lone oak, I took a cleansing breath. "This place just feels like it's mine already."

Uncle Ropey squeezes his body onto the two-person glider, the very glider Minnie and I sat on years ago after our afternoon snack of lemon cookies and soda. Now the wood is chipped and faded—the color of aged newspaper.

He starts to speak, but I interrupt. "Where's the birdbath?"

Ropey's head turns to scan the silent fountain and moss-covered patio. "Don't see it at all."

"There was a marble birdbath. I could have sworn it was here last time I visited." I scope out a pair of stones on the retaining wall that look less green than the rest, and sit down to face my uncle. "The birdbath was a clamshell. Well, a large thing made to look like a scalloped shell. Minnie and I said the mermaid left the pond to sit in it and comb her hair while all the guests slept."

Amused, Uncle Ropey pulls a cigar from his breast pocket. "I thought she would have had a rendezvous with the prince."

Actually, we'd also thought of that. "She did, after brushing her hair."

"Where have you been tonight?" he asks.

I'm annoyed that someone would steal a birdbath, but I try to focus on the here and now. "Bad date."

"You look dressed up."

For me, dressed up is whenever I wear makeup or jewelry, and my relatives know that is about the extent of getting me to look more *presentable*. Tonight I did apply mascara, eyeliner, and gold hoop earrings instead of my usual tiny studs, and even a bracelet I found at the back of my dresser in a gift box. I went way beyond my level of comfort and wore a skirt, albeit a denim one.

"So what was wrong with him?"

How to say it without sounding self-centered? "He . . . he never asked anything about me."

My uncle's eyes widen under his black-rimmed glasses. "Nothing?" He takes a drag from his cigar.

"Oh, I take that back. He did ask how I drink Diet Pepsi."

"Did you tell him—with a straw?" My uncle's eyes twinkle.

I find a small smile. "He didn't really want to know the answer. He was too preoccupied with all his stories."

"Guess his mama didn't teach him no manners."

I stretch my legs. I've always liked my long legs, an attribute I inherited from my dad, who is six-three. I note how tanned they look in the dusk. Then I think that it wasn't a completely *horrible* date. It could have been worse. At least his name wasn't Cuddy.

I snicker when I think of the tactic I used to get away.

"What's so funny?"

"I was just realizing that I left him alone at the Grille. Your niece cut the date short."

"Think he's still sitting there? All lonely? Want me to go check?"

A tinge of guilt enters, and I try to shake it off. "He didn't seem to care about getting to know me at all."

"One of Sheerly's finds?" He exhales as the scent of rich tobacco envelops the entire garden.

"Yeah, she keeps trying."

"We all want you to find The One."

I think it might be time to give up. I change the subject. "How about you? What are you up to?"

"Well . . ." Uncle Ropey takes his cigar from his mouth and lets out a yawn. "Bought a few yards of rope that I think will make some great works of art." My uncle constructs crafts with that white rope used on sailboats, a hot-glue gun, and shells. Tourists pay outrageous prices for his creations at a little shop in Buxton near the lighthouse. He prices them and then the owner of the shop marks them up at least twenty-five percent, so one shelled-rope tied in a fancy knot and framed in a glass case can retail at twenty dollars. Due to this fondness for rope art, he long ago earned the nickname Ropey.

"When I get this place," I say as I remember how it felt to sit in the glider with the sun beaming through the gaps of the thick wisteria, "I want to display your nautical pieces in every room."

"Still have your heart set on owning this place?" He gestures toward the house.

"I do. I just can't seem to figure out how to make it happen. I've called a few Realtors. No one tells me anything I can use."

Suddenly, Ropey stands, adjusts his pant legs, and announces, "I need a donut." Crushing the cigar stub with his shoe, he heads toward the gate. I wait as he makes his way around the house. I hear his car door open and close.

When he returns, he has a box of Krispy Kreme donuts. My uncle lived off these donuts until Aunt Beatrice Lou made the doctor tell him to limit his intake to only one per day. She'd read too much about clogged arteries in medical journals at the library where she works. Some are addicted to cigarettes, alcohol, or diet pills; Uncle Ropey's addiction comes in the form of glazed sugar.

The sky is streaked now with trellises of fading pink and lavender clouds. We eat donuts as we enjoy the view. I stand to peek over the wooden fence that circles the property and take in the quiet Sound, its edges thick with marsh grasses. When my uncle reaches for his third glazed treat, he makes me promise I won't tell Beatrice Lou.

"I wouldn't dare." I note how romantic the sky looks, and as a robin settles on the top of the gate, I imagine what it would be like to sit here holding the hand of a man I'm in love with. This was the garden where Minnie and I talked of boys, and now, suddenly, I'm feeling old and lonely, like I should reside at the Morning Glory Nursing Home.

My uncle rubs his fingers together and then licks the tips. I bet he did that same action as a kid. Like Aunt Sheerly tells her patrons,

"You can't take the boy out of the man." I ask him, "Any luck with the speedboat?"

The desire my uncle holds for a fast boat is not met with approval by his wife. Ever since Ropey's back started bothering him—he seems to knock it out of whack every few months—he's been told not to overdo it. Ropey doesn't agree with that. He wants to ride like the wind over the Sound, pretend his mirror lies and feel twenty-five again. Beatrice Lou would rather have him walk along the beach at least a mile each day, eat sunflower seeds and granola, and trim down to two hundred pounds like he weighed when he was twenty-five.

My uncle uses his secretive voice to say, "That's the reason I came down this way. Casey Luweigneson—he lives about a block away from here. He has an eighteen-footer for sale."

I've heard of Casey Luweigneson. His name is one you can't forget. Sheerly says he sits on his front porch and drinks Pabst Blue Ribbon while telling tales about schooners that were lost at sea. He boasts of being related, somehow, to every smuggling or looting hooligan who survived each vessel's wreckage, even claiming that his great-great-great-grandmother was once married to Blackbeard. Sheerly says his stories grow more elaborate after seven beers.

"Are you going to buy it?" I ask as Ropey brushes sugar from his lips.

"I reckon it would be a perfect match for me. Three years old, still in good shape."

"Did you check to see if any treasure chests are hidden in the bow?"

Ropey laughs at my attempt to be comical.

I offer, "If you kept the boat at his house, then Beatrice Lou would never have to know."

"Ah," he says. "There are some things that I can get away with in a marriage. But nothing that large."

I smile.

"So how's your bustling household? Zane's thumb okay?"

My household, as he calls it, consists of Minnie, Zane, and myself; we live together in a duplex in the little town of Waves. Last week Zane got his thumb slammed in a kitchen cabinet when he was trying to shove all his toys into it. Minnie hoped that maybe since the thumb was hurt he'd no longer have the desire to put it in his mouth, but such is not the case. Zane stuck his sore thumb in his mouth and complained that it stung.

"Zane is Zane," I answer as I think about how he screamed last night because we couldn't find his stuffed squirrel, Popacorn.

"The kid misses his dad."

"I miss his dad, too." My voice is soft, like the breeze surrounding us. When I think of Minnie these days, it's hard not to hear her sobs, no matter where I am.

"Maybe you and Minnie need to bring Zane over to the house."

"I can manage the kid most days while Minnie works." Manage— this is not a word I typically say; I think I might have picked it up from the man who fell off a jeepney.

We're silent for a moment, breathing in the cool, damp air. I stare up at a window on the second floor and recall another Bailey House memory. All the guests had checked out and the maid was pulling the sheets off one of the king-sized beds. She asked if I wanted to help her, and I did. Later, she complimented my assistance in front of Mrs. Bailey, and lemon cookies and raspberry cream soda were presented to me in the sunroom.

"What's up with this place?" I ask Ropey. "Do you know anything?"

"Sheerly says it's as haunted as the day is long. Spooky, so the owners left. They said Blackbeard's ghost lives in the basement." He burps, excuses himself, and burps again.

"There is no basement." I know the layout as well as I know my own duplex and have memories of so many of the rooms, including the laundry chute we used to throw Minnie's poodle purse down when no one was looking.

"Sheerly's got some story about it. I thought I heard her say the basement held a dead body."

There are times my aunt's love of a good story overrides her common sense. She makes fun of Casey's tales, yet expects her own stories to be taken as gospel truth. "Mr. and Mrs. Bailey were too old to run it and went back to live near family in Cincinnati."

"Then there was another couple," Ropey says.

"When?"

"Let's see. About the time Beatrice Lou wanted me to lose weight." He pats his stomach for emphasis. "I reckon it was about six years ago."

"What happened then?" It must have been when I was away in Charlotte, working after college at *The Daily Pulse*. I served as an intern at the weekly paper and then when they offered me a full-time position after graduation, I took it without a second of hesitation. But I do remember Minnie mentioning something about the Bailey House opening under new management. It wasn't long before I got the job with Selena at *Lighthouse Views*.

"They got scared by the ghost and left."

"Really?"

Ropey laughs, long and full, reminding me of my dad's laughter. The two are brothers, with Sheerly in the middle. "You know Sheerly. She extracts every piece of information she can from her clients as she does all that stuff with their hair." We both have learned that Sheerly Cut is more than a salon. It's a culture, a society of women. "You should dig around a bit and find out more. My guess is that people just aren't talking."

His voice sounds funny, so I ask, "What do you mean?"

"Secrets." My uncle wipes sugar off his cheeks. "This region is full of them." He lets another donut find its way into his mouth.

I know he's right; one of the first lessons of being a reporter is that there are two sides to every story, and somewhere in the middle, you'll find the truth.

I feel satisfied as the moon bobs into the night sky and we return to our vehicles. While the date with Douglas Cannon didn't go as I'd hoped, the time with Uncle Ropey has been fun. Life is a cornucopia of good and bad, and any time the good outweighs the bad, it's time to be grateful.

I know exactly what my uncle's parting words are going to be, and I'm correct. "Be careful driving home. Don't talk to strangers. Don't tell Beatrice about the cigar or the donuts."

I display a thumbs-up signal, which means that I can keep secrets myself. If ever his wife finds out about his smoking or circular night-time snacks, it won't be because she heard it from me.

As I get into my truck, Ropey tosses out, "You'll meet a good man one day, Jackie. Keep your chin up."

Driving across the Oregon Inlet Bridge toward Waves, a parade of all the dates I've had since my return to the Outer Banks to live flashes before my eyes. Not one of them has led to a second date. One did seem promising the first time I met him, but then he never asked me out again. Last I heard from the family grapevine, he moved to Chicago to run a trucking business and married a Turkish belly dancer.

"Is there anyone out there for me?" I ask God in my loud voice, the one that vibrates off the steering wheel, hits the back of the cab, and then clangs back to my ears. As I've done before, I remind God that this man can arrive on a horse, a Coast Guard barge, a sailboat, or a ferry. "Whatever you think is best," I say.

My truck bounces over the narrow strip of Route 12; thin, evenly spaced electrical poles whiz past my peripheral vision. I wait, hoping to hear an audible voice, one like Moses heard coming from the burning bush. But all I hear is the continual sound of ocean waves splashing onto the shore across the blackened dunes. Even Bodie Lighthouse's beacon seems dismal tonight, as if it can't find a man suited for me.

5

Monday mornings are reserved for staff meetings from nine until Selena Thomas, our boss at *Lighthouse Views,* feels we have "sufficient coverage." This takes hours; one Monday it took four hours and twenty-three minutes according to Bert's watch. Halfway through, Selena did stop her ranting about dishonest car mechanics—she was particularly fed up with one in Rodanthe—and ordered us lunch from The Happy Fisherman.

These staff meetings aren't at all like they were when I was at *The Daily Pulse.* Of course, that paper didn't have a colorful editor like Selena. We had Jack Brenton, who didn't believe in talking much—except on the phone to his girlfriend during his lunch in the break room. To his staff he repeatedly said, "Deadlines, deadlines," as though the most important part of being a journalist was getting the story submitted on time, not whether it was well-written, interesting, or factual.

"I know this is a recession, but tourists still exist!" Today Selena clutches her cell in one hand and a silver Cross pen in the other. The cell does not need to be up to her ear; the caller is on speakerphone and our entire staff, seated on overstuffed chairs in our small Nags Head office, is listening.

We watch the phone, quietly waiting.

"How about a quarter-page ad, then?" The caller on the other end, Roberta Hakkadok, is the manager of Blackbeard's Restaurant. I know exactly what she looks like; we were in middle school together. I've only been to her restaurant once and that was when Selena took the staff out for lunch after the death of her father. Roberta hasn't changed much since our youth; her auburn hair is still in a sweeping ponytail and her eye shadow is a pale green.

"A quarter-page ad?" Selena places the phone on an antique coffee table she inherited from her father's estate. She gives us the thumbs-up signal, a sign that she is certain she's going to get Roberta to commit to an ad in our magazine.

Roberta's voice is hesitant. "How much will that cost?"

"Didn't our advertising department send you an updated price sheet?" Selena looks at Cassidy, the head of our so-called advertising department.

Cassidy, seated beside me, nods as she chews on a granola bar. She usually eats chocolate chip, but I don't see any chips in today's variety.

We hear a pause and then Roberta's voice on the other end of the line. "No."

As Shakespeare, Selena's Yorkshire terrier, yaps twice from his perch by the office's bay window, Selena sucks in air. Her little dog doesn't bother her; in fact, she lets her pet get away with anything. However, humans, and especially those who she feels need to take out ads in *Lighthouse Views* and don't jump at the opportunity, annoy her.

"I did send her a sheet," Cassidy whispers in her defense as she crumples the Oats 'N Honey wrapper.

Selena cuts off Cassidy with a swing of her pen-holding hand. "Roberta, the ad you need for your business is two hundred dollars. That will run for the next two issues." Without waiting for an answer, she says in her most authoritative tone, "Bring in the check by Thursday. We'll run your ad as we have in the past. You'll see results, results." In her soothing tone, the one that sounds like a guitar strumming the music for "Edelweiss," she says, "Customers will flock to you like intoxicated seagulls, you'll see."

We wait until we hear a reluctant Roberta say, "Well . . . all right."

"All right, then."

"This Thursday?" asks Roberta.

"Two hundred dollars this Thursday. Just know that you're getting a bargain!" Closing the sale, Selena adds, "Thanks for your business. Tourists will know where to find you when you advertise with us." With a swift jab to a button, Selena disconnects Roberta from us.

For a brief moment we all look at each other. Cassidy, Bert, and me—the backbone of the magazine, as Selena calls us. We're already tired from this staff meeting; our coffee cups are empty, yet no one gets up to make another pot.

This is the way Selena operates—pushy until she gets the commitment. Or as Bert likes to put it: "Bloodsucking until the victim finally gives in. Then it's a regular 'Kumbaya' sing fest."

Selena walks over to give Shakespeare a treat. The little ball of champagne fur jumps off the sofa, doggie biscuit in his mouth, and scampers under Selena's desk to enjoy his reward.

In my opinion, her terrier rarely does anything to deserve a treat. It's when Selena gets a commitment from a client or praise for an article that she rewards her dog. She keeps the colorful treats in a glass jar marked "Shakespeare's Treasures." The jar sits by a framed photo of Shakespeare and her on a Jet Ski. The terrier is in front of her on the seat, wearing a lavender life vest with his name on it. Selena, also in a vest with her name on it, has her fingers on the handles and a sheepish grin, as if she just got out of bed and is still craving sleep.

Whenever people comment that a terrier is pretty small to ride a Jet Ski, and ask how the dog stays on when you speed over the waves, Selena just says, "Oh, Shakespeare loves his life vest," even though the inquirer mentioned nothing about a vest. The truth is, the moment that photo was snapped, Selena rode slowly for five hundred yards, and Shakespeare's whimper was so terrifying that the adventure of dog and owner's first ride together lasted only a few moments. Selena now leaves her pet at home with a dog biscuit and a *Lassie* DVD playing on TV whenever she takes her Jet Ski around the inlet.

Smiling at us all, Selena reaches for her legal pad. She sits on the top of her desk next to the jar of treats and says, "Now that we've got a few more commitments for advertisements, we're ready to pump this meeting up a notch. We have a lot to do."

I wish there was more coffee. I try to gauge my boss; would she mind if I excused myself to the kitchen to make some more? One morning I stood to make another pot and she stopped talking until I'd sat back down. The room was quiet, all eyes on me, until I realized what was happening. I scurried back to my armchair, vowing never to embarrass myself like that again.

"Now, kids," Selena says. To this fifty-year-old, we are all kids. "The June issue comes out in two weeks." Crossing her stocking-clad legs—legs Bert says could be models in a hose commercial—she chews on the tip of her pen. "I want us to be ready. Are we ready?"

Something makes me want to say with all the pseudo-enthusiasm I can muster, "Yes, Chef," like on an episode of *Hell's Kitchen*, but I know my boss would not approve. Instead, I nod and pretend to be taking notes. Actually, my mind is on the Bailey House. *Who is the current owner? Where can I find out if it's for sale? Can we afford it?* I scribble these questions at the top of the page. My savings account is nothing to be excited about, and Minnie is just able to pay her half of the rent and buy groceries from her earnings at Over the Edge, the surf shop near our house.

I must have missed something because suddenly everyone is looking at me. "Yeah?" I sound clueless, silly. Covering my notebook with my arms, I attempt to be interested in my surroundings.

Selena's smile dazzles. "Good," she says. "I'll need that interview for the July issue." Then her cell phone rings, and she is talking to her mother in Boston. "Ma, I know, I know!" Her accent goes from southern to northern quicker than it takes her dog to lick his paw. "Yes, it was a great article. I like that line they quoted about me, too."

As my boss continues in a syrupy voice she never uses around us, I turn to Cassidy. "What is she saying?"

"I don't know for sure. I think her mom's congratulating her on that article in the paper about Selena." That article, praising the work of *Lighthouse Views*, calling it a "stellar publication," appeared weeks ago. A copy of it hangs in a frame above our boss's desk. The photograph of Selena looks as if she was blinded by something because her eyes are wide like her dog's get when he's alarmed. I can guarantee that what they say about pet owners beginning to look like their pets is true.

"No, not that." I stop Cassidy before she enters the restroom. "What is it that Selena asked me to do?"

Cassidy laughs. "Were you bored and not paying attention again?" With her hand on the door to the women's room, she says, "Selena wants you to interview the owner of Rexy Properties. I heard he's single." She winks.

Sometimes I wonder if there are fliers circulating the Outer Banks, advertising in bold lettering, DESPERATE HALF-KOREAN SINGLE WOMAN DESIRES A MAN! NOW!

6

Aside from staff meetings, Mondays at our office are made up of discussing the previous weekend. While Selena takes another phone call, Cassidy says her family held a reunion up the northern coast in Duck. Although the food looked and smelled glorious, especially her uncle's sweet potato pie and corn pudding, she managed to stick to her diet, hovering over the vegetable platter and slices of watermelon. "I had so much watermelon I felt waterlogged," she tells us as she sips from a bottle of Aquafina.

Bert says he flew to his sister's wedding in Nashville and that he's sure she has married a loser. "He's got to be the most boring professor Vanderbilt has."

"Well, at least he teaches at a prestigious university." Cassidy was once in love with a biology professor from Duke, but that was back before her marriage to her current husband, who is a taxidermist.

"He's got nothing going for him." Bert's tone shadows disgust. "He doesn't know a thing about the Civil War." Bert is a known Civil War buff; ask him about any general or battle and prepare to spend time listening. When his parents come to visit from Raleigh, he takes them to Fort Fisher. So far, his mother and father have been to the historical landmark seven times.

"Well, I'm sure he knows a lot about other things," says Cassidy.

"He can't even tell a joke. He gets the punch line out there too early, before it makes sense. Then he wonders why no one laughs."

I keep my lips clamped, determined not to mention anything about my date with Douglas. I check my cell for messages. I'm not sure if I'm more afraid Douglas called, or that he didn't.

There are no messages.

"So how was your weekend?" Cassidy looks at me.

"Oh, fine. You know, nothing exciting."

"Another bad date?" Cassidy's brown eyes bore into mine.

"Something like that."

She laughs. "Your relatives are pretty adamant, aren't they?"

"They try."

My desk is at the far left corner of the room by a tiny window. The surface of the desk is clean except for a computer, penholder, and dictionary. Bert's is scattered as if a whirlwind just came through. Notebooks, folders, and pens are visible, yet we all know underneath are stacks of books and papers. It doesn't seem to matter that Bert's workspace is a mess; he's clearly Selena's favorite employee. Whenever I have a question about how to conduct an upcoming interview or what to leave out in a piece, Selena is quick to say, "Ask Bert. Bert knows."

Minutes later, Selena concludes her phone call, lays the legal pad in her lap, and waves her pen in circles. "We now have officially closed our ads for the June issue. Got that, Cassidy?"

Cassidy is eating from a cup of vanilla yogurt. She dips her spoon into her mouth, closes her eyes as though she's savoring the taste, and nods. She's lost about ten pounds, although she would say eleven and a half. Dieters are quite precise when it comes to pounds.

"So if Lacy Lingerie calls us at the last minute, like they have three times in a row now, it is too late for them to place their ad in this next issue."

"And Isle Bait and Tackle?" asks Cassidy.

"No more." Selena whisks her hand through the air in front of her as one would when batting at a flying insect. "Deadline has been reached. These people know we have to allow time to lay out the issue and get it to the printer." Selena lets a moment pass as she looks over her pad. She then folds her arms over it. "You are writing well."

When she smiles at me, I smile back. I don't care if she treats us like kindergartners; I've always flourished when praise is tossed at me.

"Keep it up. No worthless glop. I don't want us to start writing froufrou things like that *other* magazine!"

That other magazine she's referring to is *Hatteras Style*, a magazine Selena claims we're better than, yet clearly feels is our competition. She's constantly telling businesses that the place to advertise is with us and only us.

When Selena joins her dog on the sofa, I head for the coffeepot to make another round for all of us. I watch my boss as she pets the terrier with gentle, loving strokes. Walking over to them, I ask, "What should I know about the owner of Rexy Properties?" I hope she won't ignore me as she does sometimes when she's engrossed in her beloved Shakespeare. Once I had to wait no less than fifteen minutes as she brushed the terrier with a new doggie brush. Apparently, it was his birthday gift.

Selena glances at me and then returns her attention to her pet. "He's in his mid-thirties. Lives in Manteo in that large green house with the white fence. The house needs painting. It's hideous, actually.

Isn't it, Shakespeare?" She gives him a kiss on his nose and smiles when he licks her cheek. "What kind of man of his clout would neglect his own home? Beyond me. I feel like giving him the number of my house painter." With a sway of her hand toward the back of the office, she says, "His contact info is in the Rolodex. He's out of town a lot, but I've seen him at the Food Lion, so I know he buys groceries." Then she stands and heads toward her desk. This is Selena's way of dismissing me without saying, "That will be all," like a queen addressing her servants in a movie.

Even though we're in the century of modern electronic conveniences, Selena believes that some inventions, such as the Rolodex, can never be replaced. I have an Excel spreadsheet with local business owners' names and addresses in it, because I find a computer the best place to keep my data. Our editor still holds on to the white alphabetized cards and flips through them when she needs information.

Cassidy passes me and moans that she's hungry. "Do you think Selena will order takeout for us today?"

I note Selena's arched back as she logs on to her computer. "I doubt it." Her cell rings to the tune of "Who Let the Dogs Out," and she's laughing within seconds. I overhear her say, "Melody, you are too funny and kind. Shakespeare and I would love to be there. . . . Seven? Oh yes, that will be just fine."

No wonder we can't figure her out. Selena is either a beast or a kitten. Bert once said he thought the full moon had something to do with her mood swings, but I don't think she's that easy to predict.

At the Rolodex on the shelf by the copier, I search through the cards and then realize I don't know if the owner's last name is Rexy or what. I ask Bert.

"Davis Erickson," he says as he slams his computer screen with an open palm. He notes my bewildered expression and volunteers,

"This old thing needs a good-morning touch before it will work on Mondays."

I nod and slip back to the Rolodex. When I jot down the info from the Davis Erickson index card, I think: He's in the realty business; I could ask him about the Bailey House. In fact, I'm pretty sure I once left him a message when I was trying to get information about the bed and breakfast. That was almost a year ago, before Minnie's husband died. Since Lawrence's death, Minnie's and my dreams seem to be on hold. I haven't talked about our plans for the Bailey place with Minnie in a long time.

"Two hours and fifty-three minutes," Bert says as his cell phone rings from under his agenda book.

I'm confused until I realize he must be referring to how long our meeting lasted today.

7

When Selena opens a can of tuna for Shakespeare, I leave the office. The smell of tuna burns my nostrils and makes my stomach queasy. Once, as a joke, my roommate in college stuck a cookbook called *101 Terrific Tuna Dishes* under my pillow. I had crazy dreams that night—even though I took the paperback out to the Dumpster before getting ready for bed. One dream I still remember all these years later involved a huge bowl of tuna noodle casserole that the dean of UNC-Charlotte claimed he'd made especially for me. He held the bowl up to my face and said I had to eat it or I wouldn't graduate.

Taking my striped notebook, I head to the Sunnyside Grille. The blue sky holds an abundance of filmy white clouds, and the sun's rays sift meekly through them. Spring is here, and although the weather can be fickle, I know that soon it will be summer, my favorite season.

There was a time when I'd drive home to work on an article when the office got too noisy—or smelly—but these days, with the warmer weather, I prefer walking the three blocks from the office to the restaurant. Like Zane counts the steps up to our duplex as he pounces up them, I count my steps from the door to the office to the door of the Grille. One hundred ninety-four, if I take long strides.

Inside, I find an empty barstool near the center of the counter. I like to sit at the bar when I'm alone. When you sit on a barstool, your aloneness isn't as obvious as it is at a table with two or four chairs.

I told my mom once how much I like to listen to customers order. I think you can learn a lot about people as you hear the different ways they choose to ask for their food from a waitress or waiter. "Some people are rude or just plain strange," I commented. "And some put a question mark on the end of everything they say."

Later, Mom said that ever since I told her I enjoy listening, she became self-conscious. "I think everyone listens to me now, and I don't want to order," she said. "I don't want people to think I don't know how to speak." I hugged her, told her not to worry, that I am the only one who eavesdrops on people, so she should feel free to order as she wants. She gave me a look that still held doubt. Now whenever we are in a restaurant together, she asks Dad to order for her. I feel I've taken something from her that she'll never get back.

Buck greets me with a smile. In addition to his yellow restaurant shirt, he's wearing a black ball cap that has Sunnyside Grille printed on the front. "Hey there, Heartbreaker." He tips his cap.

"What?"

"Yeah, it was some night on Saturday, wasn't it?"

"What do you mean?" I squint my eyes to show that I'm not sure what he's up to.

"That man."

"What?"

"Your alleged date. Once you left, he wouldn't stop crying."

I laugh. "Stop!"

"It's true. He looked so forlorn, like he'd never be the same again."

I just shake my head and watch as he pours Diet Pepsi into a mason jar.

When he hands me the jar, he says with a straight face, "Anything for the Heartbreaker. I wouldn't want to get on your bad side."

"I didn't break his heart." I feel I must defend myself.

"That's not what he told me."

"You talked to him?"

Before he can answer, Buck is summoned by another customer, a beefy man with a flimsy mustache, wanting a cup of cheddar soup and fries. He asks if the soup has onions in it, saying he can't eat them because he's allergic. Buck says the soup has no onions, but the customer wants him to go to the kitchen to make sure. Buck leaves as I pull my notebook from my purse and dig around for my pen.

When my cell phone rings, it's Minnie asking when I'll be home. Zane is at Ropey's and she needs to know what time he can drop off her child at the duplex.

I think of the interview from last week that I need to type up. "I'll be home by five," I say. "How long do you work today?"

"Nine." She sighs. "Jackie, have I ever told you how much I appreciate you?"

I don't want Minnie to feel guilty that I spend a lot of my free time taking care of her son. "Minnie, don't worry," I tell her. "I'll save you a slice of meatloaf."

Buck is back from the kitchen, and I overhear him telling the customer that the cheddar soup has no onions. The man has changed his mind while Buck was talking to the cook. He wants a hamburger with no onions. Buck places the order at the computer screen.

"Actually," Buck says when he returns to my end of the counter, "your date paid and left. So, Hatteras Girl, will you be seeing him again?"

I smile. "Hatteras Girl?"

"Yeah. Do you like that name better than Heartbreaker?" His smile is exceptionally big today, just like when he was a boy with freckles and still had some of his baby teeth.

"What made you decide to call me Hatteras Girl?"

He leaves to bring a plate of fried clams to a customer. When he comes back, he refills my drink. "You are like a ray of sunshine—you enter a place, light it up, and keep it bright. You dress like you're on vacation all the time, and you love living in the Outer Banks. You're the epitome of a Hatteras girl."

My heart dances at his words, but I say, "Something tells me you're up to no good."

"What would make you say that?"

"I'm not sure I can trust you."

He shoots me a questioning glance.

"Everyone knows that you're just Jellyfish Boy."

"Jellyfish Boy," says Betty Lynn as she swings behind the counter. "That's a good name for Buck. I like it!" She stands across from me and complains about her sunburn. "I fell asleep on my boyfriend's raft yesterday and got sunburned so badly. It hurts to wear clothes. I want to wear a halter, but Blake won't let me."

"If it's any consolation for you," Buck says, "he won't let me wear one, either."

Betty Lynn giggles, her blue eyes shiny. With a graceful turn, she heads to a table to refill iced tea. As she walks past a table with two men, they both look up from their burgers to watch her.

Yet Buck hasn't named *her* Hatteras Girl, although with her fair features, she looks more like a beach girl than I do. Even today with the sunburn, she could be packaged as Malibu Barbie.

When she returns to us, she places the iced tea pitcher behind the counter, takes a look around at the handful of dining customers, and says, "If anyone needs me, I'll be in the bathroom putting aloe vera on my back."

Once she's gone, I look at Buck. He's watching the Braves play the Giants on one of the big-screen TVs above the counter. I try to think of something to say and what comes out is, "Did Blake ask you to fix the molding in the women's bathroom?"

Buck's attention turns to me. "Blake doesn't let me go into the women's bathroom."

"Even off hours? The molding is hanging off the wall."

"I'll let him know. Not sure he'll care, but I'll tell him one of his most frequent customers sees it as a problem."

"The third stall doesn't lock, either."

Buck grins. He picks up a pen and pad of paper near a stack of napkins. On a clean sheet he writes as he speaks, "Molding hanging off. Third stall door doesn't lock." Glancing at me, he asks, "Anything else?"

I lift my own pen and turn a page in my notebook. "You haven't asked if I want anything to eat yet."

After clearing his throat a few times, Buck gives me a huge smile and asks, "What can I get for you today?"

Actually, I'm still full from the eggs and bacon breakfast I made for Zane and me this morning. "I'm fine. Thanks for asking, though."

He leaves me alone to jot down the questions I want to ask Davis Erickson for the upcoming interview. *What do you know about the Bailey House?* I scribble. I cross that out and try, *Being a Realtor, you must know about the Bailey House.* As I draw a rose around the letter B in Bailey, I decide I will try to work this question into the interview. Davis could know nothing about the bed and breakfast, but it won't hurt to ask.

How much does it cost? I add a few dollar signs beside this sentence. *Do you know if it's for sale? Who owns it now? Someone mows the lawn, so who's paying that person?* If he doesn't know anything about the house, maybe he can direct me to someone who does.

When Buck goes on break, he sits on the empty stool to my right. I close my notebook and take the opportunity to ask him a question I've wondered about for a long time. "You and your dad used to work construction together, right?"

He picks at a jagged fingernail. My brother does the same thing. Growing up, Dad would see this and tell him to get the nail clippers. Sometimes Ron just bit his nail as if to say, "Why do I need clippers?"

"I see your dad's van . . ." I continue when Buck doesn't respond. "But you're never in it with him like you used to be." Even in high school, Buck went to carpentry jobs with his dad in the old gray van with Griffins & Company painted on both sides. After high school, he took some art classes at a community college, but even then he was a team with his dad; I'd see them together whenever I came to visit Minnie and Lawrence.

"We used to work together," he says as though he's talking to his hands.

I already knew this. I proceed slowly. With Buck, you never know how he will respond. "What happened?" I've heard so many stories on why he doesn't work with his father anymore. Sheerly told me they got into a fight. But then Sheerly also thinks Blackbeard's been spotted at the Bailey House.

"Now, Jackie, what could be better than working here at the Grille?"

I see the smile in his eyes. If he doesn't want to be serious, then I know I'll just have to play along. "I guess your dad never laid dollar bills for you inside the cabinets you installed or between the tiles you replaced."

He grins. "The tips here are decent."

"Construction must be hard work. I know nothing about it. Tools and I don't get along."

"I like building things. And on most days, I like tools."

"Do you miss it?" My heart hopes for a real reply, one that will disclose more than just a good sense of humor.

He picks up a menu, flips it over, and says, "Don't ever order the beer-battered shrimp here."

Not being a seafood fan, I don't think I'd ever consider doing that.

"So," he says, eyes on my notebook, "what are you working on today?"

"This week I get to interview Davis Erickson."

I can hear his tongue freeze inside his mouth.

"He owns Rexy Properties," I say. "Do you know him? He's older than me, which makes him older than you, of course."

He stands, a silent frame beside me.

"Are you leaving?"

"I gotta go."

Meekly, I murmur, "Okay."

"See you around, Hatteras Girl."

His lean legs take him out the front door, past the hostess who tells him to have a nice day.

I'm alone with my notebook until Betty Lynn returns and moans that she's in so much pain she wants to go home early. However, she knows that Blake won't let her leave until the lunch hour is completely over.

I watch her and the rest of the waitstaff carry plates heavy with hamburgers and golden fries, chicken salad, fried clams, and beer-battered shrimp. When I see an order for a Reuben sandwich, I think of Douglas and hope he's not here. Today I feel guilty for lying and leaving him alone the other night. Swallowing, I shove the guilt down my throat with a sip of Pepsi. Douglas will be fine. He was probably glad to get rid of me, anyway. I think he needs someone who doesn't love the taste of Diet Pepsi, knows what a jeepney is, and really likes to listen.

8

Davis Erickson isn't in his office at Rexy Properties when I enter at a few minutes before one. "He won't be back until Friday," the receptionist with the stick-on pink nails and lipstick of the same color tells me in a tone that makes me think I should have known this. She sits at a large, smooth desk with a disturbing painting by Picasso on the creamy wall behind her.

I guess there is no point in explaining to her that just the other day Davis told me to come to his office at one for an interview. Slowly, she reaches for a ringing phone as I stand in front of her desk. "No, no. He's not here." Her painted lips are still as she listens. Her name badge has BEV printed on it in gold letters. "He's in Ohio. That's right. Yes, I can take a message or I can give you his voice mail."

I suppose I took Zane over to Ropey's this afternoon for nothing, then. I exit the office and finger the card on which I wrote Davis's contact information. Under his office number, I've written his cell number.

As I step onto the walkway that is lined with azalea bushes, my mind deliberates. *Dare I call his cell? Is that acceptable?*

Driving back to my duplex in Waves, I think of how frustrated Selena will be if I don't get this interview. By the time my truck is parked in our driveway, I've decided that I'll call the man.

First, I pour a glass of iced tea. Minnie insists that Lipton with ginseng is the best. Of course my mom agrees. Mom was born with ginseng in her veins. When I was small, and stuffy from a cold, she made me cups of ginseng tea with other assorted herbs. She claimed that Korean ginseng was as strong as any prescription medicine. As she handed me the steamy beverage, she would insist that drinking it would not only cure my cold, but make my skin glow and my hair glossy. I wanted it to make my hair blond, but she said ginseng was not that powerful.

I prefer person-to-person interviews where I get to see the facial expressions of the one I'm interviewing. Minnie once asked if it makes me nervous to sit across from someone and ask them questions, but it doesn't. As long as I have my questions prepared, I can't lose. It's as easy for me to do an interview as it is for Aunt Sheerly to talk about hairstyles.

When my tea is gone, I head into my bedroom with my notebook. The only thing I'm uncertain of today is if it's within protocol to call Davis when we did not arrange for this to be a phone interview. Hopefully, he'll understand. After all, he's the one who told me a date and time to be at his office. I showed up; he didn't.

Davis Erickson apologizes immediately. "I am sorry, Jacqueline. I'll be glad to give you the interview now." His voice is just as warm and articulate as the first time we spoke.

"You can call me Jackie." When I called to set up the interview at his office, he kept calling me Jacqueline and I let him.

"Okay, I will, then. Give me just one minute to turn the blender off." I hear a whirling sound and then a click. "There." A pause. "Just making a smoothie."

"Oh? What kind?"

"Well, my parents have peaches growing in their yard, so this is peach."

"Where do your parents live?"

"Cincinnati. That's where I was raised. How about you?"

"Here."

"Which is?"

"Hatteras."

"Oh, that's great. You can go out on the water anytime you want to."

My mom didn't exactly agree with that. She was very big on Ron and me protecting our skin. Growing up, she reminded me that in Asia, many women carry umbrellas to shield their skin from the sun. I'd thought she was exaggerating until a Korean friend in college told me that her mother always carried a parasol during the summer months. Mom didn't make Ron and me carry parasols, but we did have to slather ourselves with sunscreen before we went outdoors.

"Did you go to school in Hatteras?" Davis's voice reminds me of Bono from U2, minus the Irish accent.

"Yeah, every single year. Then I left to go to UNC-Charlotte."

"I thought maybe they just taught the kids out on the docks."

"Barefoot," I say.

He laughs, and then I do, too.

Calling him was the right thing to do.

$\sim \backsim \backsim$

Talking with him is comfortable; I stretch out on my bed and extend my legs like Shakespeare does on the sofa at work. One topic eases into another, and soon we've discussed food we both like, personal cooking disasters, childhood pets, the differences between life in the North and the South, and movies. I'm writing some of it down, but I know I need to get into the subjects Selena wants covered in the interview. Although I find Davis's story about how his golden retriever saved his brother from drowning at a swimming hole in Upstate New York engaging, Selena isn't going to see that as important to *Lighthouse Views* readers. To segue into real estate, I ask about the Bailey House.

"What do you know about it?"

"Is this part of the interview?"

"No, just for my interest." I think of telling him how I loved going there as a child, how the lemon cookies were moist and tasty, how Ogden kept the grounds looking like a garden in an issue of *Southern Living*, but I decide not to disclose too much.

"I do have some connections to it. I know it's vacant and in need of a buyer."

My heart jumps against my chest. "Do you manage it? I mean, is Rexy Properties the one trying to sell it?"

"Possibly," he says.

"What do you mean by 'possibly'?"

"Technically, it's not listed as being for sale. However, I do know that if the right buyer came along, he or she would be considered."

His words confuse me a bit, but I switch to the question I've had for a long time. "Do you know how much it's going for?"

"Sure," he says. "Right under a million and a half."

"Half a million?"

"No, one million and five hundred thousand dollars."

"Are you teasing?" I bet he is. I clutch the phone, waiting to hear his laughter.

There is no laughter. "That's actually a little reduced. In my opinion, it's worth at least two million."

"But it's worn down. I mean, the outside of it looks pretty weather-beaten."

"Inside is gorgeous."

I hope it is, I think, and then when I realize he's serious about the price, my mind shouts: *Where in the world will you ever come up with 1.5 million dollars?* My brain searches for some way, some relative, some investment that would allow me to get that kind of money. I can't think of anything. I knew the home would be costly, being prime real estate on the Outer Banks, but I never thought the price tag would be so monumental.

Still, my veins pulsate with excitement. I've finally found someone who knows about the Bailey House and hopefully can tell me even more. "That's a lot of money, but it can be financed, right? I mean, should the right buyer come along?"

"I suppose."

"Who would I contact about it? You?"

"Depends." His elusiveness about the house bothers me, so it's a relief when he changes the subject. "How long have you been working at the magazine?"

"Forever it seems. About five years."

"You must be good at what you do." His voice soothes like a summer breeze that comes in the window from across the Sound. "Do you like interviewing people?"

"Oh, I like to interrogate."

He laughs. "Well, it's been a pleasure talking with you. I don't feel interrogated at all."

Note to Selena: It doesn't matter that his house needs painting. He's a nice guy.

Conducting an interview is one thing; putting it all together on my computer is a different beast. I sit on the chair in front of my Dell and wonder how to turn all my sloppy notes into an article that will make Selena smile.

I head to the kitchen for some more iced tea, and feeling hungry, make a peanut butter and honey sandwich. As I squeeze honey onto a slice of wheat bread, my brother's advice from the past fills my mind. "Write!" Ron would tell me whenever I'd complain about how difficult it can be to put words together in a way that conveys what you want to get across. I was on the high school newspaper committee, and some days I wondered why. "If you say you're a writer, then why aren't you writing?" Ron would say.

"Well, that is easier said than done."

Which always led him to reply, "Don't use clichés."

"You know, sometimes clichés are the only way to say something that is easily understood."

"The best writers avoid them."

"Oh, really?" With plans to major in journalism, I felt I was a "best writer."

"Yeah."

"What do you know?"

"A lot more than you, apparently."

I love Ron, in spite of his argumentative ways. He has an air about him that is refreshing. He's a magnet, pulling you in, and you always get the feeling he's arguing with you because he likes you. After all, he claims he only wastes his time arguing with people whose opinions he cares about. If you aren't important to him, he doesn't fritter away his time or words.

Ron went to Wake Forest University and now lives and works as a water ski instructor in Fort Lauderdale. Dad wonders how his degree in business administration helps him in the ocean, to which Ron replies that you always need a good business head in whatever you do. "My son plays from nine to five at the beach," Dad used to tell friends. "Can you believe he went to college so that he can do that?"

Last Christmas, Ron said to Dad, "Do you know how hard it is to teach a three-hundred-pound man to water ski?"

Our father just shook his head.

"I got him up and skiing, too. He almost capsized the boat, but he skied, thanks to my instruction." Ron was a little smug about it, but I think he made his point.

These days, Dad is more careful about criticizing Ron's line of work. When they're together, he and Ron like to play chess, a game of few words.

                                                              ◦ ◦ ◦

By the time the sun slips into a crimson-and-lavender western sky, I've not only finished composing the article about Davis, I've drifted into daydreaming about the Bailey House. The longing to enter its red door once again and walk on the Oriental carpets is so great that I consider heading over there to see if I can pry open a window. I should have asked Davis more questions. Instead, I acted like some sort of perky woman in love with her job and life, hiding the truth that on some days this very woman would sell her cherished fishermen's hat collection to own that house on Red Pelican Court.

9

Minnie prefers to drive when we go to the Morning Glory Home. Her silver Intrepid is a 2005, newer than my Ford, but I know that's not the reason she wants to drive. She feels since it's her mother we're going to see, she should pay for the gas. She also enjoys pounding the accelerator on the ride home from Nags Head to our duplex. I think it's her raw outlet after a visit, a demonstration of the frustration she feels over her mother's condition.

Minnie also likes to get to the home before lunch so that she can help feed Irvy. Just the other day as we were drying breakfast dishes, she said, "I should be taking care of Mama."

"You are."

"She's in a home." Her eyes were red at the rims. I wasn't sure if she'd been crying or if her allergies were getting to her.

"That is taking care of her," I said.

"I should visit her more."

"You do every week." I tried to reassure her that she's a good daughter.

"Zane doesn't like the home." Minnie gently wiped a plate and put it on a shelf with other dishes we moved over from her mother's house.

"Zane is going through a phase of hating germs."

"The place is clean."

"Yeah, but it smells funny. Like disinfectant."

"I've told him that takes care of the germs."

"It doesn't help when you tell him that." I wanted to say that Zane whines about many things, that perhaps she needs to be stricter with the child, but I stopped myself. I concentrated on drying a cereal bowl instead and put it away in the cabinet. What did I know? Minnie and Zane moved in shortly after Lawrence's death to have a cheap place to live, not for me to be the disciplinarian.

"I hate that Mama finally got a grandchild and yet she can't play with him."

Minnie has said this before, and I never have a good response. She and Lawrence tried for four years to have a child. Minnie never gave up hope; her own mother and father tried for ten years, and when they were both forty-four, they welcomed Minnie, their first and only child, into their lives.

Sometimes Minnie wears guilt and remorse like heavy jewelry. Today the necklace called Mama is causing her neck to turn blue. I want to take it off her neck, rub her shoulders, and tell her that things will get better.

We drop off Zane at Uncle Ropey and Aunt Beatrice Lou's. Zane perks up when my aunt says she's going to take him to the library in her yellow truck.

"We'll pick out books about trucks," she says in the same magical tone she uses when reading *The Little Engine That Could* during the library's story hour.

With a smile, Zane rushes to give his mother a good-bye hug.

The spring day is breezy, the clouds are like cotton puffballs, and I'm feeling content as we drive toward the home in Nags Head. I replay my discussion with Davis in my head. He likes John Wayne movies and old homes. He has a twenty-foot runabout boat that is brand-new, just purchased last month. He plays golf with the mayor of Hatteras once a month, and his hero is Manex Jethro, a musician who lived in poverty in Columbus until he made his big break as a songwriter and performer just nine years ago. I've never heard of Mr. Jethro, but Davis spoke like this guitarist reached for the sky and, due to his strong tenor voice and a heap of hard work, obtained his dream.

When we are a few miles from the nursing home, Minnie interrupts my thoughts. "Zane is acting a little better at being away from me these days."

I wonder if I've ever sat through an entire John Wayne movie. To Minnie, I say, "Maybe Zane's growing up."

We cross over the Oregon Inlet Bridge that takes us from the island to Nags Head, the water sparkling like a jewelry store beneath us. I love living in this area. I would not want to live anywhere else. The ocean and sky never seem to stop, giving you a feeling that there is always more to see, and more to experience.

But once we pull into the parking lot of the nursing home, my stomach starts to feel like a boulder has lodged itself between my small and large intestine. I fake a smile when Minnie looks at me as we make our way to the front entrance of the brick building with black shutters.

When we enter through the wide glass doors of the building, the smell of boiled potatoes, turnip greens, Pine-Sol, and L. J. greet us.

L. J. wears a perfume that's sweet, like Minnie and I wore in high school for school dances. She's one of the members of All That Glitters

Is Gold, my aunt Sheerly's senior citizens' band. Often she and the others give little concerts at the home, but today she's volunteering by helping the staff.

When the white-haired gentleman in a wheelchair complains she's pushing too fast, she says, "Now, Handsome, you are just too young to be complaining like an old man." She bends to pick up a handkerchief that a small wrinkled woman mobilized by a walker has dropped.

The woman takes the handkerchief and tucks it into a large pocket in the front of her gingham dress. "Thank you," she says to L. J. She then looks at me and mumbles, "Thank you."

"Irvy's by the piano," L. J. says to us before maneuvering the man around a corner. "I think she knew you'd be here. She's in good spirits today."

Sure enough, a thin woman in turquoise slippers and a matching robe sits in her wheelchair by the baby grand piano. Her right hand moves from the blue crocheted blanket on her lap to her mouth when she sees Minnie and me approach. Her mouth is open, droopy on the left side. A light moan releases from her throat.

Minnie hugs her mother, runs fingers down her sparse gray hair, and kisses her cheek.

From an abandoned card table, I pull over two folding chairs. I place a chair on either side of the wheelchair, and we sit down, Minnie on the right and me on the left.

Minnie says that within minutes of getting to the nursing home she can tell whether her mother is having a talkative or a silent day. She claims she can tell just by looking in Irvy's eyes. Regardless of whether Irvy wants to converse or just grip the edge of her blanket with her good hand, she rarely makes sense to me. Ever since her stroke four years ago, I haven't been able to understand her speech.

One and a half million dollars, I think to myself. *Can a person like me get a loan for that much money?*

Minnie's bracelets clink against each other as she reaches for Irvy's right hand. "Mama, how are you?"

Irvy's mouth moves in slow motion. "The farm is in Cary."

"Yes," Minnie tells her and quickly smiles. "Mama, do you want to go outside for a while?"

Irvy looks past her; her right eye twitches. "The farm is in Cary."

This is one of Irvy's favorite lines. There's another one she repeats whenever she's driven from the home across the inlet bridge to Sheerly's for Sunday dinner. Irvy never says a word until Uncle Ropey crosses the bridge and then, always at the same spot, just as the tires of his car hit the road again, she blurts out from the backseat, "I heard that they got married on a pontoon boat."

Uncle Ropey has heard this so many times, he is always ready with an answer. This varies from, "Well, it was about time" to "Really now? I would rather get married on a canoe."

"Mama, you look nice," Minnie says.

Irvy's lips find each other after a couple attempts, and something resembling a smile forms across her face.

When Minnie talks with one of the nurses, Irvy and I are alone.

I shift in my seat, feeling like Zane must when he gets a haircut at Sheerly's salon. Desperately, I try to see the face of the woman I knew as a child, the one who entertained us with Frank Sinatra songs on her piano. After our visits at the Bailey House, we'd walk to Minnie's cottage on the ocean side of the town. From the front yard, we'd hear Irvy playing and singing at the piano. Quietly, we'd slip inside the front door, trying not to rattle the doorknob that had a tendency to sound like BBs rolling inside a tin can. Sometimes a student would be seated on the bench beside Irvy; sometimes Irvy sat alone with new sheet music. She frequented the music shop in Manteo and particularly liked to buy selections from movie soundtracks. *Casablanca* and *The King and I* were two of her favorites.

"Hair done at Sheerly's," Irvy tells me as a pool of saliva runs down her chin.

I nod. I want to wipe her chin, but I don't have a tissue or anything with me.

"Sheerly does my hair." Talking is labor for her.

My eyes focus on a bruise on her wrist, purple lined with avocado green. It looks like a butterfly, one wing shorter than the other.

Minnie is back now, taking her seat.

I let my hands relax.

"Take me to Sheerly's," Irvy demands.

"She's coming here, Mama." Minnie finds a tissue in her purse—she keeps a pack in there for these occasions—and gently clears away the wetness from her mother's face. "She doesn't want you to travel. She'll fix your hair here."

A long pause, and I'm aware of movement around me. A silver-haired woman in a cotton duster is looking under my chair for her glasses. "I lost them, Annabelle." Her thin, spotty face is inches from mine. She lets out a breath, and my senses are saturated with antiseptic mouthwash. "Annabelle, do you see them?"

I have been called many things in my life but never by this name. Bending down, I glance under my chair. "Nope."

The woman looks at Minnie and then gestures toward Irvy. "Has anyone seen my glasses?"

An attendant in medical-green scrubs searches with her. "Are you sure, Miss Williams, that you were by the piano when you misplaced them?" he asks as his hands slide over the bench.

I feel like I do when Zane is looking for his stuffed squirrel—wanting to hurry and find the critter so I can be released from the frustration of its being lost.

The attendant ushers Miss Williams away from us, telling her that the missing glasses might be in her room.

"I want to get out of here." Irvy's right arm starts to sway with short, jerky movements.

Minnie uses her soothing voice. With fingers stroking her mother's arm, she says, "You like it here, Mama. You like the liver and onions."

"Yes, I do."

"Then you need to stay."

Irvy's eyes shut, she groans, and then, "Are they for lunch today?"

"Yes, liver and onions."

Her mouth continues to move, more saliva along her chin. Minnie wipes it with the tissue.

Irvy asks, "With banana puddin'?"

"Uh-huh."

"Yella banana puddin'."

"Yes."

After a measurable pause, Irvy says, "Not the brown kind."

"You mean applesauce."

"No, I want puddin'!"

"Yes, yes, I know."

She twists in her wheelchair. "I . . . I . . . I . . ." Her fluffy slippers have come off her feet.

"There, now," says Minnie.

Soon Minnie's mom is asleep, her wrinkled mouth open like a banana slice.

The attendant named Dicey covers Irvy's limbs with a faded pink quilt and then fits Irvy's feet back into her slippers and snuggles them into the constraints of the wheelchair's footholds.

Minnie tells Dicey that she guesses she won't be feeding Mama today. Once, she woke her mother from a nap, and Irvy was so disoriented that Minnie vowed never to do that again. Dicey smiles and says, "We'll take good care of Miss Irvy. Don't you worry your head, now."

When Minnie and I open the glass door to exit the home, the sunshine greets us with a blast of stifling heat. Normally, I'd feel bothered by the sudden humidity, especially after being in a building that was cool—but not now. I want to run, just to prove that I am agile enough to be free from the home's gray walls and brown doors, a place congested with geriatric confinement. I flex my arms a few times and in the reflection of a parked Cadillac check my hair. Still black, coarse. There is no graying or balding. I take my brush from my purse, enjoying the way the bristles run down my strands, making my hair full of life. Being almost thirty isn't bad at all today.

Inside Minnie's car, I fasten my seat belt. As she backs the Intrepid out of the driveway, I recite my verb tenses. Leave, leaving, left. Go, going, gone. The home makes Zane afraid of germs. I just like to make sure my brain still works. I roll down the window and fill my lungs with pine mulch that is being spread around a nearby hotel's grounds, the scent of turnip greens and boiled potatoes far behind.

"That wasn't too bad, now was it?" Minnie heads south on Route 12.

"No." Sorry, Mom, but I will not tell the whole truth right now.

As we continue toward the inlet bridge, I try to ignore the fact that she's following a pickup much too closely. My palms begin to sweat. Before I can say a word, the truck stops, Minnie's foot slams the brake, and we both lurch forward.

I gasp.

The truck makes a left turn; Minnie accelerates. "Why people can't use their turn signals is beyond me."

I find my breath as we pass a twenty-five-miles-per-hour speed limit sign.

Moments later, I see a tear making its way down my friend's check.

"Minnie, she is so lucky to have you." I let my words come out like a lullaby for a toddler who needs assurance that the world is safe.

She stares at a battered Buick with a Kentucky license plate in front of us. "Will you play the flute?"

We are now on the bridge, and I can see beaches dotted with people and lined with an array of billowy umbrellas and colorful chairs. Closer to us are clusters of fishermen with rods waiting for the perfect catch of the day.

"The flute?"

"At her funeral."

I almost say that she should not think this way, that her mother is not going to die, that she'll be giving piano lessons again in no time. But that's not the truth, either.

"Yes," I say and feel tears bite the backs of my eyes.

" 'Jesus Loves Me' would be good."

That's one of the first songs Irvy taught Minnie on the piano.

I find my voice. "I can do that."

"Thanks." She sniffs twice, then, "No backing out."

10

My dad started me on making lists, informing me that life goes smoother when you can read what you need to do.

Today's to-do list has the words *buy flowers* on the top. I know just the kind I want to buy for Minnie. She's always been fond of pink roses; there were vases of them at her wedding, and they were in her bridal bouquet.

Last night when I got up to go to the bathroom, wishing I hadn't drunk three glasses of iced tea at dinner, I heard muffled weeping from Minnie's bedroom. I paused at her door to listen. I considered knocking to see what was wrong, but the noise soon decreased. My desire to go back to a warm bed overruled.

This morning I woke with two thoughts on my mind. The first was that my article about Davis and his realty business is due on Selena's desk by five today. The second was the reason Minnie was crying last night. Today is an anniversary that no one wants to have on his or her calendar. A year ago Lawrence died when an angry sea capsized his fishing boat.

When Minnie leaves for her shift at Over the Edge, she lets me know that this afternoon she'll be at Sheerly's. This is a job I got for my friend when she confided in me about her need for another part-time job in order to pay her part of the rent. Minnie isn't licensed to cut hair, but she sweeps it up with the broom, makes hair appointments, collects payments, and orders hair care products. She says Sheerly is easy to work for and always sings or hums. "And the things I learn about everybody there," she says in a hushed voice. "Sheerly's clients love to share . . . a lot of stuff." My guess is that being at Sheerly's is like reality TV—much too revealing and always predictable.

After a lunch of ham sandwiches and chips, it's evident that Zane and I need to get out of the duplex. Zane is irritated about something; I can tell by the way he bangs his trucks together. The large yellow Tonka continues to collide with the smaller one as Zane shouts, "Crash, boom, you are dead!" He spells dead, only he leaves out a letter and repeats, "You are d-a-d. Dead."

The day is sunny with little humidity, a good one to run some errands. Minnie has remembered to leave his car seat for me. I take the boy with me to drop off an article at the *Lighthouse Views* office. When we get inside the office, Selena isn't in. Bert tells me that she went to talk to the owner of some new health club. Cassidy says she's lost two pounds and fourteen ounces since Monday. I congratulate her and then tell Zane, who has made his way into the men's room, to hurry. He calls from inside the restroom, "I'll only be a minute."

When he appears at the door to the men's room, I notice that the zipper on his shorts is undone. "Zane," I say, "you need to zip up your fly."

"Where's a fly?" His eyes scan over my head.

"Your fly. That's another word for zipper."

He looks down and says, "I don't see a fly," but he does zip up the gap in his shorts. Then he burps, and when I tell him he needs to say excuse me, he only burps louder.

Under her breath, Cassidy asks me, "Who does he belong to?"

"I live with him." I force a smile. "We have lots of fun."

She looks alarmed. "Does he have a mother?"

"Yes, Cassidy. You know Minnie."

She gives a tentative nod. Then she confesses that she's so hungry she could eat five burgers from the Grille.

"Want me to order you takeout while I'm there?" I ask.

"I wish. Gotta drink some water and maybe then the craving will go away."

"What about mints?" I ask. Ropey went through a whole box of Life Savers when he was on a diet. "Will some of them help?"

"The sugar-free ones are allowed on my diet. But I ate them all yesterday."

There are days that I'm grateful to be five-feet-ten with a high metabolism. "Good luck," I tell her as Zane and I leave to drive to the restaurant.

Zane says, "Good luck. Be careful of germs." He thinks this is a funny line and laughs all the way to the parking lot.

"I'm funny," he tells me as I strap him into his car seat.

"You think?"

"Yeah." His laugh reminds me of chimpanzees at the zoo.

I remember the day Minnie called to say she was pregnant. I was in my Charlotte apartment on Commonwealth Avenue, watching a car outside my window try to parallel park when my cell rang. Without any preliminaries, all I heard was, "I'm going to have a baby! I'm going to have a baby!" Minnie was on the verge of hyperventilating, she was so excited. "At last! I'd given up hope. Oh, Jackie, oh, Jackie, can you believe it?"

The car I was watching at the time was not as blessed. I saw it scrape the fender of another car, and then end up on the curb, its passenger door dented by a telephone pole.

Inside the Grille, I enjoy Buck's comical banter with Betty Lynn as I sip my Diet Pepsi. Zane spins around on the barstool next to me.

"Do you know that Buck is an artist?" Betty Lynn asks me when she comes over after filling four glasses with sweet iced tea.

"He is?"

Before she heads off with her tray, Betty Lynn says, "He paints with acrylics. We might even put one of his pictures on the wall here, right, Buck?"

Suddenly, I realize Zane is not happy with his Mountain Dew, or as he calls it, "Mountain Doom." He's tossed the straw paper onto the floor and crumpled the straw with his fingers so that it resembles an earthworm in Sheerly's garden.

With a bottom lip curved over the upper one, he sits with eyes closed. I hear the hissing in his throat rapidly make its way to his mouth. "I want . . . I want . . . I want a milkshake!"

"Zane." I'm amazed that this little creature seated next to me on a barstool, his chin just above the counter, could own such a booming cry.

A man with dark hair and eyes that flash *handsome* is seated at the end of the counter near a New Orleans poster that has a shot of Bourbon Street. In a pleasant voice, he calls Buck over for a refill and orders a bacon cheeseburger. I hear this man asking if the burger can be well done.

Quietly, I say to Zane, "Drink your soda." I smile, hoping somehow this gesture will make Zane behave.

"But I want a milkshake!"

"Zane, your inside voice. Please."

"I do, I do, I do!"

I stare into my Pepsi. Maybe if I ignore him, his attitude will go away.

Buck strides over to us. "Hi, Zane." His smile lights his whole face.

"I want a milkshake! Get me one." Zane's eyes are pits of fire. "Now!"

With calmness, I state, "Your mom said you couldn't have one right now."

"Why?" His throat has to hurt from yelling. My ears ache from listening. "Why?"

"Because she said so." I have to do better on my child psychology.

"Zane," says Buck, touching the child's arm. When he has Zane's attention, he continues. "Do you like boats? Big boats? Would you like to go on a ride?" Tenderness fills the man's voice as he says, "Maybe one day we could take a picnic and ride on a boat."

Fear hits the boy's eyes like a tidal wave. "No!"

I want to stop Buck somehow as he continues with the boat theme. "Boats are fun, aren't they?"

"No!" Zane wails. "No!"

Everyone in the restaurant is focused on this child, even the handsome man with the burger. I feel dozens of eyes staring at this scene we are making. I know they think that I'm the adult responsible for him; some may even think I'm his mother. They want me to make him shut up. I just want to sink into the floor.

Zane twitches on the stool and then slides off of it. "No!" He heads toward the dining area, the lights from the soles of his tennis shoes shooting off tiny beams.

I rush after Zane, stop him right before he collides with Betty

Lynn. Betty Lynn doesn't seem bothered by the commotion. She leans over toward my right ear and whispers, "Jackie, I want to introduce you—"

Grabbing Zane's hand firmly as his squeals sound higher pitched than a swarm of seagulls that have found tasty prey, I tell Betty Lynn we are leaving. Now. Then I push open the front door, welcome the sunshine, and don't look back.

Somehow we make it across the parking lot. "I want my daddy!" Zane yells as I open the passenger door for him and help him into his car seat. I fumble with the restraint around his waist. "I want to see him!"

Breathing deeply, I nod. Although I'm embarrassed by Zane's outburst and wish Buck hadn't continued talking to him about boats, I can't blame Buck. He doesn't realize that Zane hates any mention of boats. Buck has most likely forgotten that Zane's father died on a fishing boat.

Once Zane is strapped in, I settle into the driver's seat. A sigh escapes my lungs as I let relief bathe me. Although the truck is baking under an afternoon sun, it takes me a while to turn on the engine and the air-conditioner. Once I do, I take a long look at the little boy in his car seat beside me. Sweat beads dot his nose. Tears stain his glowing cheeks. I don't know whether to scold him or pat his hand.

"My daddy bought me milkshakes."

I think back to Minnie and Lawrence's wedding, which was held at Hatteras Christian Assembly Church. Lawrence made sure all the guests were taken care of. "Now go back for more wedding cake, Ms. Sheerly," he told my aunt a number of times. "We are celebrating today without any diets!" To which Sheerly had obliged and loaded another slice of the chocolate cream cake with the tiny toy bride and groom on the top tier. When she and her friends later sang love songs to the blissful couple, there were flecks of chocolate on her peach suit.

I have happy memories from that day, and I'm glad Zane has happy memories of milkshakes.

I lean back in my seat, grateful for the semi-cool air blowing through the vents. "I miss your daddy, too."

Zane glares at me as his arms cross his chest. "You didn't know him."

"I did."

"Then what was his favorite color?" He squints.

My memory takes me to a green tie Lawrence often wore to church on Sunday. "Green." I make my voice soft. "Like your eyes."

"He liked yellow."

I have no memory of Zane's father favoring this color, but I say, "Yes, of course. Yellow was a color he liked a lot."

"The bestest?"

I nod. "The bestest."

Zane wipes the back of his hand over his nose and sniffs. "Okay, I guess you did know him, then."

I reach over and pat Zane's dry hand. As my fingers touch his skin, he grabs my thumb. Our eyes lock, and I do what I never thought I would.

I hug this fretful, sad child.

He lets me. The next thing I know, his arms have lifted and his hands circle my head, fluffing my hair just like he does to the fur of his stuffed squirrel, Popacorn.

The drive home is silent except for the rumble of my truck's tires over the narrow road, the air-conditioning wheezing through the vents, and the sound of Zane sucking his thumb.

11

When my mother calls, Zane has fallen asleep on the living room floor, breathing softly. His head rests against Popacorn's dirty fur, fingers clutching one of the stuffed paws. His mouth curves under a button nose, and his eyelids are like rose petals—delicate and velvet. If you didn't know any differently, you could think this little boy was an angel.

Passing him, I make my way upstairs with light steps, talking in a low tone to my mother until I get into my bedroom and close the door. "Mom, how did you put up with Ron and me?" I blurt.

She laughs. "I think to myself, they are adults, they are on their own."

"No, when we were Zane's age."

"Zane." My mother says his name like it's a virus. "What he doing? Bad boy again?"

"Just answer, please." I rub my temple, hoping to alleviate the pain.

"I give you lots of timeouts in bear chair. You remember?"

I do remember that chair, always placed in the corner of the den in our house in Nags Head. I hated being sent to it, but I knew that when Mom said I must go, there was no point in disobeying. Ron, on the other hand, was able to miss many deserved sessions in that chair. He was sneaky, rarely got caught. He never stood in front of Mom, telling her he wanted a chocolate cookie right now, right this very minute, or he was going to run away to Mexico.

"Zane is driving you crazy? What he done now?" My mother's escalating voice doesn't soothe my headache.

"Well. . . ." I wonder where to start.

"Where is his mother?"

"Minnie works a lot."

"She needs to stop work and grow up with her child."

"She needs money."

"Where is her father? Grandparents? Why they not help? Grandparents are supposed to help out."

Minnie's father hasn't been part of her life since she was sixteen. As Sheerly tells her customers, one day this man "literally up and left."

"She has no living grandparents," I say to my mother.

"Oh, what happened to Minnie grandparents?"

"They died."

"Died?"

"Mom, they were old. Irvy is seventy-four years old now." I picture Irvy taking a nap in her wheelchair, her knees covered by the crocheted blanket, her arms weak and flat against her sides.

"Hard to believe so much time go by so quickly."

I sigh. Mom and Dad used to live here in Nags Head, but since they moved back to Charlotte when Dad took an accounting position with a small firm, they've lost touch with those of us who still wake each day to the coastal sun.

"You need bear chair for Zane? Give him timeouts?" I hear pages rustling and know exactly what my mother is doing. She is the most avid coupon clipper in Charlotte.

"You still have it?"

"In the attic." The sound of scissors cutting paper enters my ear along with her voice. She never rips out those money-saving squares, always cuts carefully on the dotted lines. "I keep there for memory." Then she says, "I don't want to get blind and deaf."

"What?" I'm surprised by the change in subject.

She goes into a story about her sister in Korea buying the wrong spices to make *kimchi*. She claims that her sister is going blind and deaf. She uses the Korean words for the spices, even though I know she knows I haven't a clue what they are.

"How would you cut coupons if you couldn't see?" I ask her.

The attempt at levity slides over her head. "I save ton of money."

"I know you do." I end the call then and head to the kitchen to make dinner.

When Minnie comes home at seven, she carries a vase of pink and gold Gerber daisies. "Sheerly gave these to me." Mechanically, she walks over to the kitchen sink to put water in the vase. "She remembered that today's the day . . ." Placing the vase on the counter, she reaches for the bottle of Rizatriptan, her prescribed migraine medication.

I think of my to-do list and realize that with Zane's outburst, I have failed to do what I wanted to do.

We eat in near silence; I consume the remorse of having failed Minnie once again. I was planning to tell her about Zane and his behavior at the Grille, possibly tell her that she needs to invest in a book on discipline, but decide that I'll wait until a less significant day. Zane begs for more macaroni and cheese and then asks if he has to eat the *yucky* cucumbers in the tossed salad.

Minnie only stares at the salt shaker, so I tell him he doesn't have to and add another helping of the cheesy macaroni I made to his plate.

I clean up the kitchen with calculated slowness, and then head to my bedroom. I plan to absorb the rest of my evening in editing my interview with Davis Erickson.

Later, Zane comes in to give me a good-night kiss. The wetness from it is still on my cheek when Minnie enters my bedroom. I'm stretched out on my double bed, taking a break from looking over the printed pages about Rexy Properties, how Davis got into the realty business, and what he likes to do for fun. Selena likes my interviews to make our readers feel that the business proprietors we feature are real people with "heart and soul." With that in mind, I've added that Davis enjoys boating and playing golf. His favorite meal is a rib eye with a baked potato. The guitarist Manex Jethro is his inspiration.

He certainly sounded interesting during our phone conversation, and I think I've captured some of that in my piece, so Selena should be pleased. But when I see Minnie all I can think about is the price he gave me for the Bailey House and how we'll never be able to afford it. If Mr. and Mrs. Bailey were still living, I bet they'd just *give* it to us, the way they always gave us afternoon snacks on scented napkins.

Minnie stands at my opened door and says, "I found a bed and breakfast we could get." She enters my room, closes the door so that Zane won't hear us. "I saw it online. It's called The Lexington Manor." She sits at my computer, her bracelets clicking as her fingers race across the keyboard, bringing up the Web site for me to see. "See?"

I turn my head toward the screen.

"Come on over and see it. Look, it's nice." Her enthusiasm surprises me. Isn't today her day to be sad, not focusing on a dream for the future but a dream that died a year ago?

I make my way to the foot of the bed, peer at a house shaded by pine trees, and then read the location. "Minnie, it's in Hendersonville!"

"I know."

"What would we do there?" I back away from the screen.

"Where?"

"In Hendersonville. That's like five hundred miles away from here."

"We'd run the place. We'd move there."

And leave Hatteras? Sheerly, Tiny, Ropey, and Beatrice Lou?

"What if this is what God has in mind for us? Not the Bailey House, but this place instead? Come on, take a look."

Now that Minnie is bringing the Almighty into this, I move closer to the computer to study the photos. The house is a quaint-looking Victorian framed by Carolina pine trees. A range of deep blue mountains fills the background along the horizon.

Minnie hits the virtual tour button, and magically, we are taken through a slide show of the four bedrooms. "Look, here's the Andrew Jackson Room, the James Polk Room, the William Hooper Room, and the Richard Caswell Room." Like a tour guide, she announces each as it appears in front of us. "I know Caswell was our first governor, but who was Hooper?"

"Signer of the Declaration of Independence," I say. I know this because Bert told me, as well as the fact that Hooper was buried in a cemetery in Hillsborough.

Pictures of other rooms in the house pop onto the screen. Elegant hardwood spreads over the parlor floor. A chandelier hangs over a dining room table. I take in all the embroidered pillows and quilts, the Williamsburg blue tableware spread out on a pine table where sunlight filters through the French doors in the almond-and-ivory-striped wallpapered dining room. There are three slides of high-ceilinged

porches with marble statues of bears and eagles placed between birch
rocking chairs.

"Isn't it beautiful?" Minnie turns from the screen to smile at me.

The James Polk Room has bright green carpet, and the king-
sized wrought-iron bed looks lumpy, as if there's something hiding
underneath the white eyelet spread. To the left of the antique desk
is a wicker basket with a spotted cow sticking out of it. "Did Polk
like cows?" I ask.

"What?"

I want to like this place. I do. But I don't feel that bubbling excitement that swims through my veins when I see or think about the
Bailey House.

"Look at the price." Minnie's voice gushes like she's just found
the cure for her migraines.

There it is in black numbers, a mere $695,000. A little over half
a million.

"It's not what we want, Minnie." Surely God does not have this
place in mind for us, does He?

"Why not?" There is boldness in her voice, a quality that unsettles
my stomach. She doesn't sound like the same woman who was crying
in her room last night. And I don't want to take this excitement away
from her. "Look, it's as big as the Bailey House. Over five thousand
square feet."

"But we don't have any connections to this place."

"We could start over. You know, move to the mountains. Get
away from this ocean." Today, of all days, I know she would rather
not have to face the ocean with its strong waves and deep waters.

I shake my head. "Do you know how long it would take for you
to get to the Morning Glory Home from Hendersonville?"

"Hours, I know." She sighs. "But isn't the location so quaint and serene?"

She's using words I've used to describe the Bailey House over the years. I note the blue mountains, then view the green carpet and the stuffed cow once more as Minnie speeds through the virtual tour.

Minnie looks at me.

I want to conceal it, but a frown takes over my whole face.

Sighing again, she whispers, "Okay, just a thought."

I've been too hard on her. I change my tone. "You remember the sermon last week about waiting, trusting God, and not giving up?" I stroke her hand like she does her mother's.

"Yeah, that was a good one." She leaves then. Closes the door behind her as if it's a boulder she's having trouble moving. Minnie, forceful and strong, has just crawled back to meek and sad.

I want to tell her to come back, that I was going to buy her pink roses on this day, that I love her, and that I'm just so sorry about everything.

Instead, I sit there on the edge of my bed and dab at a tear that has dribbled down my chin. I know where I want to go. Right now, it's the only thing I can think of that I won't botch up.

I could drive blindfolded; my truck knows the route.

The sun lingers in the sky while cumulus clouds display bands of violet, turquoise, and marigold as I follow the narrow route to the Bailey House.

As I pull into the driveway, I see another car there. I park behind the white BMW convertible and get out of my truck. A tall, dark-haired man emerges from the back garden. "Hello," he says, latching the gate and making his way toward me. "Nice to see you again."

12

I've never seen this man before, although his looks are quite impressive. Could I have dreamed about him once? Perhaps he was the hero in the dream where a man rescued me from hurricane winds as I was about to topple off the dock by Aunt Sheerly and Uncle Tiny's house and be devoured by a giant shark. Uncle Ropey warned me to be careful about coming out to the Bailey House alone. At night. Minnie reminds me that every woman should never be far from a can of Mace. Cautiously, gripping my keys, I say, "Again?"

"At the Grille." His smile lights up his deep brown eyes.

I just look at him.

Still smiling, he clarifies, "With the little boy."

"Oh!" I'm sure that my face turns the color of the Bailey House's front door. "I . . . um . . . yeah . . . well." Recalling those disastrous moments of my life this afternoon makes it hard to smile. This must be that good-looking man who ordered a well-done bacon cheeseburger.

Moving toward me, he extends his hand. "Davis Erickson."

I paste on a tiny smile and shake his warm, large hand. Mine feels small. "Jackie Donovan."

I can tell he's thinking because there's a pause. "You interviewed me?"

"I did."

"Well," he says, "nice to finally meet you." He speaks with such enthusiasm, as if I've made his day. He's wearing a dark blue suit. A white shirt and maroon tie peer out from the silky material. He looks like he either came from a business meeting or is on his way to one.

"I love this house," I say like a kid admits she loves Santa Claus.

"I remember you told me that on the phone when you asked about the cost."

"Yeah, I just hope that the money tree in the backyard has plenty of million-dollar bills growing out of it."

I sound silly, but Davis actually seems amused by me. He gives me a wide smile and says, "The owners want to make sure that if anyone ever runs it again they keep to their wishes."

"What are their wishes? Aren't the Baileys dead?"

"They both died a few years back."

"I loved coming here as a child. Mr. and Mrs. Bailey were the kindest people."

"You knew them?" He sounds slightly shocked.

I smile. "They were a lovely couple," I say in my finest British accent.

"They were. Great people."

With nostalgia filling every ounce of air around us, I say, "I'd like to be the one to bring this place back to its former beauty and charm."

"Would you?" He studies my face. There is another pause as I note that his eyes are, in a word, gorgeous. He then says, "Would you like to talk about it sometime over dinner?"

"Oh!" I wonder what he means exactly. Like a date? Or a business meeting? "Well, uh . . ." This time, I'm the one who sounds slightly shocked.

"How about Friday?"

"Well . . ." I have no idea if my calendar on my desk at work has anything on it for this Friday. I hope not.

"Can I call you?"

My mouth feels dry. "Sure."

"Cell phone okay?" His smile makes my heart race with all things intriguing. "I think I have that number from our interview."

I realize that it's my turn to speak. "That's fine."

When he leaves me alone with the Bailey House, I walk the premises with a grin that eventually makes my mouth feel stretched. "Davis Erickson," I say to the honeysuckle bushes and pull off a flower. Holding the bloom against my nose, I breathe.

I buy an ice-cream sandwich at the Stop-N-Go on my way home. The taste takes me back to childhood. Back when life was dreaming about things to come and believing that if you really wanted something bad enough, it could and would be yours. I remember praying for a bike for Christmas, and there it was. We prayed for Minnie's gerbil to live and it did. Later, in high school, I asked God for guidance about where to go to college, and that very day, like a kite floating straight from heaven, the acceptance letter came from UNC-Charlotte.

The ice cream provides the sweet treat I craved; I wipe my mouth with my fingers, removing the chocolate cookie crumbs from my face. I've never been able to eat ice cream without getting it all over myself.

When I get home, Minnie is crying behind her bedroom door. I stand at the solid mass of wood, my hand ready to knock. I then let my hand fall to my side and walk to my room, feeling like a traitor having enjoyed time at the Bailey House, meeting Davis, the promise of a date with him, and ice cream. A real friend would have stayed home and held her hand.

I feel guilty that I've been reminiscing about answered prayer when, after his boat capsized and Lawrence was thrown overboard, no amount of praying in the ICU helped him come out of his vegetative state and breathe on his own again. I would have forgone my bike, my college acceptance, and the life of the gerbil to give Lawrence a future with his wife and child.

In my bedroom, I put on my sleeping gear—an oversized T-shirt that Minnie gave me for Christmas years ago, back when we were both single. She commented how she liked the frilly nightgowns and how I liked the practical. "I've got my head in the clouds, and you're practical," she'd said with a smile as the lights from her Christmas tree twinkled. "And I like that practical side of you."

I run my hand over the green lettering across the front that reads, "A friend is a gift you give yourself."

"Minnie," I say minutes later at her closed door, my voice just above a whisper.

When the door opens, she's in her scarlet nightgown with the lacy bodice.

"I just met the Realtor from the Bailey Place, and we're going out to talk about the house."

She nods and tries for a smile that never quite surfaces.

I'm tempted to say how good-looking he is, but it doesn't feel right to do that on a day that holds such weight for Minnie. So I just hug her instead.

With her arms around me, she mumbles, "I was remembering how Lawrence liked to dance with me barefoot on the driveway."

"I'm sorry that I didn't buy flowers for you today."

I'm relieved to see her face of forgiveness; I leave before tears find my eyes. Then I lie in bed watching shadows weave across my walls until, at last, sleep rests against my shoulders and welcomes me into her oblivion.

⁓ ⁓

The interview is spread across pages thirty-two and thirty-three of our July issue, with a photo of Davis and his office in the top right-hand corner. Cassidy took the photo; she's the one with the camera skills. She went to his office one day and got five shots, even though she had to wait twenty minutes for him to come back from a meeting. Cassidy is used to sitting around in office waiting areas with her Nikon, killing time by texting her friends on her cell phone. She says people forget a lot of things in life, like forgetting to pick up milk on the way home from work, whether or not they've turned the coffeepot off before leaving their house, or scheduled appointments to get their picture taken.

In the picture we decided to use to accompany my article, Davis looks dazzlingly handsome, his wavy hair matching his eyes. I run my finger along his left cheekbone.

"You want the other photos for your bedside table?" Cassidy whispers to me and then winks. She's eating a fruit bar and mumbles that she detests dieting.

"How much more weight do you want to lose?" I ask.

"Three and a half more pounds. I just hope it doesn't all come back on me once I quit."

I'm nearly out the door to the office when I hear Bert's voice call out, "Hey . . . Jackie!"

I turn toward him as he lifts his head from a stack of notebooks on his desk. "Good job."

I suppose he's complimenting me on the interview with Davis. Or possibly the interview with Brenda at the car wash. Selena didn't think the car wash interview was classy enough for our publication, but I replied that if a Mercedes or Porsche goes through a car wash, then it's classy enough for me.

"Thanks," I tell Bert, whose head is now under his desk, searching for a lost pen, no doubt. Bert often drops pens, and many times I've seen him on his hands and knees, eyes to the carpet, determined to find his favorite writing pen. Usually he finds more than pens.

Today I hear him say, "Well, look at that," as he places a pair of scissors on top of his desk. "So that's where they went." He sits back on his leather swivel chair.

When I get to the Grille in the late afternoon, Betty Lynn tells me that she liked the article. "He's single, you know," she says. I know she means Davis.

Another young waitress comes by and says she read the article because Betty Lynn told her about it. "You write real good," she says and then heads over to Buck to smile at him.

As I sip my Diet Pepsi and eat a plate of crisp fries, I wish Buck would come over and tell me what a great interview I did. He's had plenty of opportunity. Instead, he says, "Too bad your parents abandoned you."

My parents didn't abandon me, of course.

They met in Charlotte at a mutual friend's and were married in a little Korean church on Bright Street in 1971. All these years later, my father never tires of telling us that the day they were married the street was bright, the lights in the church were bright, the photographer's flash was bright, and yet, even with all that brightness, my mother outshined them all.

Right after my birth, and a year before Mom became pregnant with Ron, Dad's job with the accounting firm known as Morton and Stafford transferred him to Nags Head. There my parents bought a three-bedroom cottage and raised Ron and me, paid high homeowner's insurance rates, dealt with hurricanes and a few evacuations, ate Sunday dinners with Dad's side of the family, and were always looking for an excuse to leave permanently. The excuses came, and they were twofold. The first was that I'd left for college at UNC-Charlotte. The second was that during my freshman year, Dad's company merged with another. Under the new management, Dad was frustrated. So once Ron left the nest for his first year at Wake Forest, they needed no more prompting; the decision to move back to Charlotte was as clear as a summer sky. I was in Charlotte and so were their old friends. Plus, Charlotte being the financial capital of North Carolina meant it was a place where Dad could thrive. Dad found a bank to work for and started doing some consulting work on the side. Mom was now able to shop at the Korean food stores she had so missed in coastal North Carolina. Back with her Korean friends, the afternoons of drinking ginseng tea and eating sweet bean cakes stretched into the early evening as her laughter filled my parents' new home.

I finished my four years at UNC-Charlotte, worked at *The Daily Pulse*, all with the consuming desire to come back to the Hatteras area. Charlotte is a fine place if you want to live with traffic, construction, and noise. I don't want to sound too self-absorbed, but I feel that the ocean has my name on every one of her waves. Except for the violent hurricane waves; I won't be responsible for those. When

I heard that *Lighthouse Views* was looking for a columnist, I sent my resume to Selena Thomas. The day she hired me, I called Minnie to let her know I was coming back home, at last.

But Buck pretends that my parents left the Outer Banks and left me. I like to look at it as they came to be with me in Charlotte while I was in school, and then *I* left *them* to return to my roots.

Selena calls me on my cell phone, and to minimize distractions, I take the call outside. "Jackie," she says as I blink sunlight from my eyes. "Will you pick up paper plates on your way back to the office?"

"Sure."

"Hurry."

"Okay . . ." I wonder why paper plates are such an urgent need for my boss. She's usually good about honoring our lunch breaks without disturbance.

As though reading my mind, she chirps, "Blackberry cheesecake. It's from that new deli. If we like it, you can interview the owner."

As I head back into the Grille to pay my bill, Selena says, "Oh, and get forks, too. And toothpicks."

"Toothpicks?"

"You never know when you might need one." She lets out a low laugh and then disconnects me from her in typical Selena fashion.

13

Sheerly doesn't need to know about my date tonight, although I'm sure it won't be long until she finds out. This is one date she's had nothing to do with, and although I wouldn't admit it to her, I am more hopeful because this is not someone she has lined up for me. All day at the office, my mind focused on Davis Erickson.

I'm taking Zane to Ropey's. Minnie switched shifts with someone and is at the surf shop until nine, when the store closes. She says after that she'll pick up her son at Ropey's.

At six o'clock, Zane whines as we drive to my uncle's Sound-side home on Cactus Court. Zane sticks his lower lip over the top one, then yells at me that he wanted to stay at home. I tell him that we don't always get what we want.

Ropey greets us, slipping off the porch rocker just as my truck pulls into his driveway. He stands barefooted on the pavement smoking a cigar. Beatrice Lou is out at a board meeting at the library, he tells us. Ropey smiles at Zane and says that the two of them are going to have a great time as I unfasten Zane from the car seat. Immediately, like a ball that bounces off the ground, Zane takes off across the front lawn, running toward the back of the house.

I yell, "Zane! Get over here."

"Kid has a motor that won't quit," Ropey says with a puff of his cigar and another smile. He eyes my beige capri pants and heeled sandals. "Who is the lucky man tonight?"

"We better find Zane," I say, taking long strides to the backyard. I can't see or hear the child, and this sends a few extra beats through my heart.

Ropey follows as we make our way over the recently mowed grass, slivers of it strewn across the driveway and tucked inside the flowerbeds. I look in all directions over the riding lawn mower that is parked near the open garage, and then head into the dark, dank garage in case Zane is hiding in there. I call his name, listen, and, hearing nothing, head out into the sunlight once more. I paste on a smile for a neighbor three houses down who waves, but I don't see Zane. The Sound and pier are visible, and my heart rockets to my throat. No wonder Mrs. Bailey never wanted us near the water, I think, as the potential danger that lies within the waves grips my insides. I quickly scan the area, wanting to spot a blond-haired boy with way too much energy. I call his name, then walk closer toward the Sound, looking below at the marsh that stretches before it.

"Zane!" Ropey is by my elbow.

A barking dog switches my attention to the neighbors' home to the right of Ropey and Beatrice Lou's. I know their mutt isn't fond of children. Aunt Sheerly says that dog once chased a child up the drain spout and onto the roof, but I think she was in an embellishing mode.

Suddenly, we see a little boy nearing the fence that circles their aboveground blue swimming pool.

Motioning to Ropey, I march over to the house.

Zane's eyes meet mine when I get halfway to him. He yells, "No!"

"Get back here!" I cry, and that sets Zane running, away from the pool, and zigzagging back toward Ropey's yard.

Ropey, his face red and beaded with sweat, storms after the kid.

"No, no!" Zane flings his arms up and down, propelling himself once more toward the Sound.

Ropey is slow; the donuts and cigars have not helped.

Determined to end this charade, I dash ahead of Ropey, my feet twisting out of my shoes. I gain my balance and race to catch up to Zane. Right before he reaches the pier, I grab his arm, miss, and reach for it again. This time my fingers squeeze his elbow. He falls onto the ground, pulling me down. We tumble onto the grass, inches from the swampy marsh, breathing hard.

"Zane, you're a bad boy." I sound like my mother.

Ropey stands above us, his breath coming in short pants. Removing his glasses, he wipes them with a limp handkerchief. He places them back on, adjusts them, and says, "Got my exercise for the week." Then he extends his hand, and I take it.

Standing, I see that my capris are stained with grass. I move closer to Zane, and as I walk, a pain shoots up my right leg. Wincing, I say, "Zane, get up now."

"No. I don't want to."

I pull a blade of grass off my hair, brush at a green spot on the knee of my capris. Now I'll have to go home and change clothes. I don't even know if I have anything clean; my laundry basket is plump with dirty clothes in my closet.

Ropey helps Zane up and places his hands on the boy's shoulders. "Zane, you can't do that again."

"I can! I will!" His words are loud, yet he does not try to squirm away.

I try a calmer tone. "Zane, you can play with Ropey. Watch TV. It'll be fun."

"I want my mommy!"

"She'll be here soon. Just have fun playing."

There is a sob to his voice as Zane announces, "I want my daddy."

Ropey and I just look at each other.

"I'm leaving for a little while," I say.

"No." Now the child is clutching my hand, digging his short fingernails into my palm.

Anger rises to the point that I feel I could snort it out of my nostrils. The mounting pain in my leg consumes me. I push aside my own urge to sob. I grab Zane's hand and start to hobble toward my truck.

Ropey gives me a questioning look.

Forget the date. I feel worse than I did a month ago when Selena tore into my piece on the new barbecue restaurant by the Wright Brothers Museum.

"Zane, do you like to tie ropes? Can you use a glue gun?" Ropey is treading after us, trying to find a way to make Zane stay.

"I'm taking him home." I pull Zane along, picking up the pace.

"What about your date?" Ropey calls.

I shake my head.

At home, I send Zane to his room. After a large glass of iced tea, which cools my dry throat, I call Davis. "I'm sorry," I breathe. "I can't be there tonight."

"Why not?" Davis's voice holds concern.

"Remember Zane?"

"The boy?"

"That would be him. He's got some issues to deal with. He wouldn't stay with my uncle tonight while his mom is working." I omit the part about falling into the grass and hurting my leg.

After another glass of iced tea and three aspirin, I almost call my mother and ask her to FedEx me that bear chair. At this point, I'd like to glue Zane's little butt to it.

Maybe Zane is a normal kid and I'm just not cut out for children. Perhaps I should marry someone who doesn't want any children. We could be happy together and just roll our eyes when other couples' kids disobey or throw a tantrum. Ours could be the life that looks down on parents who let their children bump into strangers without offering apologies, parents who let their children dribble juice down high chairs in restaurants and then cram crackers into the crevices.

I call Minnie, tell her everything, ashamed that my annoyance shouts so loudly at her. Her sigh fills my ear through the phone.

"I'm sorry," she says. "I hate having to work these crazy hours. Jackie, it will get better, I promise. Once we own the bed and breakfast, everything will be better."

When she gets home at nine twenty, I'm in my room eating a bowl of Cocoa Puffs. I've let Zane eat a bowl in his room, as well. Minnie walks into Zane's room and firmly closes the door.

Davis calls me later when I'm almost asleep. The sound of his voice calms the rough edges, hemming me in. "We'll go out another time," he says. "There's a great Italian restaurant in Arlington."

"Arlington? As in outside of D.C.?"

"Yeah, it'd be fun to go there together one day, don't you think? My parents took me to northern Virginia a lot as a kid."

I try to imagine him as a child. I wonder if he raced across lawns or had to spend time in a bear chair. "Do you want children?" I ask. "I mean, ever?"

"Kids are better when they belong to you. Someone else's are rarely fun."

"But do you want kids?"

"Not right now," Davis says, making me laugh.

                                   ⌒ ⌒

The next day my leg smolders with pain and I'm still annoyed with Zane. I'm mad at Minnie for having to work all the time and for needing me and others to take care of her child. Above all, I'm fed up with Lawrence for dying and leaving behind such a mess.

"God, why do these things happen?" I ask as I stand in front of the bathroom mirror, keeping my weight off my aching leg, and brush my teeth. I suppose that ultimately I'm frustrated with God for not stopping Lawrence's boat from being capsized and for not moving the motor just a little bit before Lawrence hit his head on it. Why couldn't Lawrence's arm have hit the motor instead? Or he could have missed the motor altogether, as his fishing partner, Dek Brimmer, did. Both men then would have been able to signal for help, and when the Coast Guard barge found them in the midst of the giant waves, they would have had complete relief, not despair that one was not going to make it.

There are those who say God can do anything, and I believe it. I've never doubted that He hears our prayers, even the selfish and lame ones. Ever since I was little I've held awe for God. "He made the sea and all that's in it," my Sunday school teacher told our first-grade class.

But today I do not understand how God can stand all the chaos and confusion in this world and not be so overwhelmed that He would just want to weep, and then step down here to gather his people and cradle us all the way home to heaven.

14

Bert slaps his computer while Cassidy mixes soy milk with a ginger and avocado paste. She says that the infomercial claims this concoction curbs the appetite and makes skin softer. Maybe it's as miraculous as my mother's ginseng.

I'm in the middle of writing a list of what I'm grateful for, thinking that it might help me deal with the anger and frustration that have taken hold of me. On four lines I write Mom, Dad, Ron, and Minnie. I place the names of all my Hatteras relatives after them. I toy with writing Zane's name. Then I see Minnie's face when she holds him, the light in her eyes and the way her smile spreads over her cheeks whenever he kisses her. I suppose I'm grateful that he makes her happy. I add Zane's name.

I lean back in my chair and turn on my computer. I have to admit that writing the list did help. Another point for Dad, king of the lists.

Bert asks if I know where his stapler is. "Did you borrow it?"

"I have my own," I say.

Distress lines his face; I let him borrow my Bostitch.

He doesn't say thank-you because he's aggravated that he can't find his. He continues to search under stacked notebooks and folders on his desk. Soon he's peering under his desk, but all he finds today are three paperclips and a dried-out highlighter.

Right before noon, Davis calls to ask me out for this Friday. Bert hears portions of the conversation, even though he acts like he's occupied at his computer. When the call ends, he says, "So I take it the interview with the realty man held more than what we see written in your article?"

I give him a Mona Lisa smile.

He responds with a sour look. I wonder if he's still upset over his missing stapler. Rising from his desk, he makes his way over to me. "You know," he begins, lowering his voice. "About this Rexy Properties man. I hate to break it to you, but—" He's interrupted by his own ringing cell phone.

Staring at my computer screen, I wonder what he wanted to tell me. His voice sounded concerned.

When the call ends, he's rushing out the door. Excitedly, he says, "Got an interview. Selena's going to love this."

"With whom?"

"That family from Vietnam that moved here last month. They're opening up a new restaurant on a ferryboat. Very posh."

"Maybe we'll get invited to the grand opening," I muse. One time Mom's Vietnamese friend in Charlotte had our family over for spring rolls and steamy noodles in a tasty broth, sliced scallions dotting the surface. Suddenly, I'm hungry.

Bert's last words come out quickly. "They want to use the profits to save the whales."

I interview regional storeowners; Bert's job with the magazine is to write features about history, facts, and events taking place around the

Outer Banks. At times, he'll talk to old-timers on their back porches, gleaning history about the region. He actually doesn't mind spending time swapping stories with Casey Luweigneson, but he brings his own beer, not favoring Casey's selection. Bert's good at what he does, I think, as the tires on his ancient Chevy sputter gravel, heading out of the parking lot. Even if he can't keep up with his stapler.

~⁓~

At five thirty on Friday, I'm trying to decide what to wear for my evening with Davis when Aunt Sheerly calls. A light wind blows through my open bedroom window. Alone at the duplex, I've turned off the air-conditioning and let freshness seep in. I smell grass, just cut. The sweet scent of wild onions sashays through the screen as birds call out to each other in the distance and a cat responds with its own cry.

But Sheerly does not add softness to the enjoyable scene. Desperation sucks the life out of each word as she exclaims, "How could I have forgotten? How in the world did I let this happen?"

"What?" I'm suspicious because this is how she reacted when she left her tomato pie in the oven too long, fuming with disgust at its burnt edges.

"Lord, help me."

"What did you forget?" I ask. Mom and Dad's anniversary isn't until November. Sheerly's daughter, Mary Rose, who lives in Asheville, was born in May. My birthday is a month away. None of my other relatives have birthdays around this time.

"I am really getting old." Sheerly lets out a sigh as I wonder which pair of shoes to wear. The black ones with heels add two inches to my height, but Davis is over six feet, so that would put us at about the same height.

"Why is it that getting older takes years off your life?" This line is one my aunt often repeats. No one has ever given her an answer for it. "Forgetful, forgetful," she chides.

Gradually, I find out what is making her fret. She's forgotten that today is the annual songwriting competition in Kitty Hawk, her favorite event of the whole year.

Quickly, she lays out why she's called. "Jacqueline Cate, I need to ask you to watch the salon for me this evening."

Immediately, I think that she should ask one of her employees, like Minnie. But my aunt, as if reading my mind, reminds me that it's Minnie's day off, and Minnie and Zane are visiting Irvy. My aunt doesn't realize she's asking me to break another date with a man who could be The One.

As I stare at a scruffy pair of tan sandals at the bottom of my closet, I hear Mom's voice in my head: "Family do these things for each other. Family do, and not expect anything."

I can and have dismissed my mother's voice, but this evening the word that comes into my mind—no—never makes it to my mouth. Instead, I say, "I'll be there to help out."

"Jacqueline Cate," my aunt says, "you can help me celebrate."

"Celebrate what?"

"When I win!" My aunt is giddier than Minnie or I ever were as teenagers. I ask what song she's going to be singing, but she's already hung up.

She's dressed in a pink blouse and white slacks and waiting in the parking lot of the salon when I pull up. I open the door of my truck to get out, and she's instantly by my elbow saying, "Now, the UPS delivery hasn't arrived yet, but when it gets here, can you restock all the boxes? We might be inspected next week, so can you clean a little? Just make sure the floor is swept and dust off the hairdryers."

The temptation to close the door and drive off taunts me.

Sheerly stretches up to kiss my cheek. Her pearl necklace grazes my shoulder. "Lona's under the dryer. And Mavey Marie called to say she'll be in to pick out a hairstyle for next week's rehearsal dinner."

"What dinner?"

"Her grandson's getting married in Duck on the beach so she needs a style that will withstand all the wind."

Mavey Marie's grandson used to spit in my milk in fifth grade.

"And did I tell you that Lona is under the dryer?" She slips into her pink Mercedes with the personalized plate—SHEERLY.

"You did."

"She ate French toast at Breakfast at Andrew's this morning and the food made her sleepy. Don't let her sit too long." She cranks and then revs the engine. Three times.

"I won't," I reply, although I know that Sheerly cannot hear me.

All the other relatives think she's damaging the engine by treating it like it belongs in a race car. Sheerly says Mercedes, like women, can handle just about anything.

With a wave, she's gone, driving north to Kitty Hawk, hopefully with a winning song in her head.

15

Slowly, I get out of my truck. A night at the salon is a poor substitute for a date at Evan and Julia's, seated across from the handsome Davis Erickson, a glowing candle between us. I phoned Davis on my way over here, hating to tell him the news.

"Your family needs you," he said after a while. "We'll get a date in one of these days."

I thanked him for being understanding.

Sure enough, inside the scented salon, Lona is seated under the pink dryer on the left, reading the latest issue of *People* magazine. I check her hair, feeling the locks that are wrapped around wide metal curlers.

She smiles at me, says something I can't hear due to the whir of the dryer; I just smile back.

In addition to providing the community with all their hair care needs, Sheerly also displays sayings, cross-stitched and framed, around her shop. *"The art of being wise is the art of knowing what to overlook"* hangs above the set of dryers. This saying is attributed to William James. Another plaque, stitched in blue, reads, *"Age is something that doesn't matter unless you are a cheese. —Billie Burke"*

I find a wooden stool by a tiny window, sit down, and let bits of my recent phone conversation with Davis warm me. I can see the Sound from my view; the water is crystal blue and the sky is a canvas of wispy clouds with a sun preparing to retire from a hard day of work.

When I turn off the hairdryer, Lona says, "Nearly fell asleep. Had too much to eat today." She yawns, using one large hand to cover her mouth. "That French toast at Breakfast at Andrew's is just too good to pass up. And the pancakes with all that maple syrup just make me sleepy."

"Did you eat them both?"

"Had a bite of the pancakes off of Mother's plate. They were topped with blueberries, just delicious. I did eat the whole plate of French toast." Lona takes her mother to Breakfast at Andrew's every Friday morning before she heads to the golf course in Nags Head. I know this because I've known Lona since she moved here when I was eighteen. Her first murder mystery had just been published, and the salon's regulars were eager to meet a *real author*. Sheerly's song about Lona, the mystery maven, actually has a nice beat to it.

The door's overhead bell tinkles and in walks a wrinkled woman with white hair teased into the highest beehive I've ever seen. Mavey Marie has had this hairstyle since she was born, I think. I wonder why she needs to choose another to withstand the winds of Duck. This one looks like it could stand up to any hurricane.

"I just loved *Death Dutifully Defines Dorothea*," Mavey Marie says when she sees Lona. "I liked it better than *Roger Rochester's Revenge*."

"Thank you, thank you." Lona looks up from the magazine and beams like the shining light at Cape Hatteras. After another yawn she says, "Some days I think I've lost it, can't write another."

"I just don't know how you do it." Mavey Marie sits on a chair by a shelf of hardback hairstyle books. She's wearing her favorite color— lemon yellow. She and Sheerly went to one of those color parties, and ever since Mavey Marie found out her skin tone and eyes make her suited for spring, she has bought all yellow clothing. Sheerly says she'll wear pink no matter what the color charts label her as. "At this age, do you think I'm going to change myself?" she asked us one Sunday at lunch.

"I really like that line about romance." Mavey Marie picks up a book and flips through pages of sleek hairstyles on women who look like they have overused their makeup brushes.

"Which line is that?" Lona stretches her short legs that, to me, resemble Asian radishes.

As though she's reading it from one of Sheerly's cross-stitched masterpieces, Mavey Marie quotes, "You want a man to adore you so much that his heart is only satisfied when you are with him." Mavey Marie's sigh fills the shop.

Lona nods, seeming to recall that she did write that line in a novel. "And when he closes his eyes, you are the only one in his dreams." With a sudden fling of her hand, she snorts. "I wish Sylvia would realize that. I thought I raised her to be independent and not fall for the first man who gave her a second glance." Sylvia is Lona's only child. She and I were in a church youth group together.

"Well, if she read your third mystery, she would see that Benedict was never in love with Amelia. He only used her to get to his dream of being the president of the company."

Looking at me, Lona says, "Jackie, you've always been wise. I know you won't fall in love for the wrong reasons."

I'm not sure what to say. I give her a vague nod.

"Develop who you are. How can these young girls expect to find a man when they don't even know what they want?" I don't think she's intending this question to be for me; I think Sylvia is still on her mind. "I fell for the wrong man. He left me after five years. Just like that!" She snaps her fingers for emphasis.

Mavey Marie just shakes her head, and Lona and I watch her tower of piled hair move like a barge through a sandbar.

Lona has a faraway glint to her eyes. "To thine own self be true."

"Shakespeare!" Mavey Marie's smile curves. "He did know a thing or two about life and love."

"Right now, I don't know," Lona says as she searches in her leather bag and takes out a tube of hand lotion.

"What don't you know?" Mavey Marie has opened a book on hairstyles for weddings.

"Whether to kill the neighbor off or just let him be maimed." Lona rubs her hands together. She eases the other woman's confusion by explaining, "In the mystery I'm writing now."

Mavey Marie peers over the top of the book. "Is he a good neighbor?"

"He lets his grass get too long before mowing."

"Is that all? Doesn't sound too bad." Mavey Marie adjusts the collar of her yellow blouse.

"He doesn't mow his grass because he's spending too much time with his girlfriend."

"Is she in love with him for the right reasons?"

"She doesn't know he's married."

"Heavens! Oh, kill him off," Mavey Marie squeals.

"I could let him be attacked by the wild boars in Alabama." She stares at the ceiling as though the boars and her character are fighting up there. "I could let him live." The hand lotion is back in her bag, and now she buffs her nails with a file she's found on one of the tables by the hairdryer. Her nails are clipped short, so the process doesn't take long. "I think he will learn his lesson. Sometimes people need to be put in their place."

I suggest we take the rollers out of her hair and then help her undo each one. I've helped my aunt at her shop a number of times before. Removing curlers from hair is one of the tasks she's given me to do, so I feel confident now.

Mavey Marie decides that none of the styles in the glossy book suit her. "I might just leave my hair as it is and hope for the best."

Lona stands, heads over to the mirror by the swivel chair, and combs out her hair. "I think you should just keep the style you've always had for the wedding. A wedding is no time to try something new. Eden did, and it was a disaster."

"I remember that. *Edith Eden and the Edge of Evening*, right?"

"That was the book. I was so young when I wrote it." She sighs, the comb suspended in her left hand, and peers into the mirror as though her vanished youth is stretched before her, allowing her to view it one last time.

When the cuckoo clock lets out eight chirps, my stomach feels hollow, and I wonder if Sheerly has any food to eat in the shop. I know she makes a thermos of jasmine tea each morning for her customers. Today it's on the little table beside the bay window. A jar of honey sits next to it, as Sheerly sweetens the tea with honey she purchases from a local beekeeper. She serves the drink in chipped pink teacups she got at a yard sale.

I'm looking in the back room where Sheerly keeps boxes of supplies, hopeful for at least a pack of cheese crackers, when the door opens and in walks Jolene. Jolene is one of Sheerly's most faithful customers, claiming that if Sheerly were to ever move, she'd move right along with her. Unless Sheerly moves to Alaska, and then Jolene says she might only visit her during the warmer months.

"You found yourself a good man yet?" Jolene asks me when I walk over to greet her.

I paste on a smile.

"I've been telling Sheerly about my grandson in Mebane," Jolene tells the other two women in her sweet southern tone that could soothe even a belligerent child like Zane to sleep. "He is one fine-looking boy. He loves that NASCAR and was in Charlotte last year to watch the races live."

"How old is Jack now?" asks Lona as she continues combing her hair.

"Thirty-nine in December."

"And he's never been married?"

"No." Jolene winks at me. "He's just waiting to find that right girl."

The truth is, NASCAR bores me. Sure, I grew up in the South, but my mother's Asian influence has sunk into my veins. As she puts it, we do not watch "crazy car stuff." We adore Bruce Lee and martial arts films, most certainly, but not a bunch of high-speed cars driving in circles.

"You need to go to Coronado, California." Mavey Marie's eyes find mine.

"California!" exclaims Jolene as though hearing the name of the state makes her shudder. "Why would she do that?"

"It's on the coast. Looks beautiful. Or Edgewater, New Jersey." Mavey Marie smiles. "There are more rich singles in those two places than in all of this state!"

"Now, where did you read that?" asks Lona.

"I heard it on the TV."

"I think women these days need to be careful." Lona again holds everyone's attention. "Looking for love in all the wrong places is not what God intended for us."

"Bingo," says Mavey Marie. "Girls need to not chase so much, but trust God more. Trust that God will bring the right man."

When the shop's phone rings, it's the UPS driver telling me he won't be here today. "My truck broke down in Nags Head. I'm at a service shop. Tell Miss Sheerly I'll get by there tomorrow with all her stuff."

"Where is Sheerly?" asks Jolene when I hang up the phone.

I start to answer, but Lona interrupts. "She's singing her heart out. Winning the prize and making us proud!"

I hope she wins because it will make missing my date with Davis more worthwhile.

"Can you paint my fingernails?" Jolene asks. She's looking right at me. "Sheerly does it for me every Saturday."

"Bottle of pink in the back of the shop in the broom closet," Lona tells me. To Jolene, she says, "It's not Saturday, Jolene."

"Got plans for Saturday." She smiles. "Is there any tea left?"

"What plans?"

"Going to visit my best friend in Buffalo."

"Buffalo! Isn't that up north?" Mavey Marie asks.

Jolene attempts to pour tea from the thermos that Sheerly usually keeps filled, but only a dribble plops into a cup she holds. "New York. Gonna be there for a week."

"How'd you get a best friend in Buffalo?" Lona wonders aloud.

"Went to college with her at Queens. We've stayed friends ever since. Her husband died just like mine. About the same time, too. So now we're learning how to pay bills and take care of our cars on our own. Last time, I took two of Sheerly's tomato pies up to my friend. I flew with them in a leather bag. All the way to Buffalo I smelled those pies. Her friends now call me the Southern Tomato." She eyes us all. "Isn't that sweet?" Her face holds a placid grin.

"Well, it makes a good story." Lona is all about the good stories in life. She's been known to use a few coastal folk in her mysteries— names and places changed, of course.

Suddenly, Jolene scans the room, her neck bobbing like a rooster's. "Where exactly is Sheerly?"

"The big song competition," replies Lona. "She's gonna win. I feel it. Don't you, Jackie?"

"Sure," I say as I carry the nail polish toward Jolene.

Next time, if there is ever another chance to go on a date with Davis, I will not let anything get in the way.

⌒⌒

At last, the women stitch up their fragmented conversations and decide to go home. When Lona toddles out of the shop, at last satisfied with her hair, I'm quick to place the Sorry, We've Gone Fishing sign on the front door. Sheerly has three signs she uses to state that business hours are over, and my favorite is the Gone Fishing one.

"But you hate fishing," my aunt said to me the last time I helped her close the store.

"True, but I like that sign because it's got more spunk to it than just an ordinary closed sign."

"This shop is officially closed," I now say to the walls, the pair of hairdryers, the cross-stitched plagues that silently hang, and to the cuckoo clock waiting to chirp the nine o'clock hour.

I wonder if it's too late to call Davis and suggest we go out for a bit. We could go for coffee or ice cream. From my purse, I take out my cell phone.

But then Sheerly's words come to mind. The shop is being inspected soon and I'm to dust off the hairdryers and make sure the place looks clean. I walk to the closet for the duster.

"This is what family do." My mother's words always seem to find me, reminding me that my Korean ancestors valued honor, truth, and sacrifice.

16

As Minnie and Zane leave to eat at Wendy's, I hear Zane ask if Popacorn can get a burger and Mountain Doom, too. Minnie looks at me and warns me once again about my date with Davis, saying, "Now, if he's creepy, you come home right away. Or call me. Do you have your can of Mace?"

I laugh and usher her and her son out the front door. After they've left, I note that my heart rate slows, and I am actually able to breathe normally again.

Davis flew in late this Saturday morning to Raleigh-Durham International, got his car at the airport lot, and arrived at his house only two hours ago, but he's willing to meet. When he casually suggested meeting at Blackbeard's, I sensed that he didn't really think I'm going to make the date this time. I understand; I hold a few concerns, as well.

I've borrowed some of Minnie's jewelry—two gold bangles and a pair of red coral earrings. Perhaps if I don't wear the usual hoops, this date will go better than all of the others. I've decided to wear a cream-colored shirt and a pair of black dress pants. As I spray on

Minnie's White Diamonds perfume, I smile into my mirror. The woman who smiles back could almost be called pretty.

The ringing phone makes my breath catch in my throat. I consider ignoring it but can't follow through with that thought. Hesitantly, I look to see the caller's name—Mrs. Appleton, my landlord who lives in the duplex across the street.

"Good afternoon," she says in a voice that vibrates against my ear. "I got your rent money. Did you get your receipt?"

Our landlord is an interesting woman. She insists that we put our check for our rent inside her mailbox each month, saying, "No, don't waste a stamp on it, just place it in an envelope and inside my box." Then she places the receipt for the money each month in our mailbox. Then she calls to make sure we got the receipt.

"Yes," I tell her. "I got your receipt. Thank you." I wait for her response, knowing it's coming like an afternoon thunderstorm— predictable and booming.

"Very well, then! Very well. Ta-ta."

At last, I'm on my way to Nags Head for my date with Davis. My heart hums. It appears a date with Davis Erickson is finally going to happen, although I do realize that I'm still not at the restaurant and something could detain me. A car is pulled over on the side of the road with the hood raised. Two men are deciphering the problem. As I pass them, I hope my truck isn't planning to break down tonight.

Even as I park at Blackbeard's, I have the feeling Zane or Sheerly will come rushing toward me, causing this night to end before it gets to begin. I pull a mirror from my purse and check my makeup. My lipstick is still shiny on my mouth, and none of it has smeared my teeth, so I'm feeling good. I take a deep breath, grab my purse and keys, and once out of my truck, practice smiling as I walk toward the large restaurant's front door. By the door is a flagpole with a black-

and-white skull-and-crossbones flag flapping against the evening sky. Bright petunias and asters grow at the base of the pole, forming a little circle, as if they're holding hands.

Davis, dressed in a pair of tan trousers and a blue shirt, greets me once I open the door. His aftershave is just light enough to make me want to move in a little closer when he asks how my day has been.

"Good," I tell him. So far, so good.

Davis gently touches my shoulder, shielding me from a large group following the hostess into the dining room.

Being so close to Davis and realizing that we are actually now on a date makes my head feel light. "And how about you? How was your trip back?"

He smiles. "Well, you know, air travel isn't what it used to be. They don't serve anything without charging you for it."

I nod, although I'm not quite sure what he means. I've never flown anywhere.

Finally, I'm seated across a table from Davis, a lit votive candle between us, replicas of Blackbeard's treasures displayed on shelves hanging on the walls. I turn my cell phone off, deciding no one can interrupt this night. I'm glad Davis chose this restaurant and not the Grille, the place of all my bad dates.

"It's nice to be with you," Davis tells me as he looks up from his menu, the glow from the candle casting light against his cheeks.

I feel happiness coat me like a soft melody. Somewhere within my heart, flutes are playing.

"Do you know what you'd like to eat?"

Quickly, I open my menu.

"That color looks good on you."

I feel his gaze on me but don't look up. "Thanks."

Later, I think, I will tell Minnie that he was well worth the wait.

He orders a rib eye, well done, and a baked potato. I order chicken cordon bleu, although our waitress tells us the special tonight is spinach-stuffed flounder. "It's so delicious." Her smile is much too wide.

After dinner, Davis and I share a slice of key lime pie, one of the desserts that's put Blackbeard's on the map. We take turns inserting our forks into the slice. As I chew the last succulent creamy morsel, he looks into my eyes and suggests we take a walk.

Normally, I'd ask, "Where?" but his gestures and gazes at me this evening have removed any sensibility I may have been born with. I feel like a puppy, ready to follow him over any terrain, perhaps like Shakespeare feels about Selena.

As we get up from our table, Roberta, the manager, comes by to say hello. "Tell Selena that the ad we put in your magazine," she says to me, "has given us more business."

"I will. Thanks so much for supporting the magazine." I try not to stare at her eye shadow; the green is heavier than the last time I saw her, making it look like she has two olive slices under her brows.

When we exit—Davis holding the door open for me—I turn to see Roberta look Davis over from head to toe. I imagine that soon everyone I ever went to high school with will know that I was out with the owner of Rexy Properties.

Davis suggests we take his car, leaving mine in the restaurant lot. I don't protest; I've always wanted to ride in a BMW convertible, although I think to myself that he asked me on a walk, not a drive. He lowers the top as we exit the parking lot. When we reach the Oregon Inlet Bridge, the wind flings my long hair into my face. So this is how the other half lives, I think as I clasp my hair with my hand. My bracelets jingle against my arm. Smiling at Davis, I think, yes, I could live this way.

17

He parks at a lonely bait and tackle shop in Rodanthe, and we make our way to the shore. The sun is a red smoldering coal, sizzling into the horizon. Clouds of violet and peach fill the sky, and I feel romance in the air. I feel it in my bones and fingertips. I anticipate Davis's next move, and sure enough, as we walk along the beach, he reaches for my hand. His fingers lace through mine, and I believe I've just crossed over into paradise.

Selena would say that is corny. She doesn't care for those romantic lines. "Frivolous," she says in her critical tone as she paces the floor in her black Steve Madden shoes. "The world does not need another gushy love story."

Rumor has it that Selena was engaged decades ago to a man who left her at the altar. Since then, mentions of romance have been only a sour reminder of what did not happen. Bert says she avoids all relationships and lives to protect her broken heart.

The music of the waves is like a symphony for us as we continue walking hand in hand along the moist sand. Translucent crabs, known as ghost crabs in these parts, scuttle around us, popping in and out of tiny holes. We pass other people, also strolling, but I have a feeling no one could be as happy as I feel right now.

Davis pulls me toward him, his arms now circling my waist. Facing each other, our lips meet, and as they do, my heart twirls faster than one of those ballerinas in a music box.

Davis smiles, and I note how dark his eyes are. They are like a vacuum, drawing me in. I want another kiss and lean toward his mouth. As the waves splash against the shore, his hands caress my back, my hair, and then I feel his fingers against my cheek.

We stand close together as the summer day gives herself to dusk. The wind picks up, and we huddle closer. Suddenly, with great intensity, a wave splashes against us, drenching our legs.

"Oh no!" I cry as we break apart from each other, quickly walking backward toward the dunes.

Davis groans. His pants are clinging to his legs, plastered with water and sand.

I laugh, noting that my pants are wet, as well. My sandals are squishy and caked with sand. I let out another laugh but stop quickly. Davis isn't smiling.

I try to find a way to make the night light and romantic once again. Davis walks over to a dry spot near a cluster of sea oats and with clear agitation removes his shoes and then his socks, stuffing the wet socks into the toes of his shoes. I sit by him, take off my sandals, and say, "Great. Now we're both barefooted as we should be for a walk on the beach."

Davis shakes his head.

I roll up my pant legs. "You should do this, too. We'll be like Huckleberry Finn."

"I need to get home and change clothes," he grumbles.

Not wanting our date to end, I scan the sky and note that a cloud to our left looks like a Siamese cat.

Davis says he can't see it.

Moving closer to him, I tell him to turn his head a little. "See the head, and the mouth?" My finger points upward, guiding his eyes.

"My grandparents had Siamese cats," he says, observing the cloud formation.

"Really? What were their names?"

"Buoy and Gull."

"Are you serious? The Baileys' cats were named that!" In my mind, I see those cats, each a fluffy ball perched on the glider, barely allowing room for Minnie and me to squeeze around them.

He says, "I know."

"How do you know?"

"I visited them. At the Bailey House."

"Really? You were a guest at the Bailey House? When?" My words topple like waves. Learning that his past holds similarities to mine, I feel a greater connection to him. "Which room did you stay in?"

"All of them."

Just as I am ready to ask how that was possible, he anticipates my question and says, "I'm their grandson."

"No!" I wait for him to tell me he's joking. When he doesn't, I cry, "Really, you are? You're one of their Ohio grandsons they talked about?"

Sheepishly, Davis says, "I guess I am."

Mr. and Mrs. Bailey's grandson is here beside me. I laugh as I recall seeing a photo of the two grandsons when they were in high school and Minnie and I were in seventh grade. I wish Davis would laugh with me, but his face is solemn.

"So that's why it's important to me that the future owner of the house has a love for Hatteras and this area and will keep up all the Bailey traditions."

"Yeah, I get it now." I lightly smack his arm. "You're their grandson. You could have told me sooner. You're quite the secret keeper, aren't you?" I tease. "Hey, don't you have a brother?"

"I told you I did, remember?"

"The Ohio grandchildren." I use my British accent, remembering how Mrs. Bailey spoke of the two often. "And now, you're here, we're here." My heart feels bubbly, like a glass of champagne. My mind goes back to his statement about what he wants from the next owner. "Pick me," I want to say.

With authority to his tone, Davis states, "The owner has to do things the right way."

"What do you mean?"

"Well, there was this couple from Michigan who didn't comply." Confusion strikes me. "What?"

Davis kisses my cheek again. "Oh, nothing."

"Tell me."

"It's not important." He nuzzles my neck.

"Tell me anyway." I am a sponge, wanting to soak up all I can when it comes to the Bailey House Bed and Breakfast.

"It's just that this couple wanted the house after my grandparents had to give it up and go to Ohio to retire."

"Why didn't they get it?"

Davis meets my eyes. "Not just anyone can run the Bailey House."

I nod mechanically.

"They didn't work out. I couldn't pick them."

"Pick me." This time I let the words tumble out.

"I think I have."

"You have?"

"You love it, I know. You've loved it for a long time."

"Yes," I breathe. "I hate to see it sit vacant. It needs to be opened back up again."

"You sure about that?" Davis searches my face, draws me close to himself once more.

"I want to see it thrive and be a place where others can find the great hospitality your grandparents gave." I'm a loyal Girl Scout, giving a pledge and giving it to Mr. and Mrs. Bailey's own flesh and blood, right here on the shores of the Outer Banks. I feel like history is being made at this very moment.

"Perhaps you are the one." Davis's kisses this time are stronger, like my promise has meant something to him, like he's made a decision.

18

I wake to Zane's loud noises of honking and roaring his trucks over the living room floor, but instead of getting annoyed, I feel happy. Contentment fills me as it did when I was a child pouring warm sand into a beach pail, filling it right up to the brim for a sandcastle Dad and I were building. Mom was designated to look for seashells to decorate the entranceway. Ron dug the moat with his plastic shovel, and when he dug too deep, we'd tell him to run off and pretend to be a knight.

I'm excited to start a new day. I can still feel Davis's lips on mine; the sensation is more beautiful than Sheerly's Gerber daises on a spring morning. And the fact that he's Mr. and Mrs. Bailey's grandson makes him even more significant—and more enticing.

Zane wants me takc him to Uncle Ropey's. Now. He talks to me through my closed bedroom door as I lie in bed. I know that he wants to go because Ropey bought him a new Tonka truck that is only for when he visits.

"Please," Zane says through my door. "I gots to go there, Jackic. Please."

I still remember how much my leg hurt after I chased him over Ropey's lawn a few weeks ago. Any other day I would probably shout, "Why couldn't you have wanted to be at Ropey's when I needed you to stay there?" But this morning, I am like a clam soaking up the sun on the shore with my spirit soaring higher than any kite I've ever flown.

I hear Minnie calling to Zane from her bedroom. "It's Sunday and we're all headed to church."

This means I need to get out of bed.

Breaking away from the warm seclusion of my bed, I check my phone, which I've left charging on my dresser. There's a text message from Davis: *I miss you. Dinner tonight?*

I reply that I'd like that.

Minnie smiles and then shakes her head as I walk out of my bedroom wearing one white sandal and one tan. Zane asks if he can wear mismatched shoes to church today, too.

They wait for me as I pull the other tan sandal out from under my bed.

On the way to church, Zane complains that his pants are too tight. Next he says the sun is too bright in his eyes.

"You know that song by the Commodores?" Minnie says to me. " 'Easy Like Sunday Morning?' " She sings a few lines.

"Yeah," I say.

"I don't think the writer had to get himself and kids ready for church."

"And he probably wasn't a pastor," I add. "Sunday mornings are their busiest time of the week."

Tradition has its embrace on our Hatteras clan. Lunch after church is always held at Sheerly and Tiny's.

Sunday finds the women—Sheerly, Beatrice Lou, her daughter Aggie, Minnie, and me—in the kitchen, and Zane and the men out on the patio by the grill. Irvy has been brought from the nursing home to the house by Ropey.

Once she arrives, she's made comfortable in her wheelchair and wheeled into the living room by the TV. The flat screen is always on ESPN. That's been our tradition, too. But TV programs don't seem to mean much to the old woman; her eyes are usually focused around her knees. Minnie says she thinks her mother might be remembering the past, when she wore a black swimsuit and turned the heads of young men with surfboards.

In the kitchen, painted a creamed-corn yellow with fluffy tomato red curtains, we break apart lettuce leaves and chop cucumbers and carrots for a salad.

Sheerly takes three bottles of ranch dressing from her fridge. It's the only kind Tiny will eat. She turns to me and then says, "What do you think?"

"Of what?" I pause from slicing a cucumber.

"Didn't I just say that there are tomatoes in the garden and that we could put some in the salad?"

"No."

"Oh, well, I thought it. Goodness, when you get to be my age, you talk aloud and share your thoughts when you need to be quiet, and you think you've spoken when you've only thought."

I know what she means. Often I catch her talking to herself. She doesn't know that we can all hear her when she comments aloud, especially in the middle of a church service when she decides to agree or disagree with our pastor while he's preaching.

I say, "Tomatoes from your garden would be wonderful. Do you want me to go pick them?"

"No, you're busy here. I'll get one of those men to do it." She heads to the patio door. "Last time I checked, there were three Better Boys that were nearly ripe." I see her outside, addressing her husband.

I'm sure that Tiny has been asked to bring the tomatoes inside for the salad, but he hasn't moved from his spot beside the grill. I don't want my aunt fussing at him, wondering why he seems to forget what she asks of him, yet never forgets the score when the Steelers win. When Sheerly places a quilt over Irvy's legs, I slip out the door and pick the tomatoes myself.

Ten minutes later, we eat out on the brick patio covered by a brown and blue polka-dotted awning. Sheerly has spread a plastic red-checkered tablecloth on one picnic table and a white cloth on another smaller table. In the center of both tables are vases of roses and daisies. My aunt once told me she believes flowers bring good things to life. I'm pretty sure she borrowed that phrase from a General Electric commercial.

My relatives are sweetly delusional about their cooking. They think they are fantastic cooks, but all they can really make are macaroni salad, burgers, baked potatoes, and chicken soup. None of this is really cooking—not like a dish Emeril would produce on his show. Yet we rave over the food as if it is the best we've ever tasted.

The one dish that is unique to Sheerly is her tomato pie. She's baked three of those for today's lunch, and we eat them with the burgers, tossed salad, and macaroni salad. The pies are made from the tomatoes she grows and are filled with several kinds of cheeses.

"How was the song competition?" asks Aggie. She is a wiry woman of twenty-four with brown curly hair that often falls into her face.

"I came in second place." Sheerly's face is glowing. "Oh, let me show you my ribbon!" She leaves her seat, and after a moment is back with a stiff green bow that says "Second Place Kitty Hawk Song Competition."

"Congratulations!" exclaims Aggie. "Which song did you sing?"

Beatrice Lou murmurs to Sheerly, "I told her you came in second place. She never listens to anything I say."

"She's a child," Sheerly whispers back. "They try not to listen. It's their job." To Aggie, Sheerly says, "I sang 'Love Is Your Ticket.' "

"I've never heard that one." Aggie takes a bite of macaroni salad. "Is it anything like 'Just Because You Have Wings Doesn't Mean You Own the Sky'?"

"The beat is a little faster in 'Love Is Your Ticket.' I wrote it for the competition. The judges loved it, but apparently not as much as 'Yesterday's Menu.' "

"Why would they want yesterday's menu?" Aggie asks.

"It's the name of the winning song," Beatrice Lou replies. Aggie is Beatrice Lou and Ropey's only child; she is so different from either of them that Beatrice Lou often jokes that the stork brought her.

"Oh," says Aggie, rolling her eyes at her mother. "How was I supposed to know that? No one tells me anything."

"How was your date last night?" Uncle Tiny asks, his large hands busy turning burgers over with a metal spatula. Customers at his bait and tackle shop, Tiny Tackle, marvel at the way his mammoth fingers skillfully maneuver small minnows and shrimp into boxes for them. He got the name Tiny as a joke. This afternoon the burgers look like toy truck wheels against his frame. "Did you have a good time?"

I wait for Aggie to reply. She seems to have a new boyfriend each season. She likes to hang around the local Marine bases, I think.

When I look up from my plate, Cousin Aggie is helping Zane

put condiments on his hamburger. The others are focused on me, waiting for my response.

Beatrice Lou pats my shoulder and says, "You know we all want to hear about it."

Who told them I had a date? "It was great," I say and feel my face heat.

Minnie feeds Irvy bites of tomato pie but stops to look my way. "Davis Erickson is a lucky man."

I am grateful for the way she cheers me on and is always on my side.

"So," says Sheerly, "does this mean you don't want to go out with Whistlin' Walt's cousin in Jacksonville?"

"That's right," I say. No more blind dates, I think, chewing them away as I finish my burger.

Irvy's eyes find mine from across the patio. Her expression makes my skin feel cold. It's as if she's looking into my soul and seeing all its black marks. I am not the best person there is, but I know I am forgiven by Jesus.

In her typical slow manner, Irvy says, "Did you know they got married on a pontoon boat?"

The conversation continues about how nice it is that Jackie had a good date. I smile as my relatives talk about me as though I'm not there.

"Did you know?" Irvy asks again. Her good hand jerks, as though wanting to bat at a mosquito that the rest of us can't see.

"Who are you talking about, Mama?" Minnie asks with a nervous smile.

"They were married." With effort, her head turns my way.

I see her eyes, tiny darts.

Irvy's mouth moves and then, at last, ". . . on a pontoon boat." Her hand resigns itself to rest against her lap.

"Well," says Tiny, breaking a silence that follows, "we're all glad that Jackie has found a man she likes." He resumes his place at the table and adds ketchup to his burger.

Later I ask Minnie why her mother constantly says the line about the marriage on a pontoon boat. Minnie takes a bite of the chocolate pie Beatrice Lou brought. "I don't know," she says. "Someone she used to know, I guess. Her mind is going, Jackie. The doctor tells me that she's acting more confused every day."

After Minnie feeds Irvy a slice of chocolate pie, we stand to clear the dishes. As I pass Irvy's chair, she utters, "There is a farm in Cary." Slowly, her fingers rest against my arm. I notice her carefully painted nails, the work of Minnie last week. Her bent index finger pokes into my skin. I watch her eyes, wondering what is going on behind them. Her tongue moves and hangs between opened lips. When she speaks, I have to lower my ear toward her mouth. "Will you remember there is a farm?"

I don't think that I've ever been to Cary, which I believe lies between Raleigh and Durham. But I tell her that I will remember it.

She lets go of my arm, leans back in her chair, closes her eyes, and within moments, is asleep.

19

"*Where are we going?*" I ask as my hair whips into my face. We're driving north on Route 12 in Davis's car, passing Kill Devil Hills, then Southern Shores. When we get to Duck, I try once more. "The Currituck Lighthouse? Am I right?"

Davis offers the same secretive smile he's given me several times before. This time he touches my arm as we stop at a traffic light. I feel my pulse quicken. "Surprise," he tells me. "Nearly there."

The evening sky splashes with tangerine clouds complemented by streaks of purple and white. Since Davis picked me up at the duplex forty minutes ago, I've questioned where we're headed, but he's kept his plans to himself, which makes my skin tingle with anticipation.

When we roll into the town of Sanderling, he turns his car onto a side street and then curves around another shaded with cedars and a wispy pine. He parks by a secluded dock overlooking the Sound. He strokes my hand, and then grasps it, strong fingers entwined with mine. "This is it."

"Are we going to fish for our dinner?" I ask.

"We could." Getting out of the convertible, he reaches in the back and pulls out a wicker basket. "Or we could just eat from here."

The food is bountiful, making me wish I hadn't eaten so much at Sheerly's. I most certainly shouldn't have had such a large piece of chocolate pie. Nevertheless, after we've admired the view of the water and marsh, I let him fill a paper plate with a roast beef sandwich. I see two slices of provolone cheese peeking over the edges of the rye bread. Davis opens a container of hummus and from a box, pours wheat crackers into a dish. He slices Gouda cheese and takes out a bunch of red grapes.

We sit on the dock, our legs stretched out, our plates on our laps. Davis pours Evian into plastic glasses for us. Minnie and I used to joke that Evian was only for water snobs, but right now it seems like the perfect choice.

The sun disappears into the western sky as crickets chirp their evening symphony. Bullfrogs join in just as the moon makes her appearance—as smooth as vanilla ice cream. We continue to eat and talk. I have so many questions about the Bailey House.

"Are all the dishes still in the cupboards?"

Davis's laugh is warm. "Why do you want to know that?"

"Because when I daydream, I'm serving breakfast on those plates with the gold trim and crimson swirls."

"Really?"

"Yes, and tea from those china cups with saucers. Royal Dalton, right?"

With tender eyes, he draws me close, and I relax against his embrace. "The dishes are all there. My grandparents left everything." His fingers stroke my hair. "You should wear your hair pulled back from your face," he says.

I eye him with uncertainty.

"Yeah, it looks good like that."

I've never liked my hair in a ponytail because I think it makes my face look too round, but I just smile. "Are the linens there, too? How about all the furniture?"

"All there."

"Do you know what happened to the birdbath?"

His jaw tightens. "Let's put the house aside for a while."

So we sit with our arms around each other until the moon rests straight above us. Then we eat strawberry chiffon custard from fluted plastic containers.

I know I should be heading home. Waking up tomorrow at seven is going to be difficult. I bet it's almost eleven and the drive back to my duplex is going to take almost an hour.

Davis kisses my cheek.

"I should be getting home," I murmur.

"Just a minute more," he tells me as his fingers play against my back. This time he kisses my lips.

～✦～

At the Monday morning staff meeting, I make a strong pot of coffee, hoping it will wake me up. I pour a mug and breathe in the aroma of Kenyan beans. Selena insists we have only the brand called Blue Sparkle Mountain Top Coffee at the office. She claims she met an entrepreneur from Nairobi who told her this brand is the world's best coffee. No one I know has ever heard of it.

Today, Selena has brought in our accountant—a fuzzy-haired man with a belly like a drum—to tell us about the financial state of the magazine. I'm a bit worried, but Bert says that Selena has already informed him that *Lighthouse Views* is doing okay. Selena would bail if it were headed south.

It's hard to focus on magazine logistics when my mind keeps sailing back to last night with Davis. Now I look at my cell to see if Davis has sent me a text message. He left early this morning to meet a potential client on Ocracoke Island. This man wants to discuss a set of condos he's managing to see if Davis wants to purchase them for renovation and further development. Davis isn't sure it will be a good investment, but the man is eager to sell. When Davis dropped me off at my duplex last night, he said he'd be sure to call or text me today.

Cell phones are happy instruments when they zing with new voice messages and text messages. But they can become an obsession when all you can think of is when they'll ring.

I sneak glances at mine while the accountant talks and Shakespeare dozes. I wish I could stretch out on the sofa and take a nap beside the terrier.

When the staff meeting ends, Selena heads out with the accountant, stopping to pet Shakespeare and telling us to work hard.

Cassidy opens a clear container and asks if anyone would like some pie. We are all interested until Bert asks, "What kind?"

"It's just called 'reduced sugar.' "

"Reduced sugar pie?" Bert looks like he might be sick. "No, thanks."

Cassidy gives me a questioning glance.

"What is it made of?" I ask.

Cassidy looks at the fluffy white concoction in the container. "Not sure, but it's on my diet."

"I don't think it's on mine," I say with a grin.

Bert raises his eyebrows. He grins back as I move to my desk.

I start rearranging pens and pencils in my drawer and then flip open my phone. There is nothing but the wallpaper I've set on my phone's screen—a photo I took last spring of a blue and yellow box kite that I flew. One thing on my to-do list is to fly a kite at least once a year.

When Selena returns, she hands me a list of business owners she wants me to interview for our September issue. She tells Cassidy to ask the hotel on Heron Street if they'd like to run an ad in our magazine.

"We asked them last month, and they said no," Cassidy reminds our boss.

"Ask them again," says Selena. "People can change their minds. Tell them we'll give them a good deal." She looks at me. "Aren't you scheduled to do an interview in Avon today?"

"Tomorrow. Vanessa changed the day."

Selena nods. "Just checking. You seem a bit dreamy and not your usual self." We accuse Selena of being oblivious to our personal lives, but every so often she'll surprise us by honing in on our moods, as if she does follow what we're dealing with beyond the office.

"Just tired," I tell her, which is true. Of course, I suppose I have given in to some dreaminess, thanks to a certain Realtor.

"Don't get sick. Take vitamin C," she suggests.

What I would never admit to Selena is that I wouldn't mind canceling the upcoming interview with Vanessa at Coastal Finds. Right now I don't care that each item she sells is handmade by some of the best artists North Carolina has. But Selena believes that an interview with this lady is just what our magazine needs to boost our circulation and appear classy.

I go over the questions I'm planning to ask Vanessa. When Selena leaves for the day, I wait until I hear her car back out of the parking lot, and then I head out the door. I can write much better outside of the office.

I make it to the Grille in four minutes.

~◦~◦

After a dinner of chicken tenders with Zane, he and I sit on the sofa with Popacorn and watch *Andy Griffith* reruns. My phone is by my side because I know it will ring any minute now with a call or text.

Minnie gets home, tired and complaining of a headache. She helps Zane get ready for bed, taking his dinosaur pajamas out of the dryer while he sings in the bathroom, and then goes to bed herself.

I listen to sappy love songs from the nineties on the radio and after each one check to see if there is a message from Davis.

By ten fifteen, I've decided that he hates me. I turn off my light and try to sleep.

At eleven ten, my phone rings.

20

Sleepily, I reach for my phone, knock it off the bedside table, and as it clatters onto the floor, I scramble out of bed.

"I've missed you." Davis's voice is deep and gentle, filling in all those potholes of worry that developed in my mind.

"I missed you, too."

"Have you read any of the book?"

On my bedside table is the book he lent me last night, a biography of Manex Jethro titled *When a Musician Prevails.* I touch the cover—a photo of the musician, a middle-aged man with a reddish beard and tiny eyes. "I read a little," I say. The first few pages gave the details of Manex's birth in Columbus and his meager childhood on a farm where they often had only plain oatmeal and fatback for meals.

"He's got a great story," says Davis. "He made it big."

"His childhood was sad."

"So who is your hero?"

You, I want to say, but that would sound silly. "Mrs. Bailey."

"Yeah, Grandma was a saint."

"She was. I love the way she welcomed everyone into her home.

She cared about each guest." I see her seated on the sofa in the parlor, listening to a wrinkled man in a cowboy hat share the details of his wife's last days with a malignant tumor that no amount of chemo, radiation, or surgery could cure. Mrs. Bailey rubbed his back when he pulled his hat down to cover his face, sobbing into the creased leather. Later, she brewed him one of her finest orange pekoes. I want to tell Davis that I saw the compassion of Jesus in her.

But before I can say anything else, he's telling me to have sweet dreams.

The next afternoon, I drive to Coastal Finds, Vanessa's shop in Avon. As my truck rumbles the miles over Route 12 on this overcast day, I recall how Buck teased me when I told him I had an interview set up with Vanessa. "Now, don't get carried away and let her talk you into too many of her overpriced pottery mugs," he warned playfully. "If you need a loan, I'll be glad to call the bank for you."

The outside of the shop is painted pink and lime green. The name of the shop is hand-painted on a piece of driftwood that hangs in the showcase window. Inside, the scent of peaches and cloves greets me, as well as Tina Turner. The singer's strong voice pipes through the store's speakers: "What's love got to do with it?"

As I walk around the store in search of Vanessa, I see a huge vase of red roses. They are displayed on a wide shelf near an arrangement of hand-blown glass bowls. Keeping my purse close to my side so that I don't knock anything over, I count the blooms—twenty-four.

At the counter, a young girl with a nametag that reads DONNA and Vanessa are talking about jewelry to a woman in a pair of cotton shorts, tank top, and yellow flip-flops with plastic sunflowers. The customer says she wants a silver bracelet studded with emeralds and rubies. Her grandmother apparently left her some money and she wants to use it to buy a bracelet.

Vanessa opens the glass counter, and with a delicate motion, takes out a silver bracelet shining with blue and clear jewels. Vanessa is art in perfection. Every strand of her hair is glossy and in place. She's wearing a two-piece suit, skirt and jacket with a cream silk shirt. The amount of money she spends on clothes could probably feed a small nation. And I can tell that exercising is something she likes to do. I've been told she schedules her life around sessions at the gym with her personal trainer, Fiat. Sheerly believes that Fiat is related to Arnold Schwarzenegger because he looks like Arnie did in the first *Terminator* movie.

I greet Vanessa with a smile when the customer slips the bracelet around her wrist. "I'm Jackie."

Vanessa nods my way, but I can tell that she's not finished with the customer yet. "That bracelet is one of a kind," she tells the woman. "The four blue sapphires are encased in tiny diamonds. Yesterday a man was asking about it for his wife. He said he'd be back today with her."

The sales associate marvels at how beautiful the piece of jewelry is while Vanessa tells the customer that the sapphires are imported from Madagascar.

"Really?" says the woman. "My grandmother went on a trip there one summer."

"You'll never find anything this gorgeous at this price," Vanessa tells her.

I'm eyeing a shelf of pottery with price tags that run more than I make in two weeks when the customer agrees that the sapphires do sparkle beautifully. "I love the color blue," she says. The customer lifts her arm, and we all watch as the diamonds glitter, the ones nearest the sapphires reflecting blue. "I'll take this."

Vanessa smiles at me. I see triumph in her eyes. "Donna," she says to her sales associate, "find a nice box for this bracelet. We are going to my office." She motions for me to follow her, and I do. The air around her is sweet as her heels click against the wooden floor.

I look at my sandals and wonder if I should have dressed up. I have one black dress in my closet.

We enter Vanessa's office at the end of a short hallway marked Employees Only. Warm sunlight dances into a room that is painted melon green with cream trim. Vanessa sits at an oak desk as shiny and waxy looking as her potted plants that line one wall.

I start the interview by asking if she minds if I use my little Sony pocket tape recorder during our time.

"Go right ahead." Her lipstick is red, matching the collar of her jacket.

I decide I'll start by asking how long she's owned the store. Then I ask what she likes best about dealing with the public. When she says her customers often compliment her on how clean and fresh the shop is, I think of the roses in the vase.

"I noticed the roses you have." I smile into her blue eyes. "They're pretty."

Vanessa returns my smile. "I read your piece on Davis. I think that was a fairly good portrayal of him."

"You know him?"

"Oh yes." Her laughter is light, breezy, like a day in May. "He sent me the roses this morning. His note said he hopes they make the shop as beautiful as me."

My smile freezes on my face.

She laughs. "He can't seem to accept the fact that we aren't dating anymore."

Somehow I find my voice. "Oh." I pretend to make a notation in my notebook, my fingers feeling like Jell-O.

"Now, don't be publishing this."

"Oh no," I say much too rapidly. "How . . . how long did you date?"

"Off and on for a year. With Davis it's always off and on."

"Really?"

"Yeah. We try to break it off every so often, but then, well . . ." She pauses, smiles.

I hear the sound of my pounding heart, which is almost as loud as the song now playing through the speakers. Kelly Clarkson belts, "The trouble with love is it'll eat you up inside."

"What else do you need to ask me?" Vanessa asks crisply.

I feel like I've been slapped. The sting of Vanessa's revelation, mixed with Kelly singing about why we are so vulnerable hits me. I want to find the nearest exit, which I can see is directly to my left. I want to grab Zane's toy trucks and race them all into each other just to hear the crash of metal.

Instead, I continue with my questions, faking interest in her answers about what she likes to do for fun and what her favorite meal is. The scent of cloves seems too sweet for my mood.

At last, the interview is over, and I walk on wobbly legs to my truck, waiting for me in the parking space like a refuge. I close the door, turn on the engine, crank up the air-conditioning, and breathe in and out.

Two miles down the road, I have no idea where I'm headed. I pull into a small diner's parking lot and kick my foot against the floorboard. I hit the dashboard with a tight fist as anger flares through my veins.

There is nothing I can do when it comes to Vanessa's good looks, her tiny, fit body, small feet, and, apparently, Davis's interest in her.

"God!" I cry. "I thought you sent Davis to me! I thought you were answering my prayers!" What I want to demand is, "How could you give him to me and then take him away?" but I've never spoken to God like that.

Suddenly, my thoughts jolt like a car halting at a red light. Minnie moaned these same sentiments back when Lawrence first died, and even now, a year later, she still sometimes asks the universal "why me?" question. The difference between her situation and mine, of course, is that Davis and I have been dating only a short while. Minnie lost her husband of nine years. Severed, torn, gone in an instant.

I drive home and, in a daze, take my flute out of its case and fit the slender parts together. Then I lift the mouthpiece to my lips and blow. I expect a tune as loud and fierce as the waves that overtook Lawrence's boat to come out of my instrument. But instead, the music is soft and melodic. Like an early-morning rowboat ride on the Sound, with oars that dip into the water's surface and glide over all the broken rocks lying deep underneath.

Sheerly says you never know what music the heart will bring forth. But it always seems to ring more true than our expectations.

Minnie calls to ask if I've picked up Zane from Ropey's. That's when I remember I was supposed to pick him up at six. I call Ropey to apologize and say I'll be late, but I'm on my way.

"Take your time," he tells me. "Zane is making a masterpiece. He's got rope twisted to look like a Tonka truck." My uncle laughs. I want to join in, but anything to do with happiness seems hollow to me now—and so far away.

21

"He won't eat his tuna."

At the office, the mood is heavy because Selena is worried about Shakespeare. "I even sprinkled it with parsley like he enjoys," she tells us. "He's looking frumpy." She asks each of us whether or not we think her pet has lost weight.

Cassidy stands over the sleeping terrier with a cup of strawberry yogurt. "Yeah, I'd say he's lost at least half a pound," she says, which makes Selena reach for the phone to call Shakespeare's vet.

I spend much of the morning checking my phone. The tiny screen shows no missed calls, no messages. Maybe I should just turn it off and shove it inside my desk, forget that it connects me to Davis. I write Davis's name on a Post-It and then toss the yellow square into my wicker trash can. I wish my heart wasn't so tender. I wish that I could be like Selena and swear off men altogether.

Shakespeare whimpers when the UPS truck pulls up to the front of the office but does not wag his tail. Selena asks the driver if her pet looks ill. The large man in brown lowers his head to view the dog lying on the sofa by an opened window. Selena decided he needed some fresh air. "Looks like he has a sore throat," the man tells Selena.

I can't tell if he's joking.

But Selena takes his words into consideration. "You might be right," she says, brows arched into a frenzy of concern. When the driver leaves, Selena doesn't rush to open the boxes he delivered as she usually does; instead she spends time trying to open Shakespeare's mouth. "Come on, sugarpie, let Mommy see what's wrong," she coos as the rest of us busy ourselves so that we don't burst into giggles.

I try to focus on the next assignment Selena has for me, which is to interview the owner of Rent by the Sea. This shop rents beach chairs and umbrellas, coolers and grills, and cribs and cots. I feel its owner is about as classy as a hermit crab shell mounted to the wall, but even so, Selena wants an article about the store in next month's issue. I try not to waste too much time figuring out her rationale.

At lunchtime, my stomach feels hollow; I head to the Grille. "Promise me you'll never ever go to Coastal Finds," I say when Buck asks me how I'm doing.

"Aw, Jackie, you know I go there all the time to buy fifteen-hundred-dollar mugs to drink my coffee out of."

I frown and feel my whole body sagging with the same emotion it held yesterday when I sat in Vanessa's office and heard her talk about dating Davis. I don't think I ever want to see a vase of red roses again. I also don't want to listen to her recorded voice to write my article on her and her shop. Perhaps Bert could write the article for me. When he had the flu last winter, I took over all of his assignments.

Buck squirts Diet Pepsi into a mason jar and, after sliding it toward me, touches my hand. "So what did Vanessa do to rupture your spirit, Hatteras?"

I sink teeth into my lower lip, trying to find the right words.

"Tried to sell you a diamond purse? Or was it a diamond shark fin? I heard the shark fins are popular these days. Every home needs one right above the fireplace."

"She's just . . ." I look at Buck and stop. I can't be honest with him; he'll only tease me.

He edges closer to me so that his arms are resting only inches from my hands.

I avoid his eyes and sip my drink. My notebook lies open in front of me, but I'm distracted as I watch a waitress bring plates of hamburgers and fries to a group of women at a table to the left of the counter. I bet Vanessa never eats fries and burgers. I bet her diet is stricter than Cassidy's. I bet her cosmetic drawer holds only beauty products from France, costing a hundred dollars an ounce.

"I want a bacon cheeseburger," I tell Buck. "And lots and lots of fries."

After a nod, he places the order for me at the computer. Soon he's refilling drinks at the other end of the counter.

I'm grateful that he made no comment about my need to drown my insecurities in a pound of beef and side of greasy potatoes.

But perhaps my relief is short-lived. When he comes over to me again, he says, "You know what you really need?"

Here comes the joke; I take a deep breath and wait.

"Some fun." His smile is warm.

I grip my pen and wait for the rest of whatever silly thing he's preparing to tell me.

"You're too busy interviewing and writing all the time. You need to take a break."

I search his hazel eyes to see if there is laughter within them.

"You've had a lot going on in your life. A kid who cries all the time, an overworked roommate, all those dates gone bad, and being infatuated with the wrong guy."

My voice jumps out. "Infatuated?"

"My take on it. I could be wrong." He lifts his hands as though surrendering his take on it.

"Infatuated?" The word tastes like vinegar in my mouth.

"Forget I said that."

"It's hard to do that."

"How come?"

"Because I don't see it as infatuation. I really like Davis, and he likes me."

"Okay, fair enough. Forget all that. I shouldn't have said it." Buck's eyes show he wants to get out of the hot water I've put him in.

I shift my gaze to my notebook. I feel like Ron, geared up for an argument. "Buck, I didn't mean to bite your head off." My words come out softly.

"You didn't." He smiles.

I rub my throbbing right temple, then reach into my purse for some Excedrin. I wonder if Shakespeare's vet can figure out what is wrong with me. It's certainly not weight loss; I've been eating plenty of junk food with Zane these days. None of Cassidy's reduced sugar pie for me.

"So are you interested to know what I'm thinking or not?"

Three tablets should help. I take them with my Pepsi. "I'm afraid to ask."

"I have two kayaks."

"And?"

"How long has it been since you've gone kayaking on the Sound?"

"I don't know. Years." I try to recall. "In high school."

"Well, then, it's time."

"Time?"

"To do it again."

Buck's enthusiasm makes me smile. "Okay. Why not?"

"Okay, then." His eyes sparkle. "How does next Sunday afternoon sound?"

"All right, but it has to be after lunch at Sheerly's." Buck has known my family long enough to be familiar with our weekly get-togethers at Sheerly's after the eleven o'clock church service.

"After your lunch, then. I wouldn't want to go out on the water with a hungry woman, anyway."

"Why not?"

"She'd expect me to catch her a fish for lunch, and that wouldn't work for you because you hate fish."

I laugh. Sometimes I think Buck knows me too well.

"Oh, and be sure to carry one of your fisherman hats."

"Why?"

"So I can recognize you, of course."

For Buck, I just might. My collection sits on a bookshelf in my bedroom. There are gray, beige, black, yellow, and many shades of green hats. Over the years, people have learned of my love of these hats with their special snaps and hooks and sometimes lures, and have given me some to add to my collection. Aunt Sheerly found a Greek fisherman's hat at a yard sale and bought it for me, excited that now my stash of hats had an international flair. She, as well as my other relatives, think it's funny that I hate fish but like the caps that anglers wear. "If you collect the hats, you can eat the fish," my mother said one night when she served broiled flounder—*saengsunjun.* Her child psychology was a little sketchy back when I was a kid. I reached for the box of Frosted Flakes, clearly showing disrespect to all of our ancestors. My mother hit her chest with her fist a few times and muttered something about forgiveness. I didn't care; I don't eat fish, even for my ancestors.

When I leave the Grille, my belly is content from the burger and fries. I walk back to the office, taking the longer route past pink, green, and yellow beach houses, many with rental property signs. I look to see if Davis's company rents any of them as trucks hauling Jet Skis and boats ease down the road. Pedestrians amble along the sidewalks and in and out of shops. I consider going into a candy shop to pick up some chocolate with the full amount of sugar in it for our staff, until I note the darkening sky. When the sun shields herself behind a cluster of gray clouds, I walk faster. I'm inside at my desk just before the first raindrops moisten the pavement.

22

Three days later, Selena slices and dices my interview with the owner of Rent by the Sea. Muttering about the wordiness of the piece, she strikes out a paragraph I spent twenty minutes creating. I thought she wanted our readers to see these retailers as real people, with likes and dislikes, passions and hobbies. Yet today she tells me that no one will care that the owner likes to sky dive. The enthusiasm she showed after my interview with Davis has ventured far from her today, sailed out with the morning tide. I open the July issue of *Lighthouse Views* and read my pages about Rexy Properties, trying to remember some of the compliments she gave me then. Seeing Davis's picture doesn't boost my spirits as much as I need it to today.

I know Selena's nervous about Shakespeare's recent bout of poor health, but I wish she wouldn't take it out on her staff. Meanwhile, Bert is still at the top of her list of favorites. A local furniture store came by to deliver a new desk for him. Selena claimed his previous one had a broken drawer and was older than time.

As Cassidy makes comments about his new desk, I look at my

own. It came over on the *Santa María*, I think. Yet there is no mention of my getting a new place to work.

When Bert asks if know where his stapler is, I ignore him, pretending to be too occupied to reply. I sink my teeth into my bottom lip. What point am I trying to prove? Hell hath no fury like a woman scorned? But I'm not scorned. Davis still likes me; I know he does. I'm the Hatteras Girl. I light up a room.

Right now I would like to let Zane take a red pen and color on every inch of Bert's new desk. That would certainly light up this room.

It's a good thing I don't speak my mind without realizing it, letting my emotions slip out like Aunt Sheerly does. I need this job.

⁓ ⁓

At home, I toss clothes into the washer and then hear a car engine die. Through the window I see Minnie and Zane get out of the car. Zane is able to undo his car seat's buckle too easily these days.

"Hi," he calls out to me. He bounces up the thirteen steps to our duplex, stopping on the fourth and then the tenth to tell me, "I had fun at Ropey's. We made stuff out of rope. Mine is the bestest. Can we have banana sandwiches for dinner?" His little nose is dotted with perspiration. "Did you know I'm going to kindergarten?"

"Really? That will be an adventure." My own memories of kindergarten are sketchy. My teacher seemed old and focused on the arts, something even at that age I was not skilled at. We did a lot of finger painting and making puppets. One of my puppets' head's came off and landed in Jimmy Keno's thermos of chicken soup. The teacher said it was my fault; I was sitting too close to Jimmy. I liked to be close because that way I had a better look at his soft, pudgy cheeks dotted with freckles.

"Mommy says she'll buy me new shoes. My old light-up ones are too small. I wear these now 'cause it's summer. See?" He lifts his left foot, clad in a black sandal, and balances on one leg. That pose ends when he teeters forward, and I rush down the steps to catch him.

"Careful, Zane."

He recovers much quicker than I do, bouncing up the last steps. When he reaches the deck, he opens and closes the door with several loud bangs.

I wonder if any girl will think he's cute and want to sit next to him.

Zane belches twice.

Minnie rushes past me and into the house. Soon I hear "When a Man Loves a Woman" coming from her CD player. I remember in ninth grade when she dated Jon Willowmount. After their breakup, she played Chicago's "If You Leave Me Now" over and over and over again. Each time I went to her house and asked her mom if Minnie was home, I didn't have to wait for the answer. If I heard "If You Leave Me Now" meandering down the staircase, I knew she was in her bedroom, no doubt making sad faces into her full-length mirror and singing along to her favorite part of the song: " . . . please don't go."

At her bedroom door, I pause until the song ends and then gently knock.

"Come in," she says. Standing by the dresser, she looks glassy-eyed.

I secure my arm around her waist. At five-feet-ten, I feel like a crane hovering over her short frame.

She sniffs and then lets a tear curve down her cheek. "I never wanted too much. A husband, a child, happiness . . ." She leaves my side and sits on her bed. "Or does that sound like I've wanted a lot?"

I think for a moment. Minus the child, this is what I, too, want. "No more than the rest of us."

"I miss what I had."

I nod and swallow the stone forming in my throat.

"I don't believe there will be anyone else for me."

"Well, there could be . . ."

Her eyes dig into mine. "Do you think there is only one man for one woman?"

"You mean that if you let one go, there won't be another?"

She nods, a small figure on a large bed.

"I'm not sure."

We are silent as she presses a button on her CD player, allowing the song to start once more. "I had a chance with Lawrence. That could be all I get. Ever."

We let the line "when a man loves a woman" fill the room.

"I take long showers and hope that I can wash my pain away. Just one more minute and I can handle this day. Just one more minute." She sits back on the bed. "Sometimes my shower therapy works, but on most days I end up crying out to God for one more day with Lawrence."

I wish I could send her back to when she was a little girl under the Baileys' pergola, her eyes shiny with idealism.

"Do you know what Mrs. Appleton said to me today?"

"What?"

"At least he's safe in heaven." She spits out the phrase.

I've learned that statements like that do not help when one only wishes her loved one was here beside her.

"Sometimes I dream that Rudlow is here. Holding me. Comforting me."

Rudlow is her dad; she calls him by his first name these days. I remember the day she swore she would never refer to him as Dad again, she was so mad at him for leaving her and Irvy.

"You know, Lawrence and me, we had nine years. That's a long time to be happy."

By the time the song ends, she's decided that she's going to dye her hair Golden Radiance in hopes that she'll feel either golden or radiant.

"Maybe you'll feel like both of them," I offer.

Her face is splotchy, but there is a tiny smile. "Anything is worth a try."

23

Buck does own two sea kayaks and they are here, by the edge of the Sound in Buxton, just a few hundred yards from The Rose Lattice, the place where Sheerly and her group make music on Saturday nights. Buck tells me he purchased one of the kayaks off eBay from a dentist in Myrtle Beach, and the other he received as a high school graduation gift. He asks if I want the blue or red one. The blue one has a polished look and is somehow more inviting, so I choose it.

He buckles a bright green life vest around me. Then he puts on a matching one. "Now, you've done this before, right?"

"Years ago." I hope he can't sense my nervousness. It's not the water I'm afraid of; I just don't want to make a fool of myself in front of him, or in front of anyone. I've seen too many *America's Funniest Home Videos* in which a woman gets into a canoe and immediately topples into the river.

"You'll remember." He secures his Hurricanes cap on his head. "You need a hat? I know you have lots of those fisherman ones."

"I collect them," I say. "So they just sit."

"Hats that sit." He grins. "Do you have hats that you wear?"

"Sometimes."

Playfully, he says, "Ah, I bet you're afraid they'll mess up your hair."

I had a friend in high school who owned a two-seater kayak and we'd paddle in it on summer afternoons. I always felt it was a lot of work, although it did strengthen my arm muscles. "Will I be sore tomorrow?" I ask Buck as I put on a pair of sunglasses.

"Depends."

"On what?"

"If you actually paddle today. If I have to tote you the whole way, then my arms will be sore and yours will be fine."

"Tote me? You think I'm going to act like a baby?"

Buck laughs as we make our way down the embankment to the edge of the water. I brace myself to get into the kayak I've chosen. Swallowing hard, I nod to show that I'm ready. He holds the back of the kayak until I'm seated, my legs positioned in front of me, my feet resting on the foot pegs. I have a sinking feeling that there is no way this long, skinny contraption will hold me. I wait while Buck pushes his kayak out onto the water and climbs in.

I watch as he quickly paddles with one swift stroke on the right and then another on the left. He repeats the actions, gently heading away from me. I hurry to catch up by following his method, and with one movement splash myself when the paddle slaps against the water. Laughing, I wipe drops from my face and sunglasses.

Buck smiles at me but doesn't tease. As we paddle away from the shore, me carefully following Buck, I note how peaceful the water is. There are a few ripples, but Buck did choose a good afternoon to venture out into the Sound—the wind is calm and the tide is still out.

We paddle in silence until Buck says, "Just think, you could write a book, and I could illustrate it."

I edge closer to his boat. "What kind of book?"

"Funny things tourists say, maybe. I see you straining your ears to listen to them in the Grille."

I laugh. "Cheap entertainment, what can I say?"

"Do you want to write a book? A novel?"

"You sound like Ron."

"Isn't that every author's dream?"

"To write a novel?" I dip my paddle into the glistening green water. I remember Lona saying there are days she's sure she can't write another line. I don't need that kind of pressure in my life. "No, thanks."

We are parallel, and I can see him squint into the sunlight.

"Okay, I guess I've had it wrong, then."

I smile. "I couldn't write a novel. That would involve too much dedication to one project. Plus, I'm not good at dialogue."

"What about a book without dialogue?"

"Just a narrative?"

"If that's what it's called." He's ahead of me now and makes his voice louder so I can hear him.

I raise my voice, as well. "Nope, it's not going to happen."

"You're such a dream crusher."

"What?"

"Oh, I was thinking we would do a book together. You know, illustrator and author. But you aren't biting."

"We can just kayak together instead," I say.

A flock of seagulls cries overhead; Buck is silent.

"How often do you come out here?" I ask. "Betty Lynn says you bring your sketchbook and draw."

He doesn't reply.

I turn to see his eyes on the water, straight ahead. "Hey, I didn't mean just kayak and not talk!"

He laughs. "Oh, I thought you wanted me to shut up."

I grin. "I'm not that rude . . . usually."

Suddenly, along the shore, I see the back of the Inn on Pamlico Sound, a small Buxton establishment that many tourists frequent and love for its hospitality. Looking at it nestled across a long pier, I take the opportunity to tell Buck my thoughts. "I want the Bailey House Bed and Breakfast so badly."

"Why?"

"I love so much about it." I plan to stop there, but Buck's interested look and the beautiful afternoon give me encouragement to continue. "Did you know it was built in 1910? It's had some face-lifts since then, but basically it looks and feels its age. I think it's the only bed and breakfast on the Outer Banks that's brick. Whenever I'm there, it's like being in the best bubble bath, all fresh and relaxing and . . ."

"Clean?"

"Yeah! The place is clean. Well, it was when the Baileys took care of it."

"I remember Ron told me it was run by a bunch of stuffy Brits."

Shaking my head, I say, "The Baileys weren't stuffy. Ron just never bothered to get to know them." Dreamily, I think of the garden in the backyard and wonder how many hours it would take to make it look beautiful again. I think of how Mrs. Bailey would ring a silver bell to let guests know that it was time for breakfast. Right now my stomach would love a plate of blueberry muffins with the blackberry jam she liked to make. "There are so many traditions I want to carry on."

"Which ones?"

Buck has asked, giving me free rein to talk about what I remember, and I am eager to do just that. "The lemon cookies they had there. The breakfasts, and desserts. I also would love to extend the front porch.

A lot of bed and breakfasts have a large porch with rocking chairs. I think that would really add to the charm of the Bailey House."

I'm still talking when we reach a set of short piers with two docked Carolina Skiffs, buoyed by ropes. Buck has to interrupt me to tell me to be careful of tree roots that hide in the shallow water near the wooden posts.

I follow Buck cautiously around the piers and boats.

After a minute, Buck says, "I would just say that the house is a little old, so be . . ." After a pause, he adds, "Well, you know, be smart about it. Things aren't always as they appear."

Of course I know that the house is old; I just finished telling him when it was built. Deciding I've probably talked long enough, I steer the conversation to him. "What do you like to paint best?"

Without hesitation, he says, "Frogs."

I let out a laugh. "No, seriously."

"I told you."

"What?"

He grins. "Frogs."

I guess he's serious. "Okay."

"Have you ever looked at one real close? They're fascinating."

"How?" I paddle a little faster as he heads toward deeper water.

"Tree frogs, and especially the poisonous dart frogs, are the most fun to draw. Their eyes are amazing."

"Do you paint from memory or actually sitting beside one?"

"I never sit by a frog, Hatteras Girl." His smile teases me.

"Never?"

"No, I hold my breath and stand nearby so I don't scare him away." Grinning, he adds, "Kinda like I do with you."

"You won't scare me away."

Turning his kayak with one big sweep, Buck faces me. "I've done it before. Scared women, I mean."

"Really? How did you do that?"

"Well, there was this pretty one I liked once and we talked a lot. She, too, liked art, and so I thought we were on the same page. I asked her out and after one date she never spoke to me again."

"Why not?"

"If I knew the answer to that, I wouldn't scare women away."

I wonder who she was. I try to think back to high school and who Buck dated then. There was this one cheerleader. I thought she was pretty; her eyes were a sea-moss green. I can't recall her name, though I bet Ron would remember. "Do you ever think about meeting someone online?"

"You mean like join one of those matchup sites?"

I find that funny and laugh. "Matchup sites? Who calls them that?"

"What do you call them?" He shifts in his seat, adjusts his paddle, and leads the way.

"Dating sites." I paddle faster. "Do you?"

"Are you interviewing me for something?" He waits for me to catch up to his boat.

"No."

Squinting, he asks, "Are you sure?"

"No, so answer the question."

"Only if you will answer mine."

"Fair enough."

"As for dating sites, I really haven't given it much thought." He shakes his left paddle. I watch the pellets of water drip from it into the Sound. They take turns slipping under the surface. "Maybe I should."

I follow as he guides us to a cove where the marsh grasses are high. We arrive at a sandy piece of shore that is covered in broken oyster shells. We watch a pelican swoop near one and then fly over toward a pier with docked sailboats. Buck says, "Okay, my turn."

"Shoot away."

"Based on all the dates your relatives have set you up with, you have to have some stories to tell." He leads the way away from the shore, his tanned arms skillfully and evenly maneuvering the paddle. "Have you ever been set up with someone you enjoyed being with?"

My answer comes quickly. "Yes." I don't give Buck any more than that. He doesn't need to know about the man who moved to Chicago.

He starts to ask me another question, but I slip in with, "Did I ever tell you about the guy who spilled Coke on his suit?"

"No."

"He went to the bathroom and never came back."

"What?"

"It's true."

"Did he disappear?"

"He went to the restroom and I waited for twenty-two minutes. Do you know how long that is? I sat there and sipped my iced coffee and then looked through my purse, found an old receipt, and made a list on the back of it of what I needed at the grocery store."

"What did he say when he came back?" Buck looks interested.

"He didn't. Well, I left."

"You left?"

"He was still in the restroom."

"Hatteras Girl, you have a pattern about you."

"What's that?"

"You leave men."

"If there was a man worth staying for, I'd stick around." After I say it, I think this might be a line from one of Sheerly's songs.

We paddle back to The Rose Lattice, and Buck straps the kayaks on top of his Jeep. They dribble water onto his roof and down the windows.

"Did you have fun today?" he asks me.

"Yeah." I reach into my pocket for the keys to my truck.

"Then my job is done." He ambles to his car, the sun against his back.

"Buck," I call.

He turns.

"Thanks. It was wonderfully fun." I push away the urge to say more.

"Anytime, Hatteras." Then, with a smile, he gets into his car, starts the engine, waves, and leaves.

I look out at the water. A surprising serenity fills my heart, and I realize it's been a long time since I enjoyed an afternoon as much as this one.

But like a dark cloud moving across a sunny sky, my mind is tainted with thoughts of Davis and Vanessa. I try to rub away the memory of those roses and Vanessa's words. When life gives you a perfect afternoon, you have to guard against anything that tries to steal it away. I pick up a tall blade of grass and shred it, watching the strips get carried by the wind.

On the drive back to Waves, I refuse to let any dark thoughts take over. The volume of my radio is high as Celine Dion confesses, "You gave me faith and you gave me a world to believe in." Turning into my driveway, I wait for the song's last line: "I can live, I can dream once again, 'cause you made me believe."

24

Zane is a bottomless pit. He ate a whole container of cottage cheese and then a Tupperware bowl full of pineapple tidbits as he watched *Andy Griffith* last night. When I made a peanut butter and honey sandwich for myself, he asked for half. Now he says there is no food in the house.

Bending over the counter with a pad and pen, I start a grocery list. Just as I write *cottage cheese,* my phone rings, and I see that it's Davis. The first sensation I feel is delight, but then a dark cloud pushes its way in front of the sun. My palms prickle even though his voice is upbeat, giving me details about a property in Frisco that he hopes to invest in.

I grit my teeth. "I need you to tell me about Vanessa."

"Who?"

"I interviewed her. I saw the roses."

"What roses?"

For a brief second, I want to believe that he did not send roses to her, that she's a liar.

I hate being confrontational, yet I knew that if Minnie were to hear of my predicament, she would encourage me to be bold. I try to borrow some of her strength. "The twenty-four red ones you had delivered to Coastal Finds."

Davis sucks in air. "Oh, those things? I try to keep her shop looking nice for her. She's an old friend."

"She says you two dated."

"Used to. Tell me how your day was. I want to hear how things are at *Lighthouse Views*."

His voice is tender and inviting, and I know I shouldn't, but I allow him to distract me. I begin telling him about my day at the office.

Suddenly, he says, "Let's talk about the Bailey House."

I feel my pulse rate increase.

"Hypothetically," he says, "how much could you afford to pay each month for the bed and breakfast?"

"Each month?" I know the answer immediately. I have been calculating my finances for a long time. "I could survive on a reserve of funds of $2,800 each month for about three months, and hopefully, after that, the house would be bringing in lots of paying guests."

"Sounds like you've given this a lot of thought."

I laugh at that statement. When am I *not* contemplating being the owner of the Bailey House?

"Listen," he says, "I know you want the house. It needs a good owner to run it. I want you to be that person."

My heart is doing cartwheels when Minnie comes home at six. I'm tempted to blurt out the good news, but her eyes are red, and as she sits on the couch, she complains of a migraine. I tell her that I'm going to Food Lion and will bring us back something for dinner. She thanks me, and as I leave the duplex, Zane begs to come with me.

"Oh, it won't be any fun," I say.

His lips curl to form a frown.

Using my animated tone, I say, "I'll bring you a surprise back, okay?"

I rush out the door and hope he doesn't follow me. When I pull out of the driveway, I look up at the living room window to see him standing there, curtain pulled back. His thumb is in his mouth; he waves with the other hand.

At Food Lion, I get a cup of coffee from the pot by the deli. I add sugar and stir as I push my cart along the aisles. Sometimes a simple cup of coffee brings focus to a day; something about the aroma and heat of the beverage clears the mind. Even if the coffee is only grocery-store-brewed and not Blue Sparkle Mountain Top.

Yet now as I sip my coffee, I wonder why my stomach feels like I ate a greasy bowl of chili. The neon sign over the deli flickers, and I think about the sign that's been flashing across my mind ever since I found out that Davis and Vanessa dated. *Does he still have feelings for her?* He says it's over, but she told me they tend to break up and then get back together again.

The next thing I know I've bumped into an endcap loaded with cereal boxes. The coffee splashes from the cup onto the floor. The spill spreads out toward the meat counter.

I ask the man behind the counter for something to wipe the floor with. He goes to the back and returns with a roll of paper towels.

I use my foot to wipe the paper towels across the coffee puddle and watch the white absorb the brown. This is me, I think. Clumsy. Distracted. I couldn't sell a three-thousand-dollar bracelet to a woman in sunflower flip-flops if my life depended on it.

When I hear a clearing of a throat and a crisp, "Hello," I look up to see Douglas Cannon standing beside a partially loaded grocery cart.

"Hi." My foot pauses from its motion.

"How are you?"

The shock that he has actually asked me something genuine and normal silences me for a 'moment. Dumbly, I repeat the question. "How am I? Pretty good. And you?"

I half expect him to start talking about jeepneys and sharks, but he just stands there. "Shopping for groceries?" he asks as his fingers tighten around a package of Tyson chicken thighs.

"Are you buying chicken?" I suppose one lame question deserves an equally inane response.

"Yeah."

"It's on sale."

"It is. I'm going to marinade it in teriyaki sauce and pineapple juice. I thought about making adobo, but don't think I want pork tonight."

I pick up a package of thighs and breasts. "Sounds good."

We look at each other as I wonder how I can gracefully leave this scene.

"Would you . . . like to come over?" His voice is expectant, hopeful.

I swallow. "I can't. I . . . I have to cook at home tonight."

Why is it that Douglas brings out the liar in me?

He smiles. "Maybe another time, then." He looks as though he wants to say something else, and I think, if he does, I'll blurt out that I hope he finds love and happiness, that I wish him well. He looks over my head and then at his cart. "See you around."

Part of me wants to apologize for leaving him at the restaurant that night, for lying to him, for not desiring to get to know him. The other part of me just wants to pick up the wet paper towels from the floor, stuff them inside a trash can, and hurry home.

I watch him push his cart away, stop for a block of cheese, and continue walking. I hand the roll of towels back to the butcher.

I'm halfway down the baking aisle, face-to-face with Betty Crocker's brownie mixes, when I realize I left the patch of soggy paper towels on the floor. As I round the corner, I don't see Douglas, and there is a cashier with red lipstick and a pleasant smile ready for me. "How are you today, sweetie?" she asks.

I can't risk going back now.

⁓ ⌒ ⌒

When I get home, Minnie is on the phone. She quickly snaps shut her LG flip phone as I enter the kitchen with the groceries. I set the bags on the counter and wonder about her secrecy. I sure hope she and my Outer Banks relatives aren't arranging another blind date for me.

She watches as I put cans of tomato sauce in the pantry. "Will you go with me to see Mom this Sunday after church?"

"What about dinner at Sheerly's? Aren't we all going there?"

"Well . . . yeah." Minnie moistens her lips with a quick movement of her tongue. "Sheerly told me to pick Mama up. Ropey can't do it."

I wonder if Ropey has an appointment to test drive Casey's boat that he wants to buy. Minnie and I have picked up Irvy before. Minnie has a hitch to attach her mother's wheelchair to the back of her car, but it's quite a challenge for Minnie and me to lift Irvy into the backseat and get her into a comfortable position with her legs bent and her arms at her sides. Then comes the seat belt; Minnie always tells me I secure it much too tightly.

Zane darts into the room, pretending he's an airplane. "Hi," he says and then, "What did you buy me?"

"Ice cream."

"What kind?"

"The good kind."

He smiles. "I like the good kind."

"What kind would that be?" asks Minnie.

"I'm thinking chocolate," Zane says with vibrancy.

"Well, I guess I'll have to take it back, then."

Zane gives me a questioning look.

"Because I didn't just get chocolate. I got chocolaty chunky chocolate." I draw out each word as a smile breaks across Zane's cheeks.

Zane tosses his hand in the air, and we high-five each other.

"Don't worry," Minnie says after Zane leaves the kitchen. "On Sunday, we'll get someone else to take him from church to Sheerly's so we'll only have Mama to think about."

Already I am grateful for that someone else. Bless his or her heart.

Later, after dinner and a bath, Zane has snuggled with Popacorn in his bed. Minnie and I turn on a cooking show. The chef is making egg rolls; they sizzle in a large frying pan. I think of Mom's egg rolls, almost tasting the ground beef, garlic, cabbage, and onions she puts in hers.

During a commercial, Minnie says, "I saw a grandmother and grandson today at Wendy's. I guess he was about two. He called French fries 'fire flies' and she kept smiling each time he did." She yawns and stretches her arms above her head. "I like seeing you delight in Zane."

Delight in Zane! I'm glad I'm not drinking soda, for surely it would be spewing from my mouth right now.

I massage her shoulders and back before she stretches out on the sofa like a cat and drifts off to sleep. "The grandmother was so amused by her grandson," she mumbles in a groggy voice. "She kept laughing at the way he said, 'I want a cheeseburger and fire flies.' "

She's snoring before she's able to finish her thoughts, but I know what she wanted to say. She wanted to tell me she wishes Zane's grandmother was able to delight in him.

Last week when Minnie and I visited Irvy in the nursing home, Irvy was not in a good mood. She spoke only two words when Minnie stroked her cheeks: "Dear Eleanor."

Minnie's face drained. "What, Mama? What did you say?"

Irvy pursed her lips together and repeated, "Dear Eleanor."

"Mama, I'm not Eleanor."

I tried to come up with who Eleanor was. Did Minnie know? I sat there quietly, breathing in the aroma of Pine-Sol and boiled potatoes. The rest of the visit was spent with Minnie talking to Dicey about her mother's condition. I patted Irvy's hand and smiled, but the woman let her stare settle somewhere over my head.

After we told Irvy good-bye, we walked toward the parking lot. I was swinging my arms to make sure they could move when Minnie said, "She taught me how to crochet."

"I remember."

"And now she can't recall my name."

"I know."

I reached out just as she was lifting her arms out to me. Our arms bumped against each other before we circled them around each other's shoulders. We stood hugging in the parking lot with the summer sun beating upon our heads.

As we drove home in silence, I wondered if the dementia came first and then the stroke, or did the stroke lead to the dementia? Whatever happened, Irvy is only a shell of who she used to be. Once, she taught piano to fifteen students each week. Once, she gave a piano concert of her own that was praised by the chamber of commerce. Once, she gave me the courage to play my flute, even though my music teacher didn't think I had any talent. Irvy told me I had passion and, coupled with discipline, that was enough.

I practiced for three hours and ate dinner alone that night. Mom came in to make sure I was all right. "My daughter practicing reminds me of my grandfather when he play his flute. You have his blood in you." There was pride in her voice. I felt if Irvy believed in me, I could be Godzilla and conquer every enemy.

After church, instead of heading directly to the nursing home, Minnie says she first needs to get something from our duplex. When her cell phone rings, she tells the caller she'll call him or her back soon. She doesn't disclose who the caller was, but once she unlocks our front door, she bounds up the steps to her bedroom and shuts the door.

As I walk past her room to mine, I hear her phone ring again and her soft voice. I change from my cotton skirt into a pair of faded blue shorts and my frayed UNC-Charlotte T-shirt. The humidity is cruel today. If I'm going to have to lift Irvy and her wheelchair, I plan to be comfortable.

Immediately, when she sees my outfit, Minnie suggests I wear something else.

I try to laugh it off by saying, "Minnie, I've never changed clothes just to pick up Irvy. You're joking, right?"

"Well . . ." She has no answer.

In the car, I talk about Davis, saying he wants to take me to Arlington one day soon. Just for laughs, I explain how I ran into Douglas at the grocery store, and that's when I see that Minnie has pulled up to the Grille. The Grille is closed on Sundays. The parking lot is empty, as if an invisible shroud has been pulled over the marked lines. "What are we doing here?" I ask.

Without looking at me, Minnie replies, "Irvy likes the pudding here, so I'm picking her up a pint."

"Pudding? The Grille doesn't serve pudding." I know; I've memorized the menu.

Minnie gets out of her car with her classic don't-bother-me-I-know-what-I'm-doing attitude. I've seen it before when she tried out for cheerleading and when she sent her wedding photo to *Brides* magazine.

"Minnie," I call out to her as I open the passenger door. "How are you getting inside?"

"Betty Lynn said she'd let me in."

That is absurd. I know the manager doesn't trust Betty Lynn with a crate of glasses, let alone a key to a restaurant. "She doesn't have a key."

Minnie stands at the front door and gives me a lopsided smile; for a moment, I think maybe Minnie is losing her mind, too. If she does, what will happen to Zane?

Rushing out of the car to her, I place my hand on her back. "Minnie, what are you doing?"

25

Minnie pushes open the door to the Grille with determination. I follow her into the cool interior, breathing in the faint odor of fried fish—yesterday's special. Confused as to why the door is unlocked, I wonder if the place has been robbed. Minnie shocks me sometimes. She's adamant that I carry a can of Mace, yet now she's willingly entering a dark, empty place.

Then, suddenly, there are cries from within the room. "Surprise! Happy birthday! Surprise!"

Lights flash on overhead, and people emerge from behind chairs, the counter, and Zane even jumps out from under one of the tables.

Relief spreads over me, replacing uncertainty.

There they are. Mom, Dad, Ron, Sheerly, Tiny, Ropey, and Beatrice Lou, all in front of me, smiling like proverbial Cheshire cats. Buck is here, too.

Ropey draws me to himself with a strong hug and then kisses my flushed cheek. And suddenly, I know this is why Minnie has been so secretive. My birthday is in two days, on Tuesday, and this group has planned and carried out a surprise party for me.

Across the room I see Betty Lynn, and over by the counter stands Aggie. There's no need to pick up Minnie's mom; Irvy is already here, seated in her wheelchair, wearing a mauve cotton dress, a string of fake pearls, and a pair of electric-blue fuzzy slippers. Her eyes look glazed.

I hug Dad and then Mom. I breathe in Mom's perfume—Elizabeth Arden's Green Tea—a fragrance she has worn ever since I can remember. Looking back and forth between them, I gush, "When did you get here? It's great to see you!"

"Surprised?" asks Dad. He has a piece of yellow paper sticking out of his shirt pocket; I know it's a list of some kind.

I nod.

Mom says, "We got here just a while ago."

"Can you stay with me? With us?"

Dad answers, "Sheerly asked us to stay overnight at her place. We have to head back home tomorrow."

It's funny; they look older today and yet as familiar as when I was six and wishing for a pony. I wish they would stay with me, but then again, I'm not sure I could handle Zane, Minnie, Mom, Dad, and myself all under the same roof for long.

"Thanks for being here." I kiss Dad's cheek.

Mom's smile is wide as she says, "We wouldn't have missed it for the world."

Ron sheepishly approaches me and gives me a solid embrace. "It's all about you today, so enjoy it. This kind of attention is only yours once a year and now that you're thirty, I'm not sure how much longer you'll be alive to appreciate it. Thirty's ancient."

Buck is by his side, just as he always was in middle and high school. He hugs me. "Happy birthday, Hatteras Girl. Personally, I don't think thirty is all that old."

"Thanks." I note that even my baby brother is dressed nicely for the occasion, wearing jeans instead of his usual cargo shorts. I now wish I'd listened to Minnie and put on something more festive than my ragged T–shirt and faded shorts.

L. J. opens the door with a bang and carries in a gold gift bag. She takes off her sunglasses and smiles at the gathered group. "Am I late?"

"No," says Sheerly. "Right on time."

"Great!" L. J. brushes strands of hair and perspiration from her cheek. "I had two batches of bacon cornbread in the oven that were taking their sweet time to get done."

We're ushered by Sheerly into the room in the back reserved for private parties.

Eight tables are covered in white linen cloths. In the center of each table is a creamy white vase holding sprigs of baby's breath and stems of zinnias and Gerber daisies. One long table pushed against the wall has been filled with food. On a smaller one, surrounded by paper plates, napkins, and forks, is a square chocolate cake decorated in rainbow-colored plastic kites. I wonder who made it; my relatives are not known for their baking skills.

Green and gold helium balloons attached to colorful ribbons are scattered along the corners of the room, and streamers loop around the light fixture fashioned to look like a seashell. A banner pasted on the wall reads: HAPPY BIRTHDAY!

"Did you suspect anything?" asks Sheerly as we line up at the long table to load our plates with spaghetti, meatballs, garlic bread, and a salad filled with cherry tomatoes.

I think of the past week and Minnie's strange behavior. I knew something was being kept from me, but I didn't guess it was this. To my aunt, I reply, "Oh no. Y'all are all good secret keepers."

Sheerly laughs. "We parked at the bank so you wouldn't see any cars."

"Clever."

The food is tasty, made by a catering company whose owner I have yet to interview. I make a mental note to tell Selena we need to do a piece on Italian by the Sea.

Before the cake is cut, Sheerly leads everyone in a rendition of "Happy Birthday." Then she and L. J. sing a song my aunt has composed just for me. The chorus is catchy: "Thirty years old and worth more than gold. Yes, I've been told, you are more precious than gold."

The cake is delicious, and I find out they ordered it from the Orange Blossom Bakery in Buxton.

I suppose one of the best things about having a birthday is the presents. Sheerly tells me that humans are never too old to experience that excitement that goes along with unwrapping a gift with your name on the card. On a table to the left of the food is an arrangement of boxes and bags, all in colorful birthday wrapping paper. Inside the gold gift bag from L. J. is a homemade CD of one of the All That Glitters Is Gold concerts held at the nursing home.

"Thanks, L. J."

L. J. and Sheerly both radiate happiness.

My parents give me a twenty-five-inch TV for my bedroom.

"Not a flat screen, but you like," Mom tells me. Mom loves to watch TV in bed. She sleeps with the TV on the Food Network, claiming it helps her get a better night's rest. "It's Samsung," she tells us all.

"Thanks, Mom."

"Korean," she adds. "Like us." Based on Mom's glowing smile, you'd think the Korean electronics company belonged to her.

I know Ron is groaning because I hear a muffled embarrassed sound coming from where he stands.

Aggie hands me another gift. This one is wrapped in green paper. I lift the cotton item out—a purple fisherman's hat with the words "Hatteras Girl" embroidered in pink on the front. Even though there is no card to tell me who it's from, I know who it must be. My eyes meet Buck's across the room, where he's seated next to Ron. He grins.

"Buck," I say, "I've never had a personalized fisherman's hat. Thank you."

Sheerly, Tiny, Beatrice Lou, and Ropey have chipped in to get me a gift card for Wal-Mart. "It is such a good store. I don't know what I'd do without it," Tiny confesses.

Aggie gives me a pair of earrings—gold hoops so that I no longer have to borrow Minnie's—and Minnie's gift is a promise to cook me dinner on my actual birthday. Ron's present is a pair of cheetah-spotted sunglasses.

Zane shows me his rope art—a basic white braided rope tied in a single hitch knot with two small white seashells glued to it. There is one blob of glue that is larger than one of the seashells. "Happy Birthday!" He extends the gift to me, but when I reach for it, he won't let go.

"Zane, let her have it," says his mother.

"I'll put it in my room," I say. "You can see it every day."

He seems pleased, and I am, too. My child psychology is getting better these days.

Zane begs for another slice of cake. Sheerly assists him but asks him first to say please. He refuses, his lips pucker, but when he sees

Ropey with a piece of cake, his eyes grow wide, and quickly he gives in. "Please."

As I walk by Irvy, she reaches out to me, gives me a kiss on the cheek, her faint breath caressing my ear. "Thank you for being here," I say.

After opening and closing her mouth a few times, her words come at last. "Remember Mrs. Dupree," she says.

"What?" I move in closer.

"She fell."

"Oh, I'm sorry to hear that." I wonder who Mrs. Dupree is. Perhaps a woman at the nursing home.

"Remember her." Irvy's eyes flicker and then shut. "She needs to be remembered."

Maybe I could send some cake back to the home for the woman. "Does she like cake?" I ask.

Irvy keeps her eyes closed as she says, "Mrs. Dupree fell on a Sunday."

I give up trying to understand Irvy when a fine distraction enters. Davis walks across the room, making his way toward me.

His embrace is tight and warm. "Hi, happy birthday." He kisses me, and I grow weak at the knees. He's wearing a white dress shirt and pair of tan slacks and smells of Ralph Lauren's Polo cologne. I know because he's told me that's what he wears.

I really wish I'd dressed up.

He hands me a manila envelope. "For you."

I fiddle with the clasp and then reach into the opening. Anticipation grips me as I pull out papers. I read the bold heading on the first one, then lift my eyes to meet his. They are serious with a hint of mystery.

No words will come out of my mouth. He smiles and pulls me closer.

"Is it really what it says it is?" I whisper.

"What does it say?"

I gulp. "Rent . . ." Moistening my lips, I try again. "Rent with the option to buy. It's for the Bailey House!"

"Happy birthday!" He grins.

Elated, I hug him. "I can't believe it! I can't believe it!"

Then my parents approach, and I introduce them to Davis. I'm more bubbly and animated than I've been in weeks.

Irvy is not so pleased; her eyebrows are bunched together. I catch her glaring at Davis.

At four, Buck leaves with Ron to go kayaking. "See you later, sis," my brother tells me. "I'm crashing at your place tonight. Just leave a pillow on the sofa for me."

My relatives are now all seated around one table talking about family updates. They all seem interested in the conversation. Except for Ropey. When I look into his eyes, I think his mind is on that eighteen-footer at Casey Luweigneson's. He told me last week that Beatrice Lou said she would not let him own a "death machine." After Lawrence's boat was capsized in the storm, Beatrice Lou claims she's never going to ride on one, nor be married to a man who owns one.

I load my gifts into Minnie's car with Dad's help. "Come visit us sometime," he says as he places the TV in the trunk. "Mom and I miss having you in Charlotte."

I say I will, putting the manila envelope that holds the best gift of all on top of the TV. I then carefully close the trunk and lock the car. Twice.

As we make our way back inside the Grille, I think of how I love my family, but right now I just want to be alone with Davis.

26

When I walk back into the party room, Sheerly is telling Davis about coming in second place at the Kitty Hawk song competition. I manage to extricate him and then follow him outside the Grille. He tells me he has to go to a meeting.

"On a Sunday afternoon?" I feel like Zane with a notion to whine.

"Business is always waiting to happen."

I squash the niggling thought that this business might have something to do with Vanessa. I don't want the role of the jealous girlfriend. I pull him to me, gently touch his chin and neck, and then give him a kiss along his jaw. "Thanks for the lease papers. I can't wait to read them and sign."

I walk with him to where his BMW is parked at the bank across the street and then watch as he climbs into the driver's seat. My eyes are still on him as he lowers the top, puts on a pair of Ray-Ban sunglasses, backs out and away, and until he's only a dot on the road.

He gave me lease papers for the Bailey House; my excitement is as vast as the August sky. I smile up at the wispy clouds and at a stranger riding his bike down the road. The stranger smiles back.

"Thank you, God." My voice sounds much too giddy to belong to me. "Thank you for Davis and for this gift."

While Minnie drives Zane and me home, we excitedly talk about our plans for the bed and breakfast. Zane claps his hands and sings, "London Bridge Is Falling Down."

⟳

That night, I drive to the Bailey House by myself, and when I step out of my truck, I feel like a celebrity as I give one of the front columns a kiss. "We are really going to do this!" I cry. Davis has entrusted this prime real estate owned by his grandparents to me—to *me*! The locked front door is the only thing stopping me from going inside today. I wish Davis had given me a key. I close my eyes, letting all the memories of being inside the house fill me. Davis said the furniture is covered in old sheets for protection. Who knew I could look forward to taking off dusty old sheets?

Beside the large Colonial-style home is a garage that Mr. and Mrs. Bailey used for not only their Lincoln but all the lawn tools and a riding mower. On the side of the garage is a set of stairs that leads up to a room above the garage, a room where the Baileys slept. I've always thought that either Minnie or I could have this room. Now, with Zane, Minnie will need more space. I decide to let the two of them use that room. There is a small office inside the main property on the first floor that could serve as a cozy bedroom for me.

When I get home, Zane is tucked in bed. Ron and Minnie are talking in low voices on the back deck. I greet them and then excuse myself to my bedroom.

Opening the manila envelope, I take out the pages. There it is in bold print: Rent with the Option to Purchase. I smile at myself in the dresser mirror. "Hello," I say to my reflection. "I'm Jacqueline Cate Donovan. I'm twenty-nine; on Tuesday I'll be thirty. I rent the Bailey House!"

I see that the agreement states I'll pay $2,800 each month to rent the house located at 3 Red Pelican Court. Even though that is the exact sum I told Davis I could afford, now that it is in black and white I wonder how I'll be able to come up with that. I shove the worry aside and read over the pages about five times. There are paragraphs about the closing, the rent payments, the landlord, and all kinds of legal things I only partially understand. I notice that Davis has reduced the price of the property. When we first spoke, he told me it was $1.5 million, but the contract lists the cost of the home as $1.2 million, should I desire to exercise my right to buy it. I wonder if I'll ever be able to come up with that kind of money.

It strikes me funny to think that Davis will be my landlord. What kind of landlord will he be? Surely not like Mrs. Appleton, who always spies on us and is strangely particular about where we place our check. Flipping over the lease, I let my eyes blur. I place the papers on the bed and sigh. I'll ask Davis to explain it all to me later.

There's a knock on my door. Minnie asks if I want to join her and Ron.

I shake my head in a dreamy sort of way.

She smiles. "Oh, I know. You want to read over the contract a few hundred more times."

Once she's closed my door, I send a text message to Davis. *Thank you. I miss you.*

27

As I cook breakfast for Minnie, Ron, and me, I think of the first breakfast I want to serve at the Bailey House. I've often thought about this, but now that I have the legal papers in my hand, it's as different as deciding which ice cream flavor you plan to eat as you sit at home compared to standing in front of all the varieties at Baskin-Robbins with a sales clerk ready to serve you.

Prying open an old cookbook, I flip through the breakfast section. Waffles with strawberries? Omelets? One photo has a fluffy yellow omelet with spinach spilling out over the edges, all presented on a Carolina-blue plate. I turn the pages to see recipes for banana bread and strudels. I know that a hash brown casserole would also fit in nicely on the breakfast menu. I wonder if I'll need to hire a cook to help me on busy mornings. All I know is it can't be one of my Hatteras relatives!

Once when Minnie and I were daydreaming about our plans for the Bailey House, she recommended we have a Korean night.

I stopped massaging her shoulders. "What would we serve?"

"Pulgogi."

"Who's cooking?"

"Your mom could come over."

Mom would love that. However, I'm surprised by Minnie's suggestion. The last time Minnie came over to eat a Korean meal with us, she hardly tried any of the pickled vegetables, not even the tamer ones like cucumbers in soy sauce. She did have a small portion of the seasoned beef strips—called fire beef—from the large pan set in the middle of the dining table.

Questions buzz around my head, and I find a piece of paper to start a list. There must be lemon cookies and raspberry cream soda in stock at all times. Perhaps we should follow the practice of Doubletree Hotels and give out fresh cookies upon check-in. I feel sadness seep into my heart when I realize I don't have Mrs. Bailey's lemon cookie recipe.

Not wanting to give in to sorrow, I quickly resume the list. Should we play flute music in the sunroom? Maybe buy a piano or have a music night and let Sheerly and her group entertain? Unfortunately, Irvy's piano was sold at auction shortly after she moved in to the Morning Glory Nursing Home. *Flowers,* I write at the bottom of the list. Lots of color will make the parlor bright and beautiful. My mind whirls with thoughts of special functions, dessert parties, and the possibility of having canoes and kayaks to rent by the back pier.

I hear Minnie's laughter and then Ron say, "Well, everyone thought you were pretty."

I call them to breakfast, then hear the ping of my phone. The text message from Davis reads, *I miss you, too. I'll see you soon.*

⌒⌒

"But I hardly saw you," I protest after Minnie leaves for work and my brother says he needs to head back to Florida. "Can't you stay another day?"

"Work calls. Not everyone has a flexible schedule." I know he's referring to me. I could tease that our dad doesn't think Ron really works for a living, but I hold back. Instead I say, "You and Minnie were up late talking."

His smile is large, content, too happy. Are they interested in each other?

I watch Ron get down on the floor and roll trucks across the carpet with Zane. The idea of my brother dating Minnie bothers me. I don't want Minnie to compare Ron to the love of her life every morning at breakfast and every evening over freshly grilled salmon. Perhaps they are just friends, like I am with Buck.

The coffee maker gurgles, signaling that the beverage is ready. After pouring myself a cup of coffee, I let the steam rising from the mug wash over my face.

Zane giggles as Ron lines the Tonka trucks by the wall and then pretends two are racing against each other. When he gets up to leave, Zane begs him to stay longer.

With his duffle bag in his hand, Ron tells me he had fun. "Buck and I went kayaking yesterday after we left your party and then talking with Minnie was great."

"So? Do you like her?" There are days when we never get beyond our middle school years.

"Jackie." He gives me a hug. "She's like a sister to me."

I put my arms around him. Ron is a good guy. I want him to be happy. "So you aren't interested in her romantically?"

He pulls from the embrace. "You really are the nosey journalist, aren't you?"

The words sting like a nip from a dog.

After work, I buy a dozen pink roses for Minnie and put them in a silver vase on the kitchen table. I attach a note that reads, *Our dream of owning the Bailey House has finally come true!*

Zane runs around me, banging his trucks together and shouting, "We are going to be owning the place!"

When Minnie comes home, she admires the roses and says, "It's going to be a lot of hard work, but we'll be living our dream. Do you think the mermaid still goes out with the same prince? What did we name him?"

"Sullivan."

"Did we give him a last name?"

I don't recall one and am about to say that when she confesses, "I want Zane to have a home to grow up in." There's a long pause and then, "A house."

"If I had to grow up again," I say, "I'd want to live in the Bailey House. You can't do much better than that." I imagine Zane cramming trucks down the laundry chute, racing around the lawn like a bulldozer, sliding down the banister, knocking over an ivy topiary.

I remember Minnie telling me about her ideal wedding gown while we sat next to the mermaid in the back garden. She wanted a white satin dress trimmed in dolphin sequins and pink rosebuds. Years later, when she married at age twenty-one, she opted for a satin dress trimmed in lace, laughing at her childish dream.

We all gave her glass dolphins and pink roses anyway.

28

He's late, and the fear rises in me like a hurricane wind. He isn't going to show. I think of his eyes. His lips. The way they caress mine. Yet his kisses always leave me with a feeling of uncertainty. Like he could take me or leave me.

I realize I'm no Vanessa. I've never owned a Vera Bradley purse or worn an Ann Taylor dress, and it's only thanks to a catalog that came in the mail that I know what a Coach bag is. I wonder if I'm normal—if Davis and I have a normal relationship. When I dated Louis in college, I always knew where I stood in his world because he showed his feelings with these incredible love letters that always ended in bold lines: *You are my world and I love you! XOXOXOXO!!!*

I count the windows as I pace the property.

At seven twenty-six, I'm sure I misread the text message he sent me earlier today. Flipping open my phone, I search for it in my inbox and read his words for the tenth time. *Meet me at the Bailey House tonight at 7.*

I sit on the front steps, leaning against one of the columns. I'm grateful for an easterly breeze and a cloudy sky. I again think of the plans I have for this place. The kitchen will probably need to be remodeled. It needed a major makeover nineteen years ago. The industrial dishwasher leaked and the faucet wobbled each time it was used. There were a few cracks in the linoleum.

When a familiar BMW finally pulls into the driveway, my heart feels like it's been freed from worry. The convertible's top is up, yet I can clearly see Davis inside, though his sunglasses shield his eyes.

Davis steps out of his car, and although I approach him to give him a hug, he moves away and raises one finger, asking me to wait a minute.

So I just stand there.

"No," he says to the caller. "I fixed that wall for you last week. Look at your rental agreement. No, no. Listen, the wall was repaired. That's all I can do for you."

When he finishes the conversation, his frown is immediately replaced by a wide smile. He embraces me and gives me a kiss. "How are you?"

"Ready to get inside the house."

He dangles a key in front of me.

Letting out a whoop, I grab the key and fit it into the lock on the front door. When the door swings open, I pull in a deep breath and reach for Davis's hand. "A lot of prayers are coming true for me right now," I say, my words barely audible. Excitement has been in my veins all day, and right now, I'm close to feeling overwhelmed.

We walk into the dark house together. Davis lets go of my hand and turns on the lights in the hallway and then the two brass lamps in the parlor.

And there it is in front of me, all around me—just as I remembered it, along with the musty ancient scents of a house that's sat empty for too long. I join Davis in the parlor where the furniture is covered by white sheets. I look at the walls with their familiar paintings of wild horses at Shackleford and the large canvas of painted violets in earthen pots above the sofa.

Minnie once told me the violets looked good enough to eat, didn't I agree? But that made me think back to a dandelion I ate once. It, too, had looked good enough to eat. I'd expected it to taste like parsley, and when it didn't, I drank a whole pitcher of Kool-Aid to rid my mouth of the bitterness. To Minnie, I'd said, "Those violets look like they'd taste like grape Kool-Aid."

I follow Davis through the dining room with the long farmhouse table where breakfast was served. Even the Royal Dalton tea set, now covered by a large white towel, is on the sideboard, as it always used to be.

In the sunroom, I touch the green wallpaper, and when I make contact, I'm a little girl visiting Mr. and Mrs. Bailey once again.

Then, as though choreographed to my favorite flute piece, Tchaikovsky's "Waltz" from *Sleeping Beauty,* I'm prancing around the house, upstairs, in the bedrooms, downstairs, and entering the patio from the sunroom, I walk outside and breathe in the garden—a little damp from an earlier rain—until Davis calls me back inside.

We sit at the butcher-block table in the sunroom with the front and patio doors open to let air circulate through the stuffy home. I peer under the white sheet used to cover the worn table. I can feel how it was sitting at this very table in this teak chair, waiting for Ogden to refill my glass tumbler with raspberry cream soda and giving Minnie a few kicks to remind her of her manners.

"Do you know what happened to the birdbath?"

"It broke. I told you that when you asked the last time."

I don't remember him ever saying that, but I don't dwell on his vagueness.

He reaches across the table, lacing our fingers together. I like the way his eyes look into mine.

"The bathrooms upstairs are different," I say. In addition to new paint, they are updated, more modern and functional.

"Yeah, my grandparents had them remodeled."

"Even new toilets, not those archaic ones that often got stopped up. The new sinks and round mirrors are nice, too. Are the bathtubs and Jacuzzis the same?"

"My grandma had all new ones put in," he says. "She kept this place in great shape."

I stand. "I need to check it all out again." I head upstairs once more, entering the Earl Grey Room at the top of the landing. Just as I remembered—a dresser, mirror, and next to it, an antique coatrack. From the windows framed in heavy floral silk curtains, I view the garden below. Fingering the curtains, I know that they need to be washed or dry-cleaned or whatever you do with curtains. Turning, I look at the king-sized bed with the iron legs. To the left, in a dusty frame, is a picture of the queen. Elizabeth is actually in every room. The Baileys loved their royal family.

Forty minutes later, I've entered each of the six bedrooms—two downstairs and the rest on the second floor, as well as all the adjoining bathrooms, smiling at myself in the mirror of each one. I've checked closets to make sure that there are still linens and towels in their metal storage bins. Their odors are distinctly musty, but after a cycle in the washing machine, the items should as smell fresh as they always did years ago. I've spent time opening and closing cabinets and the pantry in the kitchen, sat at the table in the dining room and the sofa in the parlor. Then I went into the laundry room with the Maytag washer and dryer and from there, into the small reading room with shelves of books and a fireplace.

I remove a few clingy cobwebs with my hands and watch spiders scale the walls. There's definitely a lot of work to do around here, but none of it should be too costly. This surveying of the Bailey House has been a perfect way to spend an evening, I think, and I make my way again to the sunroom, where Davis is talking on his phone by the opened door leading to the patio.

"I can meet you when I get back into Nags Head tomorrow. Yes, I'm out of town now," he says to whomever he's talking to, and then he ends the call to smile at me.

"All this place needs is a good cleaning, a touch of paint, and a porch," I say.

"I don't want any porch added on."

"Just a porch on the front," I explain. Mrs. Bailey had actually told me one would be nice so that guests could sit in rocking chairs and watch the sun set. "The kitchen floor needs to be repaired, too."

Davis's face is hard; gone is the smoothness it held just a moment ago. "No, nothing added or taken away. This house has to be kept just like it was when my grandparents owned it." His voice is determined, the words clipped. I think he'd make a good army captain.

"Sure," I say. There is nothing like a man who knows what he wants.

"I want you to open it up again just as it is. No changes."

I take a step and note a busy spider in the corner by the wainscoting in the dining room. "Not even dusting away the cobwebs?"

His face shines with light once more. "That can be done."

"Good. I think I'm going to hire a cleaning crew to help."

He wraps his arms around my waist and draws me close. "I'm so glad I met you," he whispers. "And I love that my grandparents' place is going to be run by you."

"Really?" I ask dreamily.

"You are going to put it back on the map again, Jackie. I believe in you."

The evening air is thick with humidity, but my heart is thick with the excitement that I am blessed beyond belief. The two things I have asked God for ever since I can remember—a good man and the Bailey House—have finally come true.

Davis begins shutting doors and turning off lights. "Time to go," he tells me as he walks toward the hallway.

"Already?"

He has his key out, ready to lock the house. "I've got some work to do. Besides, it's almost ten o'clock."

I recall our night on the dock together when he didn't want to leave. Tonight he seems eager to go.

Outside, my worry evaporates as he draws me to his chest. His arms are warm around my shoulders. Whispering into my hair, he asks, "Are you free tomorrow night?"

"I could be."

"I'd like to take you to Swift's in Kitty Hawk."

I gulp and wonder if I've ever been to a five-star restaurant. "Sure. That would be great!"

He kisses me twice. "I'll pick you up at seven, then."

As I drive to my duplex in Waves, I make up a song lyric that I think Sheerly would approve of: "There's nothing finer than to be in Carolina when romance radiates around you."

Then I realize Davis didn't give me the key. Of course, I haven't given him the papers yet.

29

Although there are some gray clouds forming in the west, the rest of the summer sky is a bright blue canvas perched over the Outer Banks. Minnie has asked me to pick up her migraine prescription at CVS, and with a Saturday afternoon to myself, I feel like driving, so I take the bottle of pills to Over the Edge.

"You didn't have to do that," Minnie says when I hand her the medicine. "But thanks." She takes a sip from a can of Mountain Dew and downs a tablet. "Zane is eating dinner with Ropey," she tells me.

"Seems he likes being with Ropey these days." It has been a while since he's run away like a wild animal or refused to listen to Minnie and me. Perhaps he's ready for kindergarten and riding the school bus next week.

"I can't believe he'll be six in November." Minnie sighs. I know she's wishing Lawrence were here to watch their child blow out the candles on his next birthday cake.

I've come to the store for another reason, too. Summer is nearly gone and I've yet to fly a kite—one of the things I love to do and that has been a tradition of mine ever since Dad bought a kite for

Ron and me to fly right here when I was six. Ron was four and grew bored with the kite when it didn't go high enough for him.

"Well, son," Dad had said, "the only way it will go higher is if we cut the string and set it loose."

"Do that, then!" Ron cheered. "Cut the string!"

I was appalled and hoped that our father wouldn't do something crazy like that. Dad smiled at his little boy, patted his head, and said, "You can do that when you get older and spend your own money on a kite." Then Dad and I leaned our heads back to admire the colorful billowy object fluttering high over our heads. Dad and I always seem to be on the same wavelength; Ron is the monkey wrench. The next time we flew a kite, we went to Jockey Ridge without him.

There are a few kites left in stock at the store, and I pick up each one. I debate about getting a kite with a sunflower on it. Then I see one with a starfish. When I turn to my right, there's Buck.

"Hi, Hatteras. What are you up to?" He's wearing a pair of khaki shorts, flip-flops, a green T-shirt that brings out his eyes, and a winning smile. No wonder customers at the Grille specifically ask for him to be their waiter, especially the teenage girls.

"I think it's time to fly a kite."

He raises his eyebrows. "Where are you going to fly it?"

"Just around the corner. What are you doing here?"

He moves over toward the wall where various items hang on pegs. "I need a whistle."

I note that there is stubble on his chin. With his shoulder-length hair and unshaven face, he looks more rugged than usual, and I consider teasing him about it. I ask, "A whistle?"

"For my kayak. The cheap one I got a couple years ago isn't loud enough."

"Why does a kayak need a whistle?"

"I know," Minnie says from behind the counter where she's just sold a paddle to a young man in blue swim trunks. "In case you're stuck and need help."

"Really?" Buck and I were just on the water in kayaks and I didn't have a whistle.

"You never know what will happen on the high seas." Buck grins at Minnie, and I wonder if the two of them should get together. Minnie looks especially cute today with her hair in a ponytail and her eyes made up to look smoky like the women in fashion magazines. I've never really thought of her as Buck's type, but now I wonder. Yet, there's something about Minnie and Buck getting together that doesn't feel right to me.

Minnie and Buck talk about kayaks while I decide to purchase the kite with a sunflower on it. The plastic casing tells me that it's made of ripstop nylon with a fiberglass frame. I turn the kite over and see that it's twenty-two dollars. For that price, it'd better last a long time and not break free like last year's kite did! I buy an extra spool of string, knowing that the amount that comes with the kite is never enough.

At the counter, I take the merchandise from its packaging, put the frame together, and then attach the string. I ask Minnie if she has an old piece of cloth around the shop for a tail. She looks in the back room and then asks a coworker. They find a dingy white cloth lined in blue. "That will work," I say. "Thanks."

As we head out of the store together, Buck with his whistle strung around his neck and me with my kite, Buck asks, "Do you let other people join you when you fly?"

"Right now?"

"Yeah."

The sun glares in my eyes. I pause to dig into my purse for my sunglasses.

Buck holds the kite for me until I find my cheetah-spotted glasses and slide them over my eyes. "Thanks."

"Are you going to make me ask again?"

"Ask? Oh, of course you can come with me." My tone is light and breezy; I like how at ease I feel around Buck.

Behind the parking lot is a railing, and in front of that lies the beach. Buck follows me, our flip-flops sinking into the sand.

The wind is stronger than it usually is, and the kite lifts easily into the air. I grip the spool of string. One time I accidentally let go and had to chase my kite across the shore.

There is something so freeing about watching a kite soar high above me, something invigorating about a piece of plastic or nylon that has no power of its own but is held aloft by the force of the wind. It reminds me of God's behind-the-scenes work in our lives.

My mind wanders to Davis, and I wonder what he's doing today. We went out to an elegant dinner at Swift's in Kitty Hawk a week ago. The wind tossed our hair as we drove with the top down on his BMW. After a while, I pulled my hair back with a clip and hoped it looked all right. I reached for Davis's hand, so happy to be with him. I talked of the Bailey House but didn't get much of a response from him. I then asked about his job, wondering how many people worked for Rexy Properties and if he liked traveling so much. Again, he only mumbled a few things and turned the conversation back to me.

As we left the restaurant, I knew something was wrong and tried to make things better by leaning over to kiss him and holding his hand on the ride back to Waves. He kissed my cheek as he dropped me off at my duplex, but his lips felt like one of Shakespeare's chew toys, rubbery and cool. Later, after I brushed my teeth, I sent him a text message. He didn't reply.

Suddenly, I'm back in the moment, realizing I've made no attempt to have a conversation with Buck. "Are you off work today?" I ask.

"Right now I am." Buck's eyes watch the kite as it rises and dips and twirls like a dog chasing its own tail.

"All day?"

"I have to go in for a shift later."

"You still like working at the Grille?"

"It's friendly."

I smile. "Friendly is important." I bunch up my toes, feeling the sand between them. I wonder if I should try to ask Buck about his dad again. Each time I see his dad in the gray Griffins construction van, I want to know what happened between Mr. Griffins and his son.

"Blake wants to promote me to day manager."

"That sounds good."

"Yeah, I guess it does." Buck watches the kite, a yellow blob against a blue sky patched with thick clouds. The string tightens as a gust of wind flutters the white cloth tail. "So how's your work? Still like doing all those interviews?"

"Most of the time." I think of the one with Davis, the way he shared with me about his childhood, hobbies, and the Bailey House, all while he made a peach smoothie. "I like writing about people. I enjoy asking the questions, digging deeper." The kite drops, but by adjusting the string, I get it to its zenith once more. "Selena can be a bother every once in a while."

Buck nods. "Yet you want to give it all up for the Bailey House."

We stand silently, watching the kite soar higher into the sky.

"I do." I expect him to give me one of his quizzical looks, but he doesn't. Instead, I feel like he understands, like he comprehends what I feel even though I haven't explained it well.

"Writing is a gift you have."

I smile at Buck, then fix my eyes back on the kite. The wind is keeping it in the air so well I hardly have to do any work. Buck steps closer to me; I can smell his aftershave, mixed with the salt and sea breezes.

"But, Jackie . . ."

"Yeah?"

"Be careful. The Bailey House is . . . old. You should get an inspector to look it over before signing anything with Rexy Properties."

"You think?" I fix my gaze on him.

"Promise me you'll get an inspection first."

He sounds like my dad.

Heavy clouds the color of espresso beans spread over the shore. I watch them looming like a flock of crows.

"Thirsty?" Buck asks after a moment. "I'm going for a Coke."

"At the Grille?"

"Nah, I think I'll try that little place near Breakfast at Andrew's."

"The bank?"

He smiles. "I think it's called Captain's Corner. Serves coffee and Coke and Diet Pepsi, so you would be in luck." His eyes hold expectancy.

"Sure, why not?" I wind in the kite, which is a struggle against the unruly wind.

Buck takes hold of the string, quickly pulling it as the kite lowers from the sky.

I wrap the string as fast as I can around the spool. I see that there's a tangle that looks like a spider's web gone awry. "Oh no. I hate when that happens."

Buck says, "Hold the kite."

I grab the frame to keep it from breaking away as Buck sits on the sand with the spool of string. He begins to detangle the mess. His hair blows in the wind while his eyes focus on the spool. I note how tan he is as his fingers work to remedy the tight web I've created.

"You don't need to bother. Let's just go."

Diligently, he grasps the string, looping it under and over a number of times.

I brace the kite and look up into the sky, which has turned nearly black now. "Let's just go," I say again as my hair whips into my mouth.

Buck continues to unclog the string until, like magic, the tangle disappears. He winds the string onto the spool, secures the end, and grins at me as he stands. "Patience, Hatteras Girl."

"Thanks," I say, and immediately, the first raindrops hit us like buttons falling out of the clouds.

Rushing over the dunes, we get to the parking lot at Over the Edge.

"Follow me," he calls as he unlocks his Jeep.

Steering my truck through the downpour, I follow him.

Water rises onto the narrow pavement of Route 12. I see Buck's taillights and maintain a slow pace as we drive over the bridge to Nags Head.

We park in a tiny lot; I make sure that there are no towing signs because I have been towed once before near here, the summer I was seventeen, and it was not a pleasant experience.

Quickly, dodging raindrops, I follow Buck into the coffeehouse just as I catch a glimpse of a gray van with Griffins & Company painted on the side. In the front seats are two men; one is Buck's father. I look at Buck purposefully, but he doesn't meet my eyes.

Captain's Corner smells of strong, fresh coffee and sugar. For a second, I think about what kind of coffee I want to make at the Bailey House every morning. I'm about to ask Buck what he thinks, but then I remember he doesn't drink coffee. As we stand in line to order, I ask him, "Do you miss working with your dad?"

"He likes to call the shots. It's best we have a little distance between us now." Buck's smile isn't as genuine as I'd like it to be. My mind's wheels spin. What happened between his dad and him?

My T-shirt is damp, so, needing to feel warm, I order a cup of coffee. Buck orders a chai latte.

"I thought you said you were going for a Coke," I tease as we sit down at a table. Then, peering at his drink, I tell him, "I don't think I've ever had one of those."

"Take a sip." He hands his Styrofoam cup to me.

The liquid is creamy, filled with milk and spices. "It's good."

"You haven't lived until you've tasted chai."

"Really?"

"You know, coffee is so overrated. Real living is in the chai."

This sounds like something my mom would say. She told me that one has not lived until she has tasted *japchae*, a vegetable and beef dish made with sweet potato noodles and seasoned with soy sauce, sesame oil, and sugar.

I sip my coffee and am glad I ordered it because it's making my insides toasty and providing the caffeine boost I crave. I look at Buck and recall him in ninth grade when I was in eleventh, a kid just outgrowing his freckles and not even close to my height of five-ten. "When did you grow up?"

"What? You expect me to still be pulling pranks at school?"

"I never expected that boy of yesterday to become a classy man drinking chai tea, a beverage not at all native to the South."

"Actually, did you know that calling it chai tea is redundant?"

"What?"

"*Chai* means *tea* in some language. Hindi, possibly. So when you say *chai tea*, you're saying *tea tea*."

We laugh. "Just like ramen noodles," I say.

This time Buck looks confused.

"Mom says *ramen* means *noodles,* so calling it by both names is essentially saying *noodles noodles.*"

He grins. "Wow, thanks for the education."

I lift my coffee cup and use it to touch the rim of his cup. "You're welcome. Thanks for your bit of knowledge, as well."

Later, as we can't help but overhear three women at a table next to us talk about heading back to Pittsburgh tomorrow, Buck tells me, "I'm going to visit my cousin in California in a few weeks."

I nod. I remember he's visited this cousin before. They go fishing together. "Do you like California?"

Buck's gaze rests somewhere over my left shoulder. "Yeah. But I'd never want to live anywhere but here."

"Wherever I lived, I'd want to be able to always see the ocean."

Buck's chin has a small dimple I've never noticed before. "I agree."

"In Charlotte, I felt like I was always looking for a body of water. Like water balances my life. Isn't that weird?"

"Not at all. I feel the same way."

I'm surprised by his response. I was braced for teasing. Buck has barely teased me at all today.

He runs his fingers through his hair. Then he peers at me intently. "I'd like to make a suggestion."

"Okay."

For a moment he's silent. "I want you to visit Kelly."

"Kelly?"

"She and her husband run a little flower shop in Salvo. Go in there and ask her some questions."

"An interview?"

"Sort of."

"What do I ask her?"

"Who they rent from. How their landlord treats them."

"Why?"

"It'll help you. You know, get a feel for how things really are."

I'm perplexed, but I try not to show it.

In a serious voice he says, "The shop is called Ocean Floral. Speak with Kelly. Tell her I sent you."

When the first boom of thunder sounds, I'm pleased to be inside a coffee shop and not on the Sound flying a kite.

Buck stands and asks if I'd like a refill.

When I say I would, he picks up my empty cup and walks over to the counter. He later returns with my coffee and another chai latte.

Rain and lightning shatter the sky as customers huddle around tables, talking above the noise outside.

Buck gets my attention by touching my hand. "See that guy there with the cast?" He looks over his shoulder.

I see a young man with a mop of damp blond hair and a cast on his left arm.

"Yeah. Do you know him?"

"No, but he was talking to another guy about an accident he was in. He says God answered his prayers because his life was spared."

"That's good." I take a satisfying sip of my coffee.

"The other car's passengers all died."

"That's awful." I look at Buck and wonder why he wants to bring this sad topic into our frivolous afternoon. What happened to the Buck who always teases me?

Gravely, Buck says, "Yeah, it is. Reminds me of how we were all hoping Lawrence would be okay, praying for his life."

I nod. "I know."

He sips his drink through a straw. "God is too often misunderstood."

"What do you mean?"

"People usually expect Him to respond differently than He does."

He isn't teasing, so I get rid of my smile. "What do you mean? Don't you think God should have spared the lives of everyone in that accident?"

"That would have been great."

I sigh. "I don't understand why some people live to say God kept them alive while others die. How does God save one person from death and allow another to die?"

"That's a question we never will get past in this lifetime."

I suppose he's right; Minnie and I can't seem to figure it out.

His eyes invite me to look deeper as he asks, "Have you ever wanted something and then when you finally got it, it didn't feel the same because in the meantime you've changed?"

"Changed? How?"

"Well, it's like you thought this part of your life you were praying for was all that mattered."

"Like me and the bed and breakfast?" I take a sip of my coffee. "An obsession?"

"Actually, I have my own example. I really wanted to get into this art school about two years before I started working at the Grille. I applied and waited. But when the acceptance letter arrived, my heart had done some changing so that being molded by God was far more exciting than the acceptance." He reaches for his drink.

"Okay . . ." I'm not sure where Buck is going with this topic.

He takes a sip of his chai as I wait for what he has to say. "I changed in the meantime. The thing that was so important to me when I first wanted it wasn't as vital when it happened. God had changed my heart in the process."

I wonder if that's how it'll be with the Bailey House and me.

"I liked the art classes," he says. "I can see how I needed them to make me a better artist. But it turned out that what I asked God for over and over wasn't the right thing for me after all."

I think of Minnie's sorrow and her prayer for one more day with Lawrence. "How do you think God stands this mess we've made of the world? Do you think He wishes He could deliver us all out of it?"

"He did," says Buck. "He sent Jesus. Remember?"

"I know that."

"He died to set us free from the bonds of this life."

"But why do we have to continue on, then?"

"What do you mean?"

"How many more generations have to carry on before God says, 'Enough!' How many more car and boat accidents?"

"I don't know, Jackie. I don't think anyone can know that. But there's a lot of good in the world, you know. You have to look at more than just the bad news."

I think of Minnie, crying alone in her room. Zane, a boy without a father to raise him.

Buck glances at his watch and stands. He surprises me by reaching for my hand. "Ready?"

"Is it time to go?" I take his hand and let him help me to my feet.

"Well, we should make a run for it. The sun is coming out."

I look through the window to see the road glistening under a sun streaming through a cluster of bright clouds. People who took shelter in the souvenir shop across the street are filing out into the day.

"Besides, I have to be at work in ten minutes." His sigh is deep.

"I thought you liked your job."

"I do." Genuinely, he says, "But I hate that we have to end."

"Buck," I say with feeling, "I've loved talking with you."

I hope he believes me because I do mean it.

30

When I get back home, Bo, our neighbor in the adjoining duplex, is sweeping his deck and blasting his music. He lifts his head, his thick black hair splaying out like a feather duster. I greet him and then enter my front door.

I shut our door and then hear Bo's voice. "I'll turn it down for you, Jackie."

"Thanks, Bo," I call as the volume from his stereo lowers, causing "Smoke on the Water" to now be only a mild vibration. In the kitchen, I pour a glass of iced tea.

I settle in to imagining what it will be like to pack up this duplex and move into the Bailey House, but another thought nags at me: What if Davis changes his mind about giving me the property?

If he and I were to break up, he could decide I'm not the best renter for the house. What if Vanessa suddenly said she wanted it? Would he tear up the papers he's given me to sign and hand the property over to her? Quickly, I call him. The phone rings four times and then I get his voice mail. I try to make my tone cheery as I leave a message. "I want to come over to your office with the signed lease papers. Let me know when a good time will be."

Earlier today, as she was making her bed and asking Zane to make his, Minnie asked why I have yet to sign the papers. I told her that it was so final, so real—in a good way, of course—yet once I signed, there would be no backing out. I would owe a huge amount of money each month. It's funny how we dream and hope and then sometimes when the dream is about to come true, right there within reach, we get scared, wanting to cower or wait.

Thinking of my conversation with Buck, I form a prayer to God, wondering why I haven't been asking for His guidance more often. I can hear my mother cry, "Jackie, you ask God for wisdom and He gives. Just like Bible tells me so."

I lie on my bed and read two chapters of the Manex Jethro biography Davis loaned me. When my cell rings, hope fills me. But it's not him. Aunt Sheerly tells me she's organizing a fundraiser.

"It's going to be next Saturday. The group wants to do this. Can you make it?" Her voice is expectant; she wants an answer now.

When she refers to "the group," I know she means All That Glitters Is Gold. But I'm not sure why she wants me at her fundraiser. "Next Saturday? What time?"

"The Rose Lattice at seven. I think we'll be able to raise a lot of money for the Bailey House."

"A fundraiser for the bed and breakfast?"

"That's right. It's our usual night to sing there, so there will be the local crowd. We'll advertise and see if we can get more people to come. I'm going to see if folks will donate some items for an auction."

"Wow, this sounds great." Given the opportunity, my family can really get things done.

"I'll be handing out fliers here at the shop and at Tiny's store.

Beatrice Lou has some posters she and Aggie made for the library. We can invite everyone."

When I put my phone back into my jeans pocket, I feel grateful that my aunt wants to raise money to help Minnie and me make renovations on the house.

I call Minnie to tell her the good news.

"Have you given the papers to Davis yet?" She sounds just like she did this morning.

"No, but I will."

"Has he given you a key yet?"

"No. He will, though." I wonder why my tone sounds so defensive.

"I'm anxious to go inside again." Then she tells me she has to help a customer and hangs up.

31

I make my signature as flamboyant as I can and force a smile. This rent with the option to buy agreement is a dream coming true. So why do I feel so tense about it?

I head to Davis's office to give him the signed contract so that he can add his signature to it. When I didn't hear a reply to the voice message I left, I called him today. He answered and said to come by anytime.

When I walk into his office, my stomach does a flip as I see that Vanessa is there. She's wearing a beige dress with a white collar and a necklace of rubies. Her dress looks like it was made for her to model. No amount of makeup or tailoring will ever make me as beautiful as this woman. I wish I had at least put on dress pants, but I'm in a pair of worn denim capris and a large Breakfast at Andrew's T-shirt. The shirt was a promotional tool—the owner of the restaurant gave a box of them to our staff about four years ago.

Davis smiles, but my heart feels like someone has poured vinegar over it. Even so, I return his smile over Vanessa's silky head. He looks at her, then walks from his desk over to me. He gives me a hug, and though I hope for a kiss, there is none.

Taking the signed papers in his hands, he lays them on top of his desk.

"Add your signature and it's final," I say. I wonder why my voice has to crack now.

Davis studies the pages, flipping through them over and over again.

"Is something wrong?" My mouth feels as if I've swallowed sand.

Vanessa straightens the gold pendant on her necklace. Her perfume lingers like a bad omen. For a second, I think she might shout, "I want the Bailey House! Let me rent it!" And then it would all be over for me because I know in my heart that Davis would choose her.

I avoid her eyes as Davis picks up a pen. I only breathe after he signs in two places.

"I hope you will be happy with the house," Vanessa says when Davis has finished. "Seems like a huge undertaking." She crosses her legs; her skirt exposes a toned thigh.

I look at Davis. "Do we need to get it notarized?"

"Nah," he drawls, "it's all good." He waves his hand between us. "We don't have to be so formal about this."

"Okay." My smile feels weak. "Do I get a copy?"

"Did you bring a check for the first payment?"

I've been so intent on the contract that I forgot about the required check for the first month's rent. I find my checkbook at the deep end of my purse, open it to a blank check, and scribble in the amount.

When I give Davis the check, he points out, "You didn't sign it."

My face burns with the heat of embarrassment even after I sprawl my signature across the bottom line.

Within minutes, he has made copies of the documents on a Hewlett-Packard printer that sits behind his desk.

"See you later," he says as he hands the copies to me.

Leaving the office, I feel like I've done something wrong. I reflect on the words we exchanged and conclude that I said nothing out of line. Clutching the pages, I walk to my truck.

I saw the way he looked at her.

Inside my truck, I turn on the air-conditioner, and with each wisp of cool air that blows through the vents, disappointment mounts. The Bailey House is legally mine to rent, and right now all I can do is ask questions. What is she doing in his office if she says it's over? How can he tell me that she's just an old friend?

When Minnie calls, her pleasure at hearing that the house is ours diminishes my worries. We talk about how much our room rates should be, and she agrees that omelets and banana bread would be a fine first breakfast to serve.

~~~~~~

I drive through the minuscule town of Salvo and see the shop with the crooked sign: Ocean Floral. A week ago, Buck asked me to stop by here and talk with Kelly. That same day, he asked me to promise to get an inspection of the property before signing anything with Rexy Properties. Since I failed with the inspection suggestion, I will at least try to find Kelly.

The scent of flowers is strong when I open the door with a tinkling bell. The store's interior feels damp, but the colorful flowers dazzle the floor and shelves.

At the counter, a woman in a floppy white hat arranges yellow roses and baby's breath in a glass vase. Using shears, she clips off the end of a stem and a few stray leaves.

"Hi," I say. When she acknowledges me, I add, "I'm Jackie Donovan."

She gives me a tiny smile, her round face and cheeks showing youth. "Hi."

I wonder why Selena hasn't suggested that we interview the owners of this shop. I note the bins of white daisies and zinnias. As I think of how pretty vases of each would look on the tables in the Bailey House, I ask if the store delivers.

"Yeah, we do."

"Are you Kelly?"

She nods, the hat bobbing like a buoy. "And you're from the *Lighthouse Views*, right?"

"I am."

Softly she says, "I recognized you from the photo of your staff."

I watch her continue with the arrangement. I didn't think anyone ever looked at the photo of our staff that is in each issue of the magazine.

"You wrote the article about Davis Erickson."

"Yeah. Do you know him?"

Hesitantly, she says, "My husband and I rent from him."

"Oh, so do I. I mean, I will. I just signed papers for the Bailey House." My enthusiasm cascades around the room almost as brightly as the yellow roses shimmer in the sunlight.

With a solemn look, she nods.

The door opens and two women breeze in, exclaiming how nice it feels to be inside a cool place. "We'd like to order flowers for a wedding bouquet," the shorter one says as she approaches the counter. She appears to be about twenty-five.

"I can talk with you in just a minute," Kelly replies, adding another rose to the vase.

The older woman looks at me and says, "My daughter is getting married next May on the beach. I think it's a crazy idea, but I'm just the mother."

"Oh, Mom." The daughter lets out an exasperated sigh. "It doesn't matter where you get married as long as you're happy."

When I imagine my own wedding, it takes place in a church sanctuary like Minnie and Lawrence's. I can almost hear the organ play and see myself in a flowing gown, taking small but confident steps toward the altar. Yet I have no idea who the groom will be. A month ago I might have pictured Davis standing beside me, but now I can only imagine him with Vanessa.

"Good luck," I say and then bend over to get a whiff of sweetness from a bin of gardenias. If I ever do marry, I want these flowers.

When Kelly talks to the two women, answering their bouquet questions, I leave the shop. Confusion sets in on the drive home. Why did Buck want me to stop by and speak with Kelly? I feel as if I'm viewing one of those detailed pictures where the instructions are to find ten hidden items. What have I missed?

32

On Saturday, The Rose Lattice in Buxton, a modest restaurant that serves up fried food and music every weekend, is drawing a crowd. I'm amazed at how many people my aunt has gathered for this event. Minnie and I aren't the only people who want the Bailey House to reopen, I guess. I see people I've never met, only seen on TV. There's the man who gives the weather forecast on the local news and the mayor's sister. From a cluster of women, I recognize the owner of a Hatteras realty office, the one who had no clue about the Bailey House when I inquired three years ago. Tiny and Beatrice Lou smile at me from across the restaurant floor, and Ropey invites Zane to sit with them.

Zane asks me, "Is that okay? Will you be lonely?"

I don't tell him that I would love for him to sit away from me, as far as he can. I'm supposed to be delighting in his little-boy ways.

As Zane scampers toward my relatives, Buck comes over and gives me a hug. He's wearing his Hurricanes cap and a hint of aftershave. "Thanks for being here," I say.

"Of course. How could I miss an event featuring the Hatteras Girl?" he teases.

"It doesn't feature me," I say. "Sheerly planned it all."

We find seats together on the back row behind women I've seen at Sheerly Cut. I think these three women come in every Tuesday to get a cut and color. They also drink cupfuls of the hot tea Sheerly provides.

Then Whistlin' Walt, who gained his nickname because of his ability to whistle any tune while delivering the mail, joins the ladies. He looks a little heavier tonight without his postal service uniform and hat. The ladies don't mind. They ask how his mother is doing, and if he thinks it's going to rain tomorrow.

On a typical night, the Lattice has tables and chairs, waitresses and cooks. Tonight, the chairs have been placed into rows, there is a cover charge at the door of five dollars, and punch, cubes of cheddar cheese, crackers, and sugar cookies sit on a large table behind the chairs.

Sheerly welcomes us to the evening through a mic she holds with ease in her manicured hand. As she speaks, conversations are reduced to murmurs, people shift into chairs, and then the room is quiet.

All I can think of is Buck's left shoulder. This shoulder, clad in a T-shirt and smelling of aftershave, is touching mine.

Sheerly, tiny yet filled with pep, announces to her audience before her, "We are gathered here to join in raising some money for a landmark that signifies the epitome of our region. Here's to the Bailey House!"

When the music starts—two guitars and a saxophone—Sheerly's soprano voice fills the room. Within a few lines, I recognize the song, one she wrote about being a hair stylist, called "Mama Don't Like My Hair." My nose starts to itch. I scratch it with my left hand so that my right shoulder remains snug against Buck's left shoulder. I glance over at him; his eyes are on the band.

Sheerly, L. J., Little Clemmens, who is only five-three, and Jack Junior, an elderly man who used to be a pilot with the Air Force— the entire cast of All That Glitters Is Gold—stand before us and belt out the song:

> "Mama don't like my hair, says it's too red;
> Mama don't like my hair, says it's not for me;
> Mama asked the stylist and the stylist said,
> 'It's the fashion, and you gotta let this fashion be.' "

We clap, and I feel the movement from Buck against my own arm. *This is ridiculous,* I think. Davis is the one I'm interested in. He's successful, handsome, savvy, and not just working as a waiter at some restaurant, being vague about a carpentry job he used to have with his dad.

When the next song starts, I shift in my seat so that our shoulders are not together in any way. I glance to my left and then try not to stare. Waving at me a few rows over is my cousin Aggie, and seated next to her is none other than Douglas Cannon. His right arm is draped around her shoulders, and she looks content, like the woman dining on the New Orleans poster at the Grille. I give Aggie a smile.

She pushes strands of wavy hair away from her face and smiles back.

"Buck," I whisper, directing his attention to the couple, "look. They seem happy."

"Who would have thought it?" Buck says with a grin, before turning to focus once more on the band.

Later, over punch and cookies, Buck tells me he's flying out to San Diego on Monday to spend time with his cousin.

"How long will you be gone?"

"Two weeks."

Two weeks. I stuff a cookie into my mouth and wonder why I suddenly feel sad.

Vanessa approaches us. She's wearing a cream-colored dress with a tan leather belt that emphasizes her tiny waist. "Hi," she says to Buck and me. In the evening light, her silver earrings shine like the chrome on a polished car, the chrome on Davis's car. Even the air around her smells sweet—peonies on a warm spring night.

"Hi," I say, trying to block out the memory of the last time I saw her at Davis's office.

"This is a great fundraiser." She takes a glass of punch from the table.

Somewhere in my head, I hear my mother's advice: "Be appreciate, be appreciate, Jackie." I hope my smile looks genuine as I say to Vanessa, "Thanks for being here."

"I admire you," she says. "I think it's wonderful you're going to open up the bed and breakfast again."

"Thanks." She really isn't a bad person, I tell myself. I just don't like the way Davis looks at her, or that he sends her flowers, or that they used to date.

Sheerly ushers us to our seats once more, and we listen as she and the band sing a song she wrote about the Bailey House. She says the band has only practiced it once, earlier today, so to bear with them. The lyrics are about the region of Hatteras wanting to put the lovely landmark back on the map under the shimmering sun. The chorus says, "Dreams are made to live."

An auction follows, and I'm surprised by how many donations

my aunt has collected. The most unique is an acrylic painting on canvas. The painter has named it "Frogs by the Marsh on a Summer Afternoon." The two green tree frogs are perched on the edge of a chipped pier beside a dense marsh. Their eyes are vibrant red.

"You are so talented," I whisper to Buck.

I consider bidding for the painting, but when the auctioneer starts the bidding at two hundred dollars, I keep my hand in my lap. I'm renting a bed and breakfast. Time to start being frugal.

Within two minutes, the painting sells for four hundred two dollars to an art dealer from Maryland. He's a tourist who just happened to come by The Rose Lattice after picking up a flyer about the fundraiser.

Buck says, "You have to love the Outer Banks tourists. Each time I see one of those oval black-and-white OBX car stickers, I'm thankful. An OBX lover keeps our jobs from vanishing."

This is a lesson we all seem to be learning.

After the auction ends, and before the art dealer carts the painting to his vehicle, I view Buck's frogs. I like the way he shaded in the pier so that it looks like the sunlight is casting a slight shadow over the frogs and marsh. With a closer look, I see he's added a spindly-legged spider near the grasses and a feathery turquoise butterfly in the right-hand corner.

"Did you go to see Kelly at Ocean Floral?" Buck asks before heading out the door.

"Yeah, why did you—?" Zane bolts around the corner and runs into my legs.

"Jackie," he says over my groan, "can I ride home with you? And can we stop at Food Lion and buy some chocolate ice cream?"

"Sure," I say. "Why not?"

Zane doesn't just want ice cream; he finds cereal, pretzels, and sour-cream-and-chives chips to add to the shopping cart. I agree to one bag of chips for him but remind him that the last bag of pretzels he opened, he spread out on the living room floor and used his trucks to flatten them into the carpet.

"So no pretzels today, Zane."

"I cleaned it all up," he says as he crams his hands into his pants pockets.

I distract him by telling him to get some juice while I give in to temptation and grab a bag of white corn tortilla chips to put in the cart, deliberately placing the bag under the container of ice cream.

As we leave the grocery store, walking out into the windy evening, my gaze catches two people entering Movies and Tunes, the DVD rental store at the end of the row of shops. The man, tall and handsome and much too familiar, smiles at the woman in a cream-colored dress. He opens the door for her—one hand on the door, the other hand lingering along her back, fingers moving up and down. The familiar gesture makes me freeze.

"What's the matter?" asks Zane as the store's door slams and my own heart knocks against my chest.

When I don't move, he says, "Come on, Jackie. The ice cream is going to melt." He tugs at the loaded plastic bag in my right hand.

For a moment I want to run inside the DVD store and scream, "I caught you!" like we used to do when playing hide-and-seek. But I'm not a child anymore, so after strapping Zane into his car seat, I revert to an inane act of adult behavior—I gun my engine. Five times.

Then I back my truck out of the lot as though I'm trying out for the speedway.

Zane giggles. "That's cool, Jackie!"

This is how short-lived joy can be. I was feeling joy about the fundraiser, yet now I give in to the angry feelings brought about at seeing Davis and Vanessa so happy together.

Suddenly, I realize that if someone saw me seated next to Buck at The Rose Lattice, rumors could start then, too. "Oh, he's just a friend of the family," is what I could say. I could launch into the story about catching him spying on Minnie and me when we sat in my bedroom talking about school dances and boys.

Darkness forms around us, and lights start to blink on. As we head north, the truck in front of us towing a red Bay Liner moves slower than frost on a December morning. I'm ready to bang on my horn but then I reconsider. I can't show anger now. Zane is watching my every move. Mom would tell me I'm an adult and I need to set a good example.

"Let's sing a song," Zane suggests, his face shiny with eagerness.

"Why?"

"Singing makes you feel better."

And so we sing "London Bridge Is Falling Down," and somewhere in the middle, I know that there is no way to repair what has fallen down, my fair lady.

After Zane has enjoyed a bowl of chocolate ice cream, Minnie sends him to bed. Then she wishes me a good-night and closes her bedroom door. Within minutes, I hear faint music from her room and wonder if she ever has a night when she doesn't think about Lawrence.

I change into my nightshirt and turn on my new TV in my bedroom. Mom said that having one would be nice. I flick the remote, searching for something to watch.

"He was in love with another woman," a distraught female with bleached blond hair claims.

The hostess of the talk show asks how she found out.

"He started wearing English Leather."

"Really?" the poised hostess says. "And that made you realize he loved her and not you?"

"Of course!" says the blonde. "He never wore any cologne when he was with me."

I turn off the TV and decide to do some laundry. There's something about washing clothes in a machine. You add the detergent, turn on the cycle, and imagine that in the time it takes to get your clothes from grungy to clean, you can feel fresh, as well.

I used to think life was just that simple.

I used to believe a bowl of cottage cheese and a bag of chips would get you through any crisis.

In the kitchen, I scoop some small-curd cottage cheese into a cereal bowl and search for the tortilla chips I bought today and hid from Zane in the back of the pantry behind the cans of green beans. Like a treasure, they are there. I take my meal into the living room and, avoiding Zane's toys, ease onto the sofa.

And I'm relieved to find that food still serves its purpose of comfort for me.

33

Sheerly calls to say that the fundraiser netted over two thousand dollars for the bed and breakfast. "The actual amount, once I got all the donations tallied, is two thousand fifty-two dollars. Jackie, this is tremendous. I just love how giving the people of the Outer Banks are. They all want to see you succeed, you know."

I find Minnie in her room, her eyes focused on her computer, and tell her the good news.

"That's great! I wish I could have been there." I know that she asked for time off, but the surf shop is short-staffed these days.

"What should we use the money for?" she wonders aloud. "You said you paid the first month's rent, so maybe something else?"

I hate to think that all the hard work put into the fundraiser is not even going to cover one full month's rent. I'd love to add a porch to the house like Mrs. Bailey told me she wanted someday. I wish Davis would want this for the house, as well, instead of being so insistent that *nothing* can change.

Minnie's attention returns to her computer screen. "Guess what. I met this guy on Facebook. He lives in Roanoke."

I wait for more.

"But I'm not ready to go out with anyone." The words come out in a rush. "Still, he says I'm cute."

Of course. Most people would agree with that.

"I feel like I'm cheating."

"What?" I almost choke on my Diet Pepsi.

"On Lawrence."

"But . . . how?"

"I'm corresponding with a man, Jackie."

"I think Lawrence would forgive you."

"I can't forgive myself. Not yet." She closes the page she was on and moves to her bed. "I still don't believe there's anyone else for me. I mean, people tell me that I'm young and should find someone else." With a long sigh, she draws her knees to her chest and gazes out her bedroom window. "I wonder why people are so quick to put a life together again."

"They're uncomfortable," I say. "They want you to be better so that they can feel better."

"Really?" She looks at me as though I've said something profound.

"Yeah, I really think so. People don't know how to handle grief. They think that after the funeral and a few cries, you should be back to your old self again."

"Jackie?" She studies a worn patch on her bedspread. "I don't remember what my old self was like."

⌐⁀⌐ ⌐⁀⌐

For as close as I live to the beach, actually walking along it or sitting beside it is not something I regularly do. This September evening is different. Perhaps it helps that the tourists are almost all back to their homes in Michigan, Kansas, or Iowa, preparing for autumn and then snow and ice, and more snow. The seagulls own the shores again, gliding across a pale sky. A lonely fisherman stands by a checkered canvas chair, his line dipped into the foamy water.

Davis hasn't called me since I dropped off the lease papers. Since I sighted him with Vanessa, I've felt distanced from him. I'm not sure where our relationship stands. He constantly occupies a corner of my mind, and sometimes I close my eyes and feel his arms around me. I would never admit it to anyone, but I have scribbled his name and mine together inside a lopsided heart in my notebook.

An elderly couple in matching straw hats strolls toward me. From my position on the sand, near a lanky growth of sea oats, I can see that his stomach sags underneath his blue Hawaiian shirt. She has thighs that are streaked with varicose veins. He reaches for her hand as they stop to take in the view, their feet brushed by the playful waves.

My heart cries, "I want that!" I want to be them in forty years.

I watch them continue their walk; they stop to point at a dune. This time she grasps his hand. He turns to smile at her, and my heart fills with a yearning stronger than any I've ever known.

When I look out over the horizon and ponder my future, it is Buck's name I see written in the wispy lavender clouds. Each letter appears to be formed with deliberate flair. Slowly, with the changing light, the clouds turn to gray—a sky poised for a night of twinkling stars and a bright round moon against a charcoal backdrop. When did he go from being just my brother's friend to a man I care about deeply and miss when he's gone?

I let out a sigh that is barely audible over the pulsating tide. I wish Buck were here right now. I have this mad desire to run over to his apartment and tell him that I want to go for a kayak ride or to the coffee shop for chai. But he's gone to California to visit his cousin. Why didn't I tell him how much he means to me before he left? What if his plane crashes and he never knows?

Opening my phone, I stare at his name in my list of contacts. Buck Griffins. His given name is Alexander—a name his parents called him until he went hunting with his dad and instead of shooting deer, sketched a pencil drawing of a buck. Who would have known that the skinny kid who hung out with my baby brother would one day capture my heart?

I wonder what to say in a text message to him. *Miss you? Wish you were here? Can't wait to see you again?*

Closing my phone, I stuff it into my pocket. I'm a writer; I should be able to come up with something interesting to say. Maybe something clever like *Don't fall for any of those California girls. Because, really, the Beach Boys are right; southern girls do keep their boyfriends warm at night.*

As the clouds sprawl into a mass of twilight, I think of how Davis and I walked along the beach holding hands, and then shared our first kiss. I contemplate telling Minnie how I feel, asking her to help me decide. Yet when darkness takes over the shore, I wonder why I feel secure about one man and uncertain about the other.

34

I bake banana bread and imagine serving it at breakfast to guests at the Bailey House. This afternoon I want to create a Web page for the bed and breakfast so that people from around the world can read about the property and see what it has to offer and maybe decide to stay with us. Cassidy could take photos for the site once we're done with the cleaning and renovations; I know she'd make each room look inviting.

I hear the front door open. Minnie stands on the threshold as if she doesn't know whether to come in or go out.

"Hey," I call out to her. "You're just in time. I'm baking today." I take the bread out of the oven with a worn oven mitt and the aroma fills our duplex.

She enters the kitchen, and I note how pale she looks.

"Are you okay?" I go to her and rub her back with my free hand. "Baking keeps me from worrying about Davis, so I think it's good therapy. I've only—"

"Mom died last night."

I almost drop the banana bread.

"Dicey called to tell me."

When I open my mouth, no words come out.

"She's gone . . ."

I feel the slow-motion rhythm of a bad dream, one where I know I'm supposed to run from the predator, but my legs won't move. "But . . . how?" We just saw her last week and she was fine—well, fine for Irvy.

"She had another stroke. Massive." Minnie's voice does not sound like the one I'm familiar with. When she called to tell me that Lawrence had died, her words held a different pitch from the way they sound in the kitchen today. She was hyperventilating then, just minutes from being sedated. Now she repeats, "Massive." Her eyes move past me and focus somewhere over my head. "She died right away."

Zane enters the house, his Popacorn clutched to his chest. He walks over to me slowly. "Mommy's sad."

Minnie stands in the kitchen like a child lost in a crowd. I put down the banana bread and go to hug her, but she turns and makes her way up the stairs. I start to follow, but Zane is against my thigh, his head on my stomach.

He whispers, "Everyone dies."

Wobbling, I walk over to the sofa. As my head spins, Zane crawls into my lap. Leaning his head against my chest, he tells me, "Please don't die today."

I assure him I have no plans to do that anytime soon.

My tears slip into his hair as we listen to Minnie's sobs, unable to be contained inside her bedroom walls.

With the death of her husband and now her mother, I wonder if Minnie has anything left. I'm afraid if I go into her room I will see only a lonely puddle on the carpet.

Rubbing Zane's arm, I draw him closer. He doesn't protest. We sit until daylight gives way to darkness. Then he tells me he has to eat something or he might die.

I slice the loaf of bread, now cold. The delighted feelings I held while mixing the batter are long gone.

⌒ ◦ ⌒

I am zipping up a black dress that makes me feel like I don't belong in it when my phone rings.

It's a number I don't recognize, but I answer anyway.

Buck's deep voice fills my ear. "Hi, Jackie."

"Hi, how are you?"

"Do you need me to come back?"

"What?"

Slowly, he says, "My mom told me Minnie's mom died."

Word travels faster than clouds move across the sky in the Hatteras wind around here. "It's horrible. I mean, it was so sudden."

"How is Minnie doing?"

"She's too calm, too still."

"Yeah, she's been through a lot. Death is always difficult."

"It's so final." The second the words leave my mouth, I feel stupid. "I mean . . ."

"I know what you mean."

I want Buck here. I want to see his face, to watch the way his hair falls onto his shoulders, to have him tease me, to hear his laughter.

"I'm glad that Minnie has you."

I nod into my phone.

"You're a good friend for her, Jackie."

My eyes turn watery; I blink and feel tears curve along my cheeks. "How are you doing?"

ALICE J. WISLER

"Oh, having lots of fun. Fishing in the Pacific. Too bad you aren't here to eat some of my fish."

I'm happy that he's able to tease me across the miles.

"I'm sorry that y'all are having such a rough time. Doesn't seem fair."

I toss out a line my mother often told Ron and me when we'd complain about rain when we wanted to swim, or having to complete chores when we wanted to play. "Yeah, well, they say life's not fair."

When our conversation ends, I feel like I have a protective coating around me, like talking with Buck has given me strength to handle the gloom of this day.

⌒ ⌒

"Call me crazy," Beatrice Lou tells us at lunch on the Sunday after the funeral. "All of you, go ahead."

Not even her daughter Aggie seizes the opportunity.

Actually, we're all excited. Ropey is the proud owner of an eighteen-foot runabout, a used yellow Stingray. He has docked it at the pier by his home, and each morning he opens the shades to make sure it's still there.

As we eat slices of coconut cake on this cool afternoon, a southerly breeze flutters against Aunt Sheerly's flower bed of chrysanthemums. The white blooms make me think of Davis, they being the color of his BMW. I shiver and Sheerly asks, "Cold, honey? Need my sweater?"

I let her place her white crocheted sweater around my shoulders. I've learned that there are times it's nice to just let people do for you even if you don't need them to do anything.

Beatrice Lou says, "Don't you think I knew he was asking Casey about that boat all summer? I know he made trips to Juniper Lane to check it out and was eyeing my truck, wanting to put a trailer hitch on the back of it." She clicks her tongue against her teeth. "I don't know how he thinks he can keep secrets from me after thirty-three years of marriage."

I bet she knows about the cigars and donuts, too.

Our smiles are gentle toward her. We look for Ropey to congratulate him, but he and Tiny have taken Zanc and gone for a cruise around the inlet. At first, we all thought Zane would not set foot on the boat due to his fear from the way his father died. But Zane said he is in kindergarten now and that he would like a ride. Ropey put an orange life vest on the boy and, holding his hand, guided him onto the boat.

"Ropey is as cool as a cucumber about owning a boat again," Beatrice Lou says, her gaze focused over the water beyond the dock by Sheerly and Tiny's. "The power of it, the expense." There's a pronounced sigh and then, "You know a boat is a hole in which you toss all your money."

I look at my aunt, expecting to see fear in her eyes—doubt, remorse, and bitterness. Instead there is resolution, acceptance, even something that looks like love.

"Men and their boats." Sheerly wipes her mouth with a paper napkin. "I do wonder if there is a bond as strong on God's green planet."

I smile and touch Aunt Beatrice Lou on the arm. Her skin feels cool. "You are such a good soul," I tell her.

"Well, when he crashes into rocks because salt water has impaired his vision, tell me that. Or when his back gives out and he comes crying to me, we'll see how good of a soul I am."

I almost say, at least he'll be crashing while doing something he loves to do, but I stop myself. Minnie told me that a few people gave her that line after Lawrence's death. *At least he was fishing when he died. He loved to do that."* Minnie says she has yet to find any warmth from that sentiment.

And now her mother is gone. Today, we women take turns hugging her. Even Aggie comments on how lonely it feels now that Irvy and her wheelchair are no longer here. Then she goes into the house, and Beatrice Lou tells us about Aggie's most recent date.

"Douglas?" I ask.

My aunt nods. "He's wealthy and available," she says.

So I've heard.

⌒⌒

That night I pick up the biography from Davis and read another chapter. The author says that most of Manex Jethro's songs were written by his blind girlfriend. However, he never gave her credit for any of them. I find that annoying and read the chapter again to make sure I've comprehended it all correctly. Instead of crediting the lyrics to the woman who penned them, Manex always told people he came up with them. This girlfriend was just as poor as he was, yet he never let others know about her, even when he began to earn millions of dollars.

I head out to the deck and watch the night sky.

"He is my all-time hero," Davis said about this man. Did Davis not know about the blind girlfriend, or did he ignore that part?

All-time hero. My skin itches, and I'm not sure if it's due to mosquitoes or mental irritation.

I take out my phone and text him. *When can I get a key to the Bailey House?*

By midnight, there is still no reply.

35

Sheerly gives Minnie three days off to go to the nursing home and "tie up the loose ends." Basically, this means picking up Irvy's belongings and signing some papers. Minnie says it shouldn't take more than a few hours, but Sheerly reminds her that "these things take time" and not to rush the process. Then she describes how she felt when her own mother died. "I felt lost, like nothing mattered. I cried each time I picked tomatoes from my garden. How Mama loved a plate of sliced tomatoes, sprinkled with salt."

After heading out the door, Minnie comes back into the house to retrieve her car keys that she's left by a vase of limp carnations—funeral flowers.

"I'll be here when Zane gets home," I call out to her as she makes her way down the stairs to the driveway. I don't know if she hears me.

When she backs out of the driveway, I take my flute from the closet and start to play a few weak notes. I think back to the day Irvy asked me to give a little concert with her. She said it would be at her home for a few close friends. For some reason, I agreed to it.

That Friday evening in March, day lilies, tall and tilted, were placed in wide vases around the foyer. We sat in her living room as guests ate little cheese-and-olive hors d'oeuvres and drank punch. I was proud to be giving a concert. Our school had plenty of band concerts in which I played, but this was my first private event. I chose my clothes carefully—black pumps and silky hose. My dress was just above my knees and as black as coal. Minnie brushed my hair for me and put a garland of artificial pink rosebuds around my head.

I played with all the confidence I had within me. Irvy was her usual poised self and played her piano with vigor. I sure hoped I was doing all right, but I was too nervous to make eye contact with her. My fingers pressed hard against each key as I breathed into the mouthpiece; my eyes did not shift from the sheet music.

Later, after her guests left and the last car took off from her driveway, Irvy gave me a white envelope that had my name printed on it. Inside was a twenty-dollar bill and a perfumed card. The sloping words on the card read, "Always play, always practice, always perfect."

"She liked your playing," Minnie told me the next day at school. "Everyone did."

Now I play "Jesus Loves Me," which I also played last week at the funeral. I hit a wrong note and stop. Suddenly, a jubilant piece comes out. "The Hallelujah Chorus" suits me well today, for Buck is due back. My heart flutters like a sandpiper wanting to soar. With every note, the darkness of Irvy's death creeps out of my heart, until at last, the wings spread wide and it flies away.

In her room, Minnie tells Zane to be careful. He has one of Irvy's veiled back hats on his head, balancing it while walking over a strip of scarves he's laid over the floor. I remember how Irvy sat in the second pew at church wearing that very hat. She wore it in the fall with a peacock blue suit, her feet encased in sleek heels.

Minnie has brought Irvy's belongings from the nursing home to our duplex. Now I imagine she'll add Irvy's things to Lawrence's. As she opens the heavy chest that holds mementos of her late husband, I pray that this chest won't have to have any more items added to it anytime soon.

Pausing at the doorway, I wait until Minnie motions for me to enter the bedroom.

Zane has lost interest in the items and picks up two toy trucks and begins to drive them into the hallway.

Minnie's cheeks are flushed, her eyes dull, and I wonder when the last time was that she ate a good meal. She hands me a square maroon box, tattered, with dingy hinges. "Open it."

Gently, I peel back the lid and am greeted by an aroma of furniture polish and vanilla. Inside the velvet interior are index cards with writing on them. I take one out. It's a recipe written in sloping letters for shortbread cookies. The next is for chocolate cake. Then there's one for lemon cookies. But not just any ol' lemon cookie recipe; across the top of the card is written *The Bailey House Lemon Cookies*.

When I look at Minnie, her face shines. The sorrow from the day seems to have evaporated, even if only for this moment. "We found it."

"This is it!" I read through the ingredients and the instructions. The key for me is the icing made from powdered sugar. Not every lemon cookie recipe has this, and this card tells how to frost the cookies after they are baked, exactly like Mrs. Bailey always frosted hers. I knew that Irvy and Mrs. Bailey were good friends—apparently they were the kind close enough to share recipe cards.

"So now that we have the recipe, we can make them for the new

243

and improved Bailey House." Minnie amazes me. Even with everything going on in her life, she spends time thinking about our plans for the bed and breakfast. "When is the house going to be ours, Jackie? When can we start working on it? I'm ready." Minnie closes the box of recipes and rests her fingers across the lid.

I think of the signed contract, the time I spent with Davis at the Bailey House, the worn walls and kitchen tiles, the need to do a zillion things to the place before we can possibly open it again to the public. I start to tell her that there's a lot of work to do, but her face is so intent, her eyes so full of something I haven't seen in months, I just let my smile be my answer.

She grins back at me. "You know, not since Lawrence's death have I felt this . . . this . . ."

I wait for her to finish.

" . . . hopeful."

I decide to make her favorite dinner—grilled pork chops, corn pudding, fried okra, and baked potatoes. Before setting the table, I whisper to Zane that he needs to help Mommy by being a big boy and not complaining about our meal tonight. He looks at me and says, "I'm going to kindergarten, so I can be big."

Minnie eats her dinner with enthusiasm, commenting on how delicious it all tastes. She thinks we should make a batch of lemon cookies, but I tell her I'm too tired for that.

"Another time, then. I'm so glad Mama had the recipe."

"Me too."

"Today I talked to a woman who owns a cleaning business. I got her card. I guess we need to start thinking about people to hire to do the lawn care and cleaning at the Bailey House." There is lightness to her voice and movements; gone is the weighty shroud she once wore.

Zane and I look across the table at each other and smile. After the dishes are cleared, I give him a big bowl of ice cream, even though he's eaten only half of his pork chop and folded the okra into his napkin.

But he never whined.

36

Buck is back from California, and the Sunnyside Grille is a place I want to be again. Through the grapevine—or more accurately, the salon—Minnie heard that Buck was due to arrive home last night. Buck's mother was at the salon two days ago getting a perm and disclosed this information. I nonchalantly nodded when Minnie told me this news, acting as though it didn't matter to me whether Buck came back or not. But Minnie seemed to know that it did.

This afternoon, when I enter the restaurant, I see two waitresses I don't recognize. Buck has told me staff members come and go quickly. I glance around the restaurant—tables filled with chattering customers, the computer where the waitstaff enters orders, Pepsi glasses and skillets on the shelves, New Orleans posters on the walls—but I don't see Buck. Then he pops up from behind the counter, and my heart dances. I look for a vacant seat and find one at the end of the bar.

When Buck comes over, he grins at me and asks what I'd like to eat.

"A bunch of fries with lots of salt," I tell him. My salt craving tends to be stronger when the weather grows cooler.

He nods, but his eyes don't have their usual gleam.

I try to tease him. "Can you ask the cook if the fries are fried in vegetable or canola oil?"

Buck doesn't react. "I can do that," he says in a monotone. Quickly, he walks to the soda fountain and fills a mason jar with Diet Pepsi for me. He got his hair trimmed and it looks good, but I was getting used to him looking like he did before.

When he hands me my drink, I ask how his time in San Diego was, but he's gone, headed over to the other side of the counter to take a young couple's order.

Panic causes my blood to chill. Did I say something wrong? And why do I care? Technically, I'm dating Davis. I know we haven't spoken in a while, but he's a busy guy. I take a large swallow of my soda, feel it go down too quickly, cough, and reach for a napkin.

"You okay?" Buck brings me a large plate of fries, steam rising from them. "Be careful, these fries are extrēmely hot," he says in his best Betty Lynn imitation.

"Something went down the wrong pipe."

Betty Lynn calls him over, and his attention is no longer on me.

Methodically, I chew a French fry. Looking for the saltshaker, I watch as Buck serves plates of the daily special—clams and shrimp with garlic mashed potatoes and coleslaw—to the couple.

"Need anything?" he asks me when he walks by again.

Something is wrong. He hasn't called me Hatteras Girl once this afternoon.

"Salt." I try to make my reply lively.

Buck brings a saltshaker to me, places it in front of my plate.

"Thanks, Jellyfish Boy." I hope that my teasing will make the light come into his eyes again, but he just nods and turns toward the kitchen, disappearing behind the set of swinging doors.

Something inside me wants to jump up, follow him, and blurt, "I'd love to go kayaking with you again. When are you free?"

When he comes back to the counter, he brings a plastic container of tartar sauce for the couple with the seafood. He walks right past me and I want to cry out, "Buck! Buck! Here I am! Did you miss me?"

Buck doesn't know that I saw his name in the clouds the other evening as the sun set.

⌒⌒⌒

I head back to the office, reaching the front door just as heavy rain pours from the sky. Only Cassidy is here, arranging the layout of advertisements for the November issue. "I'm getting a head start," she tells me when I say that the October issue isn't out yet. "I'm tired of being behind schedule and hearing Selena's voice pounding in my head. Sometimes I even hear her in my dreams, you know."

Later she tells me, "Did you know there was a study showing that people on diets dream more than those who are not?"

"Really? I wonder if their dreams are all about food."

"I think so. Mine are."

At my desk, I pretend to type an interview at my computer, but I'm really making a to-do list for the Bailey House. Minnie mentioned getting a person to clean, and in addition to that, we'll need a landscaper. I smile, thinking how serene it will be to see the back garden of the bed and breakfast cultivated properly once again, with the honeysuckle bushes clipped and the flower beds cleaned out. Thinking of how dingy the walls of the house are, I stop and phone a painter who owns a shop on Shady Sea Lane. He's not in; I leave a message.

Taking a break from my computer, I stare at the downpour through the window by my desk. Tree limbs sway under the torrents, and the sky is a sheet of dark gray. The rain beats the windowpane like an angry fist. My mind feels as heavy as the weather.

While I told Davis that I can spare $2,800 each month from my savings, that was before. Now that I've seen how much work needs to be done on the property before we can welcome any paying guests, I'm worried I won't have enough money. What exactly is the landlord supposed to pay for versus the tenant?

Repairs I write on my to-do list. I delete it and type it in capital letters. Minnie has told me she has $2,000 in savings we can use for rent. Then there's the $2,052 brought in by the fundraiser—will that be enough to complete repairs and updating of the house? I doubt it. Will Davis help pay for cleaning and repairs? I know he wants nothing added or taken away from the old home, but surely he would agree that the place needs paint.

I doodle in my notebook as I think, drawing tiny circles and then petals of geraniums. How will I be able to put work into the house if I have to keep writing for *Lighthouse Views* in order to make the rent? Should I quit my job? Should Minnie keep one of her jobs? We probably won't be able to work once the guests start to come. *Time and money.* I write both words next to my flowers. These are the American people's two big stresses.

Cassidy says she's heading home.

"Really?"

"It's almost five. I get to eat a slice of lemon cake tonight. It's made from yogurt, rice flour, and lemon extract. Can't wait."

She isn't joking; her face shows that she's really eager for this piece of cake.

"You look great. Don't you get to go off your diet soon?" If she lost any more weight, we wouldn't be able to find her.

"Maintaining." She says the word like a drill sergeant. "Don't want to gain anything back. Plus, after months of diet food, I've grown used to this lifestyle." She walks to the door. "See you tomorrow."

I am about to tell her to be careful outside in the rain, but my cell rings and I see that it's Davis.

"Hi, Jackie. How are you?"

"Great." Just the sound of his voice warms me like a cup of hot tea. "How about you?"

"I am swamped." He sighs for emphasis.

"Really busy, huh?" I brace myself for what is coming next.

"Look, I'm not going to be able to make dinner tonight."

My voice is small. "Oh, okay."

"Try to stay dry."

Right before he hangs up, I say, "When can I have a key?"

"A key?"

"To the Bailey House. I want to get started on things." The last time I visited the property on my own, the shutters still had not been removed as Davis had promised he would do.

"Well, I can meet you there if you want to look at it again."

"I don't mind going there alone."

"Well . . ."

The pause is too long for me. Does he think I can't be responsible in a place that I now rent? "I want to walk around inside again. Make plans. You know me, I love going up and down those stairs."

"Sure," he says at last, but I can't tell if he's smiling into the phone or not.

"Can I come by your office and pick up the key?" His office closes at five, but I can come by tomorrow morning.

"Of course."

"In case you aren't there, could you leave the key with your receptionist?" I can't seem to remember her name, but I recall it starts with a B.

A long pause; I'm tempted to chatter to ease my discomfort, but I wait. At last, he says, "Okay."

Somewhere in my head, the U2 song "With or Without You" plays. *"I can't live with or without you."* The line is stuck in my mind. I think it found its way there for a reason.

37

In the silent, dusty house that smells of mold and despair, I sit on the banister and let a tear slide down my cheek. "This is my dream," I moan. I officially rent this house, and now all I can see and feel is the mess it's in. The water stain on the ceiling in the parlor seems larger than it did when I was here with Davis. The kitchen floor has buckled in places, and there is a dripping noise I can't detect the source of. How much will it cost to restore it to a functioning bed and breakfast? Scenes from *The Money Pit* flash before my eyes.

Clearly, Davis has let me know that I can't change a thing. Yet there is no way I can open an establishment to the public that looks this dilapidated. We can use the money Sheerly and her group raised to pay for a new faucet in the kitchen and maybe an industrial dishwasher, but what about the more costly items?

Holding my cell in one hand and wiping tears with the other, I debate whether or not I should call Mom and Dad and admit failure. I see my mother's face looking sternly at me, telling me that we, as a family, don't stay defeated, that we rise up because we know God always helps those who ask.

Although Davis told me he'd leave a key at the reception desk, Bev could not find it when I stopped by. While she searched in between answering the phone, my rage soared. *Does he want me to have this house, or not? Did he only give me the papers in a moment of passion?*

Bev said that there was one more drawer she'd look in and perhaps it would hold the key. As she talked to a client, my thoughts tamed. I like Davis Erickson. He's handsome, educated, established in his career, and is the Baileys' grandson. He said I'm the one to run the Bailey House, and I believe that, too. Yet he doesn't seem to realize that this place needs work before it can reopen. So that it can begin making money I can then use to pay him rent.

Suddenly, bringing the crisp autumn air in with her, Vanessa walked into the office. Dressed in a black dress with a string of pearls glistening around her neck, she waved at me.

What is she doing here? my mind screamed.

She gave me a small smile and said, "Good luck with the Bailey House."

"Thanks." Bev held out a key to me, and I grasped it.

"You are lucky to be in love," said Vanessa.

"In love?" *Would it be strange if I asked, "With whom?"*

"If there is one thing I can tell, it's love in the eyes." She spoke with clarity and authority—a saleswoman well aware of a product.

Love in the eyes? Sounds like a line from a song by Sheerly.

With Vanessa's words fused into my heart, I walked out of Davis's office, ambling to the right and then to the left, almost forgetting where I'd parked. I pulled my keys out of my jeans pocket, and with that motion, confusion left me. I remembered Vanessa smiling at me across the room at the fundraiser when I was seated next to Buck. That was when she must have sensed something between us.

Now I walk around to survey the home once more. I want to

hear music and laughter, but only dust, dingy floors, and that stain in the parlor's ceiling cry out to me. Minnie and I hope to have the place restored and operating by Christmas, starting with a celebratory open house. Yet here it is September and we have so much work to do in order for that open house with lighted topiaries and lemon cookies to take place.

My head is in my hands when I hear familiar footsteps across the floor. "You need to come home." Minnie stands before me; her solemn eyes look into mine.

"Why?"

"Buck is coming over to see us, to see you."

I wipe my eyes, sniff. "Buck? Why?"

"He needs to tell you something."

Has Buck ever come to my house before? What news would be important enough to bring him? "Why?"

She won't look at me now. "Come on, we need to get home before he gets there."

"What about Zane? Where is he?" I look at my watch. Ropey was to bring him home from a boat ride a half hour ago at six. And I was supposed to be there to let Zane in—the responsible adult. "Is Zane okay?"

"Ropey and Beatrice Lou have invited him for dinner."

I remember when he used to refuse to stay at their home. And when he was petrified of boats. "Did he like the boat ride? Did he do all right?"

Minnie sighs and helps me off the banister. "Yes, he loves that boat almost as much as Ropey does. I try not to think about it too much. I just suck in all my fears."

We walk to the front door, and my mind flashes back to the two of us entering the large house with our school bags. "Remember how whenever we came here, Mrs. Bailey was so happy to see us?"

"Yes, and you always let me in the door first."

"Do you know why I did that?"

"Because I had to be first."

I halt in my tracks. I can't believe she knows this about herself.

"I had to be first to get married and to have a child."

"You did?"

"You had everything, Jackie. I wanted something that you didn't have."

My lower lip quivers, and I wonder if I'm going to cry again. "You were the beautiful one!"

A serene look crosses her face, not her argumentative look that I've grown to anticipate over the years. "You had a mom and dad who loved each other and a brother who was so cute."

"You got a date with Benny Saforrn."

"He never liked me. He only used me to get to Tina Plymouth."

I want to hug her, but I also don't want to cry anymore.

So I let her lead me out of the Bailey House. She waits as I lock the door. "It was nice being back inside," she says.

Then we walk to our cars. Slowly, I follow her down Route 12. She still likes to be first.

⌒〜⌒

Minutes after we pull in to the driveway, Buck arrives. He's still in his Grille shirt. The sun hits his face and I think how handsome he is.

We all enter the duplex and find room to sit amongst Zane's toys.

Minnie looks at Buck as I imagine the worst. He's going to tell me he's moving to California. Or that he's in love and getting married at Second Methodist. I gulp and think it's a good thing I bought a big box of tissues the other day.

Buck shifts his feet and won't look me in the eye. I feel discomfort in his gestures and in the air around the living room. I want to blurt, "Hey, let's all go have dinner at that new Chinese place in Nags Head." But we've all just driven from Nags Head to gather here, in my duplex.

Minnie runs her tongue over her lips and after drawing a deep breath says, "Buck knows something about the Bailey House."

38

The ceiling fan shakes like an old woman's hand.

Buck clears his throat.

Dear God, I silently pray, *you know I'm a wimp. I can only handle so much. I'm not strong like Minnie. Don't let anything hurt her anymore. She's been through enough.*

Buck's eyes catch mine from across the room where he sits on a dining room chair. He makes no attempt to smile.

My fingers knot into a ball.

"This is about Davis," he begins.

Minnie nods from where she's seated on the armchair.

"What's going on?" I ask.

Buck clears his throat again. "I don't know how much you already know, Jackie, but Minnie thinks you need to know everything."

I swallow as my skin feels like pins are scratching its surface.

"Davis is the Baileys' grandson. He was given full ownership of the Bailey House when his grandparents got too old to take care of it."

"I know that," I say.

Looking at me, Buck says, "Years ago he had a buyer for the place."

Minnie nods when Buck pauses.

"Well . . ." He draws a deep breath. There are lines in his brow, something I've not seen before. "I was working with my dad then. We were working on the Bailey House. A couple from Michigan was all ready to buy it, but they wanted the upstairs bathrooms remodeled. As my dad and I did the work, we discovered a lot more needed to be done."

"A lot more? Like what?"

"For one, there was water damage that showed up in the ceilings and walls. The drywall was crumbling both in one of the upstairs bathrooms and in the smallest downstairs bathroom. Rotting, actually."

"So?"

"Dad and I told Davis the problems we found and said that we'd fix them. Davis refused."

"What do you mean refused?" My voice is louder than I like it to be.

"He said the couple wanted new bathrooms and that was what Dad and I were contracted to repair. Nothing more."

Minnie holds on to her stern look as Buck continues.

"That house has structural issues. What it needs is for these to be repaired, not just plastering over them like Davis wanted us to do."

"What are you saying?" I ask.

"Dad and I got into an argument and that's why we don't work together anymore."

For a moment we are all silent.

Buck says, "Davis didn't want us to let the word out that the Bailey House needed thousands of dollars worth of repair. He basically told us to fix what he'd asked us to fix and no more. And when I said that he needed to repair pipes and drywall due to leaks throughout the place, he said that we were not to do that and not to tell anyone about it."

"Why?" My mind spins. I look to Minnie and then at Buck. "Why was he trying to cover it up?"

"He knew that I was adamant that the place be properly restored; anything less wouldn't be up to code. But Davis didn't want to spend the money."

I see the car he drives and the price of the meals he orders at restaurants. I never thought he was cheap.

Buck looks at Minnie and then at me. "I'm sure you've noticed that the railing is missing. With seven steps leading up to the house, there needs to be a railing."

I'd forgotten about that railing that led up to the house. As kids, we slid down the wooden banister—when Ogden wasn't looking. "What happened to it?"

"I think the railing was probably destroyed in the last hurricane. Davis hasn't bothered to replace it, even though the house doesn't meet code without it."

My hands are clenched as disbelief jabs at my mind.

"Davis threatened me if Dad and I told on him." Buck's voice is hard, as though he has to force the words out. "He said he'd make life unbearable for us. He has a lot of clout in the area. He could have ruined my dad's business."

I feel a dull pain pulsating in my temples.

"Dad said to let it go and just repair what Davis wanted us to. I said that buyers needed to know of the damage the house had. Dad didn't agree, and I said I couldn't do it."

"Do what?" I ask.

"I couldn't work for a guy who lied and ignored safety issues."

I feel my muscles grow taut, as if I want to hit something. "Davis told me that the bathrooms were remodeled when his grandparents owned the place, just years before they left for Ohio to retire."

"No." Buck shakes his head. "Dad did those."

I think of the new toilets, sinks, mirrors, and floors in each of the upstairs bathrooms. They looked nice. "He did a good job."

"Dad does good work. But I don't see how he let Davis convince him that it was okay not to do it right."

"He wasn't really covering up, was he? I mean, your dad just did what Davis wanted and contracted him to do. It wasn't his responsibility to fix the whole place. He was only the contractor."

Buck shifts in his chair. "I saw it differently then. Over the years, I've tried to see it Dad's way. Dad and I don't talk about it nowadays. I thought I was done with having to worry about the Bailey Place." His expression softens. "Then you came along, determined to open it again." After a pause, he adds, "I think his wife wanted him to sell the place, but he wouldn't."

"Whose wife?"

"Davis was married."

"He was?" Wouldn't he have told me something like that? I look to Minnie, who seems just as confused as I am.

"On a pontoon boat."

Right as the words come from his mouth, I hear another voice, the one that repeatedly said each time we drove over the inlet bridge, "He got married on a pontoon boat." Irvy did know more than I gave her credit for.

"Yeah, about seven years ago. He met her in Ohio. They were married here in the Sound on this huge pontoon. They divorced after a year or so."

"And you knew?"

Minnie looks shocked to hear me raise my voice.

"Sure, lots of people knew. Your relatives probably knew."

I realize then that I haven't been very open with my family about Davis. I let the frustration wipe its ugly hand over me and then say, "I wish you'd told me."

"Hatteras, I didn't want to talk about Davis with you if I could help it."

"But you could have said something."

"I told you to get the place inspected before signing, remember? I hoped that would have then led you to see how much work the place needs." In a softer tone he adds, "Besides, Davis likes coming to the Grille. He's been a regular since way before I began working there. Blake thrives on his business and the business of all his clients."

"I would have chewed him to bits if I had been you," I say hotly.

"And you were dating him. I didn't want to be negative about him."

"If you dated someone deceitful, I would tell you."

Buck seems to think about this. "Well, that's my fault. I guess I'm not good with confrontation." He rubs his chin, looks down, and then up at me again. "Obviously I stink at these kinds of things."

"But you are telling Jackie now," says Minnie, trying to smooth things over.

Buck lets his eyes hold mine. "I hope it's not too late."

Before he leaves, he hugs Minnie.

"Thanks, Buck," she says and gently pats his arm.

Then he turns to me.

There is a second when I'm uncertain of what he's going to say or do, but when he wraps his arms around my waist, the uncertainty dissipates as the ease of how well we fit together surprises me.

His face is only inches from mine. "I didn't want to have to tell you all this," he says. "I guess part of me assumed that Davis would confess the truth, since you two were dating."

I wonder if anyone has ever felt more foolish than I do right now. Davis's face appears in my mind. I lower my gaze, squeeze my eyes shut, hoping to shoo it away like a fly at a picnic. I lift my face to Buck. "Please be more honest with me from now on."

His eyes are solemn and distant. He lets go and moves away from me.

Minnie says, "Well . . ."

Buck and I stand silently as she climbs the stairs with her phone. Within seconds she's made a call to Ropey, telling him he can bring Zane home now.

When Buck exits the duplex, I stare out at the driveway from the living room window, listening to the longing of my heart. Buck's Jeep pulls out and is gone. A voice inside my heart reminds me that he's proven once again that he's a good man—honest, sincere, and moral.

When I turn from the window, I'm gripped by another emotion. This one is not silent. I kick a plastic ball Zane has left under the coffee table. The sphere hits the wall and bounces back at me with a force that causes me to kick the toy again.

I want to head over to Davis's house and force him to admit to everything. Then I realize with a jolt that I don't know where he lives. He's never invited me to his house, nor has he taken me to Arlington, as he promised he would.

I've never even had a ride on his pontoon boat.

39

I think decks are built for contemplation. I bet many politicians and judges have made decisions after being on a wooden structure, suspended above whatever lies beneath. I stand on our deck, looking at the rosebush in the dirt below. A couple minutes ago I noticed my neighbor Mrs. Appleton watching me with a pair of binoculars.

Minnie joins me under a spattering of stars accompanied by a moon that looks like a polished bowling ball. She's put on a sweatshirt and asks if I'd like one, too. "Getting chilly." When I don't comment, she asks, "You okay?"

"I will be." I feel like the ache in my heart has spread throughout my whole body, even my fingertips.

Minnie stifles a yawn and begins to rub my shoulders, sort of like I massage hers sometimes. "You know, I never liked Davis."

"I know."

"He just seemed . . . well, he was too busy all the time, you know?"

She's right; his phone did seem to keep him occupied. He also was too prideful, evasive, and interrupted when I talked, but I fell for him despite those things. "I know you didn't care that much for him. I thought it was because you might be jealous."

She sighs and lets go of my shoulders. Then she leaves me alone with a darkness that hangs heavy over my bones.

I think of our kisses, our embraces, of the meals we shared, of the conversations. These all dance around my mind until I see Vanessa's exquisite face. But that sight isn't what makes my mouth taste the bile from my stomach. My jealousy about Davis and Vanessa isn't even a blotch on my skin anymore compared to my anger toward Davis alone.

How could I have been so quick to fall for this handsome business-man who has no integrity? My parents would be appalled to know that I trusted someone so deceitful. I picture them shaking their heads and muttering, "We raised her to be smarter than this. Where did we go wrong?" Mom might even consider taking the bear chair out of the attic and giving me a timeout. Even Lona's characters in her mysteries learn not to love men for the wrong reasons. Have I been so blind because of the Bailey House? I've idealized the house, and I've idealized Davis. I expected perfection from the beloved Baileys' grandson.

Desiring sleep, I head inside and try to find a comfortable posi-tion on my bed. First, I try lying on my side, but the mattress feels lumpy, so I shift to my back.

When my mother can't sleep, she pounds rice into tiny balls and fills them with sweetened red bean paste. She says that in her village of Damyang-gun, she was the queen of making sticky rice balls or, as they are known in her language, *gyungdan*. Growing up, I knew she'd heard some disturbing family news from Korea when I found her in the kitchen turning rice into clumps on a floured cutting board, forcing them into shapes she could control. The outcome was always a treat for us—delicate circles with bean paste sweetened with cinnamon and coated on the outside with toasted and ground black sesame seeds or a dusting of sweet mugwort powder.

Sadly, I have no idea how to make rice balls. Maybe I will ask Mom to teach me and then serve them at the Bailey House.

If it ever opens.

At midnight, there are noises in the bathroom. Zane mumbles, bumps into something, and lets out a murmur.

Entering the bathroom, I see him by the sink. "You okay, Zane?"

His face is solemn. "I lost Popacorn."

"Did you look under your bed?" Suddenly it hits me that a dark room and an even darker space under a bed is not a happy place for a kid. I enter his room. "I'll help you find him."

Getting on my knees, I look under the bed. All I find is a lonely sock. I then scan the floor. Finally, I search the closet. There sits the stuffed squirrel, as if he wasn't hiding at all but that we just weren't looking in the right place. I pull out the fuzzy creature and hand him to Zane. "Why is he there?"

"I don't know. Maybe the trucks wanted him to be there. They get lonely in the closet."

"I see."

He kisses his stuffed animal. Then, "Jackie?"

"Yes?"

He whispers, "I think I'm okay now."

I guess he wants me to leave. Funny how I wouldn't mind staying by his bedside for a little while longer.

I pull the downy comforter up to his chin. His eyes are closed before I leave his room.

The duplex is silent, but outside I hear a barking dog and the echo of a foghorn. I see Buck's smile, hear his laughter, and want to feel his hand holding mine.

In my own bed again, I count my breaths, and then, closing my eyes, picture a sun-baked seashore of bright shells and attempt to count them. I flip to my back, then my stomach. I wonder if Cassidy counts calories when she can't sleep, and if that helps any.

It's very hard to pull myself out of bed the next morning. Before Minnie and Zane leave, Minnie tells me not to worry about Zane.

"Why don't I need to worry?" I ask as I measure three cups of water and pour the liquid into the coffee maker. I turn the pot on. Coffee should help clear my head.

"Because after school Ropey will meet his bus and then take him fishing."

The coffee maker gurgles.

"Jackie," Minnie says, her face just inches from mine, "did you hear me?"

"Oh no!" Surely I didn't forget.

"What is it?" Minnie asks.

"I forgot."

Zane enters the kitchen, his book bag lopsided on his back. His eyes are bigger than his stuffed squirrel's as he notices my poor attempt to brew a pot of coffee.

Minnie is oblivious to my error. "Zane is going to Ropey's after school today—"

But I cut her off as I see the steamy water fill the coffeepot— clear—without a trace of coffee in it. "I can't believe I did that."

We all watch as the rest of the water splashes into the pot to create a drink of only hot water.

Zane says, "Just stop at Starbucks for your coffee, Jackie. They know how to make it there."

When Minnie and Zane leave, I open and close the refrigerator, not sure what I want to eat. There is leftover macaroni and cheese, a baked potato in aluminum foil, and half a grapefruit. The container of cottage cheese has three curds left in it; Zane needs to learn to throw empty containers away.

I take out my striped notebook and tear out a sheet. Stretching my hand over it, I smooth the torn edges, and then sit at the dining room table to write.

Where do I stand? I've signed the lease papers, so I owe rent on the house. Davis is a liar—and probably a cheat. He may still be in love with Vanessa. Why was I so quick to think he and I were made for each other? Even Irvy was trying in her limited way to warn me about him. Davis told me he'd never been married; I recall that conversation as we sat on the pier eating roast beef sandwiches. Or did he only say, *"I'm not sure marriage is for me"*? That night, I took that statement to mean that as a single man he wasn't sure he wanted to get married. Now I realize he could have meant he didn't want to ever be married again.

"I don't want to be deaf and blind," my mother said to me on the phone. I feel I have been both with Davis. I should have been seeing things the way they are, not viewing them with a heart gone soft with romance and visions of the Bailey House clouding my good sense.

"Slow down; good things take time. Don't be quick to give away your common sense or your heart." These are lines from one of the first songs Sheerly ever wrote. I find it appropriate that I'm reminded of them now.

On another sheet of paper I write at the top: *List of what I need to do.* My pen starts to swirl along with my mind, but instead of a list, all I come up with is: *Wait upon the Lord.* I read the words twice.

But I have waited and waited.

"You must be still and listen," my mother often told me when I was growing up. *"We have hard time—you and me. We want to hurry up. But God tells us in the Bible to be still."*

With determination, I head to Rexy Properties. But Davis is not there.

At first I tell Bev that I'll wait. I pick up a flyer with pictures of properties for sale around the island; one home with a pool is listed at two million dollars. Another has seven bedrooms, two pools, and a whirlpool and has been reduced from 3.25 million to three. Placing the flyer back on her desk, I decide to sit. I hold my cell phone, debating whether or not to call Davis. After six minutes, I leave.

Outside the sun is only a shadow of what it was this summer. Autumn looms as I stand under an oak with rust and gold leaves. And suddenly I realize Davis is not the man I want to see today.

Sometimes a person cannot continue to keep her emotions inside, letting them silently brush against her heart like waves on the shore. Sometimes there's a call for speaking up, and out. So as I drive to the Grille, I form a plan. I am going to boldly ask a certain waiter if we can go for a kayak ride and then, as we paddle around the coves, I'll let him know how I feel about him. Girls do this in the movies. I've seen enough to know how it's done. I'm not coy, and I've had enough of blind dates. I'm taking the initiative and asking Buck out on a date.

When I enter the Grille, I freeze when I see Davis seated on a stool at the right side of the bar. A large man almost hides him, but I spot him anyway. He's wearing a light blue Ralph Lauren shirt and eating a well-done cheeseburger.

Buck catches my eye as I pause for a second, and then once I see his smile, I make my way toward Davis.

There are times when you know something important is about to happen in which you will play a large role, and yet you have no idea what you are going to do or say. Life is unrehearsed, Sheerly says in one of her songs. My mother phrases it this way: *"You never can know how you will be."*

I find my feet moving toward Davis, buoyed by a wild boldness unfamiliar to me.

40

Davis looks my way and then takes a sip of his iced tea. I watch his fingers ease their way around the mason jar, those fingers I have grown to know and love the way they feel against my skin.

When he flashes his broad smile, I hear myself saying, "I know, Davis."

He says, "It's good to see you! How are you?"

As he slips his arm around me, I step back. "I know everything."

His face shows no worry lines, no fear. "What do you know?"

From the corner of my eye, I see Buck's face, drained and shaded with disbelief. He's holding a towel. Neither the towel nor Buck move.

"I know that you aren't the man you want us to believe you are."

Davis looks so strong, so tailored in his black pants and button-down blue shirt. I recall how it felt to rest my head against his chest. "I'm not sure what you mean, Jackie."

"You haven't been straightforward with me. You hired men to fix the Bailey House, but when they found serious problems, you ignored them." My calm tone has escalated.

I expect Davis to glare at Buck or stand up and punch him like in a scene from a film. He does neither. He is the epitome of serene, like a glassy lake on a spring afternoon. He takes another sip of his drink. "Don't believe everything they tell you."

"Why not?"

"There's no proof."

I now know what novelists mean when they use the phrase "her blood boiled." I feel mine rapidly churning with heat. "You made sure there wasn't. You used your power to silence people." *And to make me be a toy in your scheme to get a renter—a renter that would do just as you wanted.*

Davis laughs, sinister and cool.

His response gives me strength to say, "You're a . . . a disgrace."

He touches my elbow. "Jackie—"

I pull back. The large man turns to look at me, but I don't even care that he's there, listening in. "No."

Davis uses a soothing tone. "Jackie, really, let's not do this here."

"What you've done is deceitful."

"Sweetheart, you are beautiful."

He's never called me either of these things before, yet, at this moment in time, he's using them as if he's turned into Humphrey Bogart. I don't think my mother would approve.

"How could you be like this? How can you be so . . . so callous?"

His face holds a smirk, one I haven't seen before.

"Why can't you be a decent landlord?"

"You know you love me." His words are out of place.

"Love?" The word sounds empty, as empty as it did coming from Davis's mouth. "I don't love you."

He grimaces. For a second, I think he might break down, get angry. Instead he says, "You are in love, and you know it."

The next words fly from my heart straight out of my mouth

without consulting my mind. "I do love someone." His smug look only makes me bolder. "And it's not you."

Davis spins in his seat to face me. "You are such a confused and misguided child."

"Child!"

His smile insults me.

"You know something? I can't believe that your hero Manex Jethro never gave any credit to his girlfriend for all those songs she wrote for him. He made his money and never gave her any of it."

"What are you trying to say?"

"Who has heroes like him? His girlfriend was entitled to some of his wealth."

"They broke up."

"That's not the point. She still wrote all those songs you like so much. She still deserved some credit. After he broke up with her, she had nothing."

"Her loss." Davis reaches for his tea.

I leave the restaurant because I've never hit a man and I don't want to start today.

41

I don't know where to go, but I know I can't be alone right now. I need someone to reassure me that I'm capable and sensible, that I'm not going to end up in the Morning Glory Nursing Home anytime soon. I wish I could talk to Buck, but I'm not sure of my feelings toward him right now—and besides, I can't go into the restaurant again. Minnie's at the salon, and her shift doesn't end until five.

Seated in my truck, I feel that a trip to the salon might be just what I need. There is safety in the familiar walls of my aunt's shop with the German cuckoo clock, the cross-stitched wall hangings, the warmth of women's chatter, and the thermos of hot tea. And Aunt Sheerly, with all her wise sayings, might be able to help me.

Inside Sheerly Cut, my aunt puts her scissors down to give me a hug and ask if I want my hair trimmed today. "I could give you lots of layers," she says, running her fingers through my long, straight strands.

"No thanks."

Beatrice Lou offers me a cup of jasmine tea as I sit in one of the empty chairs. My aunt's just had a perm; her graying curls look stiff, and the air around her is heavy from a bottled solution.

Minnie stops sweeping hair to ask me what's wrong.

I wonder how she can tell. I fake a smile for each customer—Mavey Marie, the woman seated under one of the pink hair dryers, a round-faced woman with a baby, and Lona in the pink leather chair, her head a mass of spongy curlers. When Minnie sits next to me, I whisper, "I confronted Davis." Then I take a swallow of tea and burn my tongue.

Beatrice Lou comments to the woman holding the infant in a purple dress and matching bonnet, "Such a cute baby. What lovely blue eyes she has."

The young mother, a jacket pulled around her thin shoulders, smiles sweetly at my aunt and at her child. "Thank you."

"How old is she?"

"Seven months." She watches as her baby sucks her fingers. I recognize this woman, but I can't decide where I've seen her before. Perhaps she's a cashier at Food Lion.

Firmly, Beatrice Lou says, "Enjoy her when you can still control her."

The young woman's eyes widen.

Sheerly laughs. "I think God wants to humble us and that's why He gives us kids to raise." She unfastens one of the rollers, freeing Lona's curled hair. "I used to think I knew all the answers. Then I had kids." Busily, she unclamps another roller while Lona peers at her reflection in the mirror. "When your kids become teenagers, they will show you that you know nothing."

"Ain't that the truth?" Beatrice Lou says with extra volume to her voice.

Minnie whispers over the other conversation, "You okay?"

Mechanically, I nod.

"Want to go to the back room to talk?"

"Later," I say.

Minnie gives me a concerned look but resumes her sweeping, and then answers a ringing phone.

Sheerly walks over to the set of pink dryers and, after checking a petite woman's head, snaps the dryer off. She removes the dryer from over her and invites her to sit in the chair next to Lona.

"I miss having young kids at home," Mavey Marie tells us. "Funny, while they were there, I only dreamed of what I would do once they left the nest."

"What was that?" asks Beatrice Lou.

"I wanted to redecorate. Did you see the shop near the vet in Waves?" She makes sure all of us are looking her way as she reveals, "I designed the colors in there."

"That little cute shop that sells hammocks?" Sheerly takes more rollers out of the tiny woman's hair, which is starting to resemble sheep wool.

"That's the shop," says Mavey Marie as her own hair bounces from its beehive abundance.

Beatrice Lou puts in, "Dreams are vital. They keep us going. Sheerly's dream was to own a salon, right?"

Sheerly nods. "I had no money. Just a dream. Then one day the owner of this salon let me rent it for only two hundred dollars a month." She smiles knowingly at Beatrice Lou. "God provided."

"I had a dream to write. Some days I wonder why I dreamed that one." The women laugh as though Lona is a guest comedian on *The Tonight Show.*

Beatrice Lou sighs. "My Aggie is twenty-four now, and I still wonder what she's up to."

"Wasn't she going to be a lawyer?" Lona asks.

"Oh yeah, then a psychiatrist, and then a mortician." Beatrice Lou pours another cup of tea.

I wonder if she's going to tell us about how Aggie is dating Douglas now, but she doesn't.

"She needs to find her passion," says Mavey Marie.

"Like Jackie has with the B & B. How is that coming?" Lona peers at me from the mirror she's seated in front of.

As I wonder how to answer, Beatrice Lou interrupts. "Sheerly had a fundraiser for it."

"Hated to miss it," says Lona as Sheerly combs soft piles of curls on top of the woman's hair.

"It went great," Sheerly says. "The gang sang our hearts out."

"Raised a lot of money?" asks the woman with the sheep wool hair.

"We sure did." Sheerly grins at me.

Lona then says to all of us, "I don't know why I can't write today. My main character is supposed to be optimistic and fun. Today she's sounding a lot like me."

"How's that?" asks Beatrice Lou.

"Tired. Tired." She slips her handbag over her shoulder. "I think I need caffeine and a greasy burger."

"Go to the Grille," I say, placing my empty teacup on an end table near my chair. "And while you're there, punch someone for me."

This is not how I planned to tell them about Davis Erickson, but sometimes I surprise myself.

Disbelief fills every pore of Minnie's face as she stares at me over the counter. She was in the middle of calling someone but lets the phone find its way to the cradle.

Sheerly's hand with the large metal hairbrush is suspended from her side like a raised sword.

My words crawl at first, and then tumble and leap all over themselves.

I must be making sense, for there are looks of understanding and disgust.

"Davis Erickson?" Sheep Wool and Sheerly's eyes lock through their reflections in the mirror.

Slowly, I say, "Yeah, he's been covering up all that damage at the Bailey House."

Sheep Wool presses her lips tightly. "Oh, mercy! He's our landlord. We weren't supposed to talk about it. We love the location, don't want to move."

Lona is no longer interested in her hunger and a burger. She plops down in a chair beside me; her purse swings onto her lap.

Minnie says, "This is where I heard the first rumors, Jackie. Remember, Sheerly, the other day when that couple came in and said something about reading about Davis in *Lighthouse Views?*"

Sheerly shrugs her shoulders, looks at me as if she should have told me what she'd heard the other day, shows guilt that she didn't.

Minnie sees her guilt. "At least Jackie knows now," she says. "The couple knew that Buck and his dad were contracted to repair the Bailey House. As more and more information came out, I realized I had to talk to Buck to see if it was true. That's when I knew you had to hear it from him." Minnie is looking at me now.

I sigh. "Well, I let everyone in the Grille know that Davis is a liar."

The baby starts to fuss and the mother turns away from us to nurse her. After her baby is soothed, she says, "We rent from Rexy Properties, too." She stops herself, toys with the collar of her daughter's dress, and then continues, her eyes on her child. "The owner just keeps painting over a water leak in our apartment. He won't fix it, although we've asked him to."

She seems hesitant to say more, so Mavey Marie prods, "Where does your husband have his business?"

"In Salvo. It's called Ocean Floral."

Sheerly says, "This is not good at all."

"Ocean Floral?" Now I recall where I've seen this woman before. "I was supposed to talk to you about who you rent from. I went to your shop." She looks different without her white floppy hat.

"I know." She keeps her gaze on her child, as though studying her head. When she raises her eyes to meet mine, she asks, "You're friends with Buck, right?"

"Yeah."

"He told me you might be stopping by. But when you did, I realized you write for *Lighthouse Views*." She shifts her eyes toward the floor. "I was afraid."

"Afraid?" Mavey Marie repeats.

"Yes."

"Well, honey, you can tell us. We don't bite."

Kelly nods, as though she now has the courage to share. "My husband wouldn't want me to jeopardize anything by speaking badly of Davis." She sighs. "We argue all the time about what to do. I want to move, but my husband says we can't afford it. This recession hasn't helped." Her baby starts to cry, and she pauses to comfort her.

Lona shakes her head. "I never liked that Rexy man. Now I know why."

"But what makes you afraid?" Sheerly steps closer to Kelly.

"Well." The young woman chews on her lower lip. This action seems to give her confidence because when she speaks, her voice is bolder. "Davis threatens to raise our rent. He reminds us all the time how he didn't make us give him a security deposit. We were strapped for money when we first opened the shop and he said he'd make it easy for us. That was then. Now he holds that over us."

Sheerly clicks her tongue against the roof of her mouth. Beatrice Lou follows; the two of them sounding like hens who just got their feathers ruffled the wrong way.

With her child resting quietly against her, Kelly continues. "The lady next to us told us that a woman fell when Rexy Properties didn't fix the railing for her duplex. She broke her leg."

"She should have sued." Lona shifts in her chair.

"Mrs. Dupree was advised not to sue by Davis. I heard he threatened her." Kelly stops, perhaps thinking that she's talked enough.

"Mrs. Dupree?" I say. "Did you say Mrs. Dupree?"

Kelly winces. "Yes . . ."

And in spite of all the confusion of this day, I laugh.

The women are surprised; puzzlement lines their faces.

"Irvy!" I say to Minnie. "She told me at my birthday party to remember Mrs. Dupree."

Sheerly clicks her tongue once more.

"I thought Mrs. Dupree was a brand name for spices," Minnie confesses. "You know, like McCormick. Weeks before she died, she started bringing that name up. I thought she was talking about nutmeg and sage."

"And now you know what she really meant," says Sheerly. "Bless her heart. Your poor mama was trying her hardest to help you out."

When the cuckoo clock clucks two, I realize it's much later than I thought. Even with my flexible schedule, I need to get back to the office. I stand to leave the salon. Sheerly's embrace is tight as she tells me she's proud of me for confronting Davis.

Minnie says she'll pick up Zane from Ropey's and then some barbecue for our dinner on her way home. "So don't worry about cooking tonight, okay?"

I'd forgotten what it was like to be taken care of by Minnie. Before Lawrence died, she was freely motherly toward me, helping me through life's bumps and detours. Seeing the old Minnie makes me hug her twice.

42

I pull into the Lighthouse Views parking lot and note that it's empty except for Selena's convertible.

Shakespeare wags his tail as I enter the office. He's looking healthy once again thanks to some pills that took care of a parasite the poor canine picked up. Of course, Selena was horrified to think that her beloved pooch would get something as nasty as a parasite.

I hurry toward my desk and turn on my computer, an attempt to busy myself with work and take a break from thinking about Davis and the Bailey House.

After I give Selena a weak "Hi," she immediately asks, "What's the matter?"

I shake my head.

From her desk she says, "Everyone went to see the sandcastle art in Buxton. Did you not get the memo?"

This sounds vaguely familiar.

"Bert said he sent it to all of you. One man has created a whole village out of sand, including dragons and mermaids. Sandy Catering is selling hot dogs and drinks. Sure you don't want to go?"

I wait for the computer screen to light up.

"Want lunch?" She walks to my desk and stands in front of it. "I can pick up some salads from The Happy Fisherman."

"I ate." I know I did; I just can't recall what it was.

Selena looks me up and down, like Betty Lynn used to look at my dates. "What's going on? What is it?" She waves her pen around.

I can't pretend any longer. I give her a quick glance. Standing, I walk over to the couch and hear her footsteps follow me. Shakespeare nuzzles my leg as I sit down. "What do you know about Davis Erickson?"

"Davis? You interviewed him. You wrote the article."

"That's not what I asked."

"Oh . . . well, he's good-looking. Owns Rexy Properties. House needs paint. What do you want to know?"

"Did you know that he owns the Bailey House Bed and Breakfast?"

"Well," says Selena. "Well." Her pen waves in front of her face. "Is that it?"

I gently pet Shakespeare, my mind going a thousand different directions. "It has problems he's tried to cover up."

Selena sits beside me on the sofa. "Tell me what you are trying to say."

My words only come out in partial sentences. "Water damage. Rotting wood. Things not visible to the naked eye."

"Who told you this?" Selena has always been keen on wanting to know our sources of information.

"I'm the new renter of the house."

Selena hasn't petted her dog the whole time I've been talking.

I take a moment to ask, "Do you want to know the real story?"

When she says that she does, I summarize what Buck shared

with me, throwing in the extra bits and pieces I heard at Sheerly's today and explaining how unmoved Davis was when I accused him earlier at the Grille.

Selena stands. Her hands are like anchors against her hips. "Okay. Listen. If he—if Mr. Deceitful—ever tries to ignore problems again— No, no. Let me put it this way." She clears her throat. "If he ever denies any of what you have just told me, or tries to stray from the straight and narrow ever again, then I will become his worst enemy."

My eyes grow wide, like Zane's do when I tell him if he doesn't brush his teeth, he'll grow fangs.

"I will use my powers."

"Powers?"

"The magazine! He will be front-page bad-businessman news. You make sure he fixes all the problems at the bed and breakfast ASAP. On his dime." She snaps her fingers, and Shakespeare jumps. "Or he will be sorry."

I have a deep feeling that he will be.

"We gave him a great story months ago when you interviewed him. Should he not change his ways, we can do another story. This one will not make him look good. Could put him out of business."

I believe her. Selena will put on her boxing gloves should the need arise. Personally, I think that she has hit a man before.

Moving to her computer, she brings up the North Carolina General Assembly's Web site. "Aha!" Her cry vibrates throughout the office. "It states here that the landlord is to comply with the current building and housing codes."

Standing in front of her computer screen, I read the section from the North Carolina statutes under the heading: "Landlord to provide fit premises."

"You say he just keeps painting over leaks and ignoring structural damage? Hmmm. Doubt a housing inspector would label that safe and look the other way." She turns to me and adds, "Go to the Rolodex and find the card for that inspector."

"Inspector?"

"Peace of Home."

"Peace of Home?"

"I know it sounds like a silly name for a housing inspector, but that's what he goes by."

When Cassidy and Bert return from the sandcastle show, Bert begins to tell about an idea he has for an interview. Selena's hand motions him to go no further. I don't think she's ever told him to hold his tongue before. Quickly, she fills him and Cassidy in on the news about Davis.

Cassidy shakes her head, but Bert turns to me. "When he called to ask you out that one time, I was about to tell you to be careful."

"What do you mean, Bert?" Selena asks.

"My cousin works for Vanessa. Her name's Donna. She's always telling me how Davis is trying to get Vanessa to get back together with him."

"So he was dating Jackie and her at the same time?" Cassidy's tone is one of shock, like when she found out how many calories coconut milk has.

Selena snorts. "Despicable!"

"He gets rid of people when they don't cooperate," says Bert. "That's why he and his secretary are the only people who still work for Rexy Properties."

I bite my lip. Perhaps Selena is right; Bert does seem to know everything.

"Where I come from," Cassidy says, "we'd call a man like him 'sleazy.' "

Selena, still perched over her computer, reads the statutes. She gets our attention by saying, "All landlords are to make sure the electrical and plumbing in the rental property is in good and safe working order." Leaning back in her chair she gives us an assignment. "Let's put together an article on Davis and his despicable ways."

"To print in the magazine?" My voice is hoarse.

"To use as a teaching tool. We'll be sure to send him a copy." Selena's grin dances across her face. "If he doesn't agree to make some changes, then we take the next step."

"What's the next step?" I know I must ask, even though I'm pretty certain of the answer.

"We'll print it! We'll put in there everything that he's done in the past. I bet with your interview skills, we could uncover a lot more than we already know. And when we do, no one will ever rent from him again." She clasps her hands together as if she'd like to wrap her fingers around someone's neck.

Bert lets out a low whistle.

Cassidy takes a bottle of Aquafina from the fridge. "Did your relatives set you up with this man?"

"No," I say. "They had nothing to do with him."

"At least you can't blame them this time," says our boss. She then unscrews the lid of the jar and takes out a sausage treat for her dog. As she sits beside Shakespeare, she raises the morsel to his mouth, which is already an open crevice, waiting in happy anticipation. "We'll hang out all his dirty laundry," she says with obvious satisfaction. "Oh, poochie," she croons as her terrier chews and then rapidly licks stray crumbs off the sofa. "Your mama is so smart. Sometimes she surprises even me."

43

Once after one of my blind-dates-gone-bad, Sheerly told me that, for as much as she sings about love, she has yet to understand just how it happens. What makes a man and woman fall in love? Is God behind it? Is it something deep within that clicks due to hormones or genetics? Or is it something we just fall into, like the way the wind carries a sailboat down the Sound? Perhaps, she concluded, it is a combination of all those.

Today, Buck and I paddle his kayaks to an inlet on the outskirts of Rodanthe. On a narrow shore, we search for shells, drink Fruit Punch Gatorade, which is Buck's favorite, and Diet Pepsi, which is mine. We sit on a wobbly dock with our bare feet dangling over the edge as the afternoon sun warms our legs and backs. And most of all, we smile at each other as if we can't believe how happy we feel just being together, just breathing in the same space.

Hours later, we paddle back to where our vehicles are parked. Before leaving, Buck reaches for me; our embrace is warm and lingering. He leans toward me; I want nothing more now than to kiss Buck.

When our lips touch, it's as though my feet have stepped off the ground and my head is floating somewhere on a cloud of cotton candy.

"Wait," he says when we finally pull apart and I take a step toward my truck to go home to Minnie and Zane.

He hands me a large plaid notebook. "I noticed your old one was almost out of pages. I think," he tells me with a smile, "you need to make the switch from stripes to plaid now that you're the manager of the Bailey House."

~⌒ ~⌒

I carry the notebook to the Bailey House on this late-October afternoon.

Buck calls me as he leaves the Grille after his shift, saying he'll meet me at the house.

When I see him step out of his Jeep—tall, fit, hair tossed by the wind—I have a desire to run across the driveway to greet him and run my fingers along his jaw, touching the stubble that I know is there. But I hold back. I took things too quickly with Davis; I don't want anything to ruin what I have with Buck.

Buck and I take our time walking throughout the interior and around the exterior of the bed and breakfast as he points out the things that need to be repaired. With the handle of a wooden spoon he finds in one of the kitchen drawers, he taps the wall by the toilet in the tiny restroom that only has a sink and toilet. The wall caves in; he taps it a little harder and the lumpy gray mixture inside emerges, damp plaster spilling onto the tile floor.

The smell of concentrated mold makes me hold my nose. "Yuck," I say. "How long did he think he could just patch things up and pretend the place didn't need proper restoration?"

"Seems like he didn't think that through. He was only worried about making money," says Buck.

"Can you do it?" I ask. "Can you repair all this?"

He grins. "I like tools. Remember?"

I remember. That conversation seems so long ago, way back when he was just my brother's friend and not the man with bright eyes who makes my heart go fuzzy with warmth each time I see him.

"I'll be glad to make it the way it should be."

"Will you ask your father to help?" I sound like a little child.

"We might be able to do the project the right way together this time."

I have been praying that Griffins & Company will let Buck work with the team again.

"The Home of Peace or Peace of Home or whatever the name of that inspection company is will be here tomorrow. We'll see what else the inspector finds wrong with the place, and then you and your dad can get to work."

Buck nods. "Your attitude is great, Hatteras."

We enter the sunroom for the fourth time. This room always draws me in, always presenting me with an invitation to enjoy its beauty. The wide windows and the way the ceiling slopes gives the room a cozy feel.

"Zane wants to place his artwork here," I say, pointing. "He says he has lots of knot-work he's created at Ropey's. He showed some to his kindergarten teacher and she said he was a budding artist."

"Zane? Is this the same kid who pitched a fit at the Grille?"

"I guess we all grow up."

Just this morning, Zane showed me some braided rope he had

glued onto a piece of wood. It looked an awful lot like the birthday present he gave me. "We can place it in the Lawrence Room," I told him.

His face lit up. "Lawrence? That's my daddy's name."

"We can name the sunroom that. It can be filled with things you like." I'm not sure why I let the moment carry me away like that.

Now, as Buck and I stand in the sunroom with the sun sliding behind a cloud, I say, "I want to call this the Lawrence Room."

Buck nods. "Minnie would like that."

"I bet Sheerly would cross-stitch a plaque for us. 'The Lawrence Room.' " I turn to Buck.

He reaches for my arm and pulls me against his chest. I like the way my cheek fits so nicely along his shoulder. "What do you think?" I murmur into his shirt.

"About us?"

"Well, I meant the room, but forget that for now. What do you think about you and me?"

His arms feel secure around me, as though they belong there. "I hated every date you went on with other guys."

I swallow. "You want to know what I think of that?"

"Yeah."

"I think you should have told me. You could have said, 'Hey, I like you, Hatteras. Why don't we go out?' "

"And have you laugh in my face and never come back to the Grille again?"

Serenity fills my voice. "Oh, Buck, I wouldn't have ever done that."

His arms tighten around me. "Really?"

I look up, expecting to see humor in his eyes. There is only a soft sincerity.

"Tell me again," he says.

"About?"

"The man you are in love with."

I draw a deep breath. "He's sweet, cute, draws frogs, and surprises me."

"How?"

"I never expected to feel this way about . . ."

I close my eyes. His lips meet mine as I think about my repeated prayer to God to send me a man. *He can arrive on a horse, a Coast Guard barge, a sailboat—or maybe even a kayak.*

The truth is that he didn't ever need to arrive. He's always been there, right in Hatteras. Like the waves, sea, and sun—all along. Like me and the Bailey House. He was waiting even before I realized that waiting for him was what really mattered. My eyes open. I touch his jaw with fingers that feel like they were created to do just this.

We kiss slowly as the sun finds shade behind a flock of clouds.

"You are a funny creation," Buck teases. "You love fishermen's hats but hate to eat fish and hate to fish."

"Is there anything wrong with that?" I laugh.

He smiles. "You are always right in my book, Hatteras."

In the distance a foghorn sounds, a familiar drone that makes me think of changing seasons and how humans strive to find ways to keep up with them. The tourists who have returned to Upstate New York are probably already wearing wool as they chop wood for their furnaces. Down here we are still in light sweaters, although our recreational boats have been winterized, and many shops have closed for the season. Yet what connects each person is that thing Sheerly sings about—love. When you're in the season of newfound love, it just doesn't matter if your summer clothes have been replaced in your bureau by winter ones. You don't care what the weather does because you're with the person you love.

Sheerly has a song with these lyrics: "Wait for the perfect moment. Wait for that magical day. You will feel it in your heart. The season of love is here to stay."

Selena would think that was corny and syrupy, but then again, Selena is not in love.

Today feels like it belongs to a woman who recalls being a little girl at this very house and thinking that love just happens to you when you are busy doing something else. Now I can't help but think that that little girl wasn't so far off the mark.

44

Minnie is blasting Eric Clapton's "Lady in Red" when I enter our duplex. The music is deafening; I wonder if she's borrowed Bo's speakers.

Zane is at the dining room table doing his homework, either ignoring the loud song or in need of a hearing aid.

"Homework?" I cry. "Aren't you only in kindergarten?"

"I'm big now," he tells me. "Mrs. Cravensport says I'm not supposed to cry."

"Who is Mrs. Cravensport?"

"My teacher at my school."

"Oh yeah."

He chews his bottom lip and carefully traces the dotted letter B on a sheet of wide-lined paper. "She likes me."

"I'm sure she does."

"Yeah!" He grins and then presses his pencil against the page to form the letter C.

Peering at the sheet, I see that he's writing the alphabet. "But you do know that there are times to cry," I say.

"Of course." I've never heard this child sound so certain. "But not when your chicken nuggets get eaten by angry crabs."

"Did that happen to you at school?"

He shakes his head. "No, not yet. But if it does, I won't cry."

I head upstairs where the music is louder. Minnie is replaying the same song. Her door is closed. She hasn't cried since Irvy died, and I hope she isn't now. I hear her singing along to the music.

I enter my room to see that Minnie has laid two letters on my bed. The business envelopes are to the right of each piece of stationery. I glance at them, wonder what they say, and then reach for one.

The first letter is from Irvy's attorney in Nags Head. The letter states that land in northwest Cary—ten acres—has been willed to Minnie from Irvy. Another letter is from a Realtor who wants to buy the land for a new development. He has heard that Minnie now owns the land and is trying to get her to sell. He makes it clear that he knows that Irvy did not want to sell the land, but perhaps her daughter will think otherwise. He will be offering "top dollar."

Rushing into Minnie's room, both letters in my hands, I find her putting on red lipstick. She sees me, turns the music off, and grins wider than she has since Lawrence died.

"So," she says, "I guess I'm the proverbial poor little rich girl!"

"Irvy owned all this land?" I let the letters from the attorney and the developer shake in my hand. "Did you know?"

"No. No more than I knew why Rudlow up and left us. My parents seem to have a lot of secrets."

"How much do you think the land is worth?" I ask.

She stretches out on her bed. "Can you believe it? Art wants to build a strip mall on it."

I cannot believe it. "Who's Art?"

"The developer." She motions toward the letters with fingernails that have been painted ruby.

"Really?" I ask, still stunned.

"Really." She smiles.

"All those times your mom said there was a farm in Cary, we thought she was insane."

Minnie nods. "I just wanted her to stop."

"We should have been saying, like Sheerly did the other day when we learned who Mrs. Dupree was, 'Bless her heart.' Your mama was trying her hardest to help us out."

"I know, but she was also calling me Eleanor, so I was sure she was losing her mind."

"So there really is a farm in Cary." There is wonder in my voice today.

"That's what they say." Minnie flashes a smile, the red lipstick bright against her fair complexion. "Apparently Mom's grandparents owned it and now she does. No, now I do." She crosses her legs and leans against the headboard. "Four hundred thousand dollars, Jackie."

"What?"

"That's what Art said he would pay me. It's been a fantastic afternoon!"

I flop on the bed next to her as we giggle just like we did in middle school as we sat on the glider at the Bailey House while Ogden trimmed the honeysuckle. Our laughter is genuine, freeing, childlike.

Irvy knew what she was talking about all along.

⌒⌒

We make lemon cookies. I prop the recipe card with Irvy's hand-writing on it against the canister of flour. Zane helps, and we don't scold him for knocking an egg onto the floor or for dipping fingers into the mixing bowl and licking them.

The cookies are soft and round when they come out of the oven. We eat dinner as they cool on racks, and then sit at the kitchen table to frost them with the powdered sugar and lemon juice glaze. Zane pops three into his mouth as crumbs coat the top of his shirt.

"Zane, don't you want to put some icing on them?" Minnie asks.

Zane shakes his head. "I don't like that yellow stuff on them."

Minnie and I spread the glaze on each cookie and, after ushering Zane to bed, sit in front of the TV with a plate of the treats.

Picking up a cookie, Minnie takes a few bites. "What do you think?"

I reach for a large cookie and sink my teeth into it.

"Delicious," we say at the same time.

"We can serve these as guests check in. What do you think?"

"I think I have the strangest life," Minnie says as the weatherman tells us the five-day forecast.

"Strange?"

"I mean, who would have known that Mama had this money tied up in a farm?"

"What are you going to do?"

"About what?" She stifles a yawn.

"The land."

She smirks. "Hold on to it and raise cows."

"Seriously."

"You should know that answer. It's going to be used for the Bailey House." She reaches across the sofa and grasps my hand, the same way she did her mother's. "We were born to run the Bailey House, you and me. Mrs. Bailey is smiling down from heaven at us now, don't you think? 'So glad you've come round to restore my house.' Do you hear her?"

I think I might.

Minnie gives a contented sigh. "Oh, Jackie. I want to build something good. If I have to work hard, I want to put hours into something that can be mine, that can be ours. We can do it, right? With this extra money? Buck will help." She stretches out on the sofa and flexes her toes. "I think it's time to give my two-week notice."

I'm grateful to see her so happy. I'm also the daughter of an accountant, and therefore my mind begins to think about numbers. "Minnie, what would you think of us using a chunk of the money as a down payment? You know, buy the house instead of rent it?" I stop myself. This is Minnie's inheritance and I'm acting like it belongs to both of us.

Minnie peers at me. "Will he sell it?"

"You mean will Davis sell the house to us? Yes, I think so. We have a rent-with-the-option-to-buy agreement."

Minnie says, "Or we could use the money for rent and repairs."

"Selena tells me that according to the law, Davis should be the one to pay for the structural repairs if he's our landlord."

"Really? How are you going to get him to do that?" Minnie looks doubtful.

"Buck and Selena both say that as landlord, the law states he has to maintain the property and keep it up to code."

After she eats another cookie, she says, "I'll talk to Mama's attorney again. I think his name is Johnson. I'll make sure we get some good legal counsel."

Something about her words makes me feel reassured.

Minutes later, I ask her when she plans to tell her bosses she'll be quitting, but she's softly snoring, her head on a blue pillow her mother crocheted with Eleanor decades ago. Eleanor, I have since learned, was Irvy's mother.

I fall asleep to the wind whipping over the roof and pulsating the windows. My dream features a Colonial-style home with twelve-foot ceilings, a sunroom, and a picture of the queen in each of the six bedrooms. The two Siamese cats in my dream sit on the glider under the pergola and respond to the names Finally and At Last.

45

Bert says he can't remember the last time Selena actually worked all weekend on a piece for the magazine. "I can't believe she spent all this time on something that may not ever be read. She even declined a golf game with the mayor on Saturday."

Selena may have written it, this article describing Davis Erickson as a "Hatteras Landlord Gone Bad," but she wants me to deliver it. She says it will be read by Mr. Erickson and followed, or else. We know what she means.

"You take this over to him," she tells me as she pets Shakespeare's ears. "If *Lighthouse Views* is going to eventually lose you to the bed and breakfast, I want to make sure that I'm entrusting you to a safe and protected environment." Then she gives me a smile as I thank her for making my battle her battle.

Davis is seated at his desk talking on his cell when I enter Rexy Properties. I see him from Bev's post at the front, just to the right of the Picasso. She's on the phone as usual, tapping her nails against a coffee mug. I march right into Davis's office, my stomach twisting with nerves. As I place the pages in the center of his desk, I wonder if he'll hang up, but he only nods in my direction, avoids my eyes, and continues his conversation.

I don't have to wait for him. The waiting days are over.

As I walk toward my truck in the parking lot, dampness from the overcast day surrounds me, making me wish I'd worn my jacket. Quickly, I get into my truck and start the engine so that I can turn on the heat. I warm my fingers by the vent as tepid air shoots through it.

"Hey!"

I turn to see Davis coming out of Rexy Properties; his long strides carry him to me. "What is this?" He waves the papers in his hand.

I roll the window down and ask, "Did you read it?"

"She's going to put this in the magazine?"

"She will, if you can't abide by the North Carolina property laws."

"She won't!"

"I work for her, and she will. Unless you start to really be a landlord who takes care of his property and tenants."

"A threat?" His face looks as fierce as the afternoon sky.

And for the first time, my palms do not prickle from sweat.

"Are you threatening me?"

Repeating Selena's words from this morning, I say, "A taste of your own medicine, Davis." I know he's thinking that this won't and can't affect him. That there is no way our little plan could force him to do what he doesn't want to do. But the cold truth is, Selena knows a lot of people in this town.

And what will really destroy Davis will be my aunt Sheerly. She has this tendency to make up songs about people and sing them on Saturday nights at The Rose Lattice. Her songs have been known to travel up and down the island faster than a hurricane wind. You don't want her singing about the evils you've done.

"I'm having a crew come in to do the needed structural repairs at the Bailey House," I say, surprised by the authority in my tone. "You know, the railing outside, the plumbing, those crumbling walls that you've kept painting over." I could go on, but my head is getting a little heavy. "I'll send you the bill."

Davis lets out a sigh. I'd like to think there is remorse in his eyes, but I think they only show that he's sorry he got caught.

⌒⌒

As Buck and his father work in the Bailey House's kitchen on a mid-November afternoon, I take a walk around the property. I stand back to look at the house, framed under an autumn sky, and suddenly, I think that we can't do it. I can't do it. Change is good sometimes, such as Zane growing out of his tantrums and my relatives no longer seeking out eligible men for me. Yet sometimes there is no logical reason for change. Minnie, Buck, and I originally thought we should give a fresh name to this bed and breakfast since it is now under new management. Buck suggested The Fisherman's Hat, and I had to hug him for that. But the more I watch the men of Griffins & Company restore it, the more I'm certain that it just doesn't seem right. The Bailey House will remain the Bailey House, a landmark on the coast of Nags Head, as it has been for decades in our community.

46

We decided the first day of December would be a good time to christen the remodeled Bailey House with friends and family. Sheerly suggested that we each bring a dish of food to share.

The wind is fierce, and we have to adjust the thermostat in the large house. I'm thankful that the heat works. Regardless of the chilly evening, our hearts are warm. My mom and dad have driven over from Charlotte. Minnie and Zane arrive, and then Ropey, Sheerly, Tiny, and later, Beatrice Lou. L. J. is excited as she enters the parlor, admiring the décor and breathing in the smell of fresh paint. She waltzes into the kitchen, gushing about what a wonderful job *handsome* Buck has done. She'd like new counters in her home's kitchen, and new cherry cabinets, and then she says, "Oh, get me a new sink, too."

Before our potluck dinner, she and Sheerly sing a song they've written for the christening of the bed and breakfast. The refrain talks about waiting on God and how prayers are sometimes answered in a different way than we expect. We clap at the end; Zane goes a little crazy and claps louder than anyone else.

Uncle Tiny suggests that we all join hands and pray. We do this, closing our eyes. My hand feels warm encased in Buck's. We are all silent, standing there as the wind whistles outside.

Finally, Tiny says, "Ready when you are, Jackie."

I realize he expects me to pray. I do; my heart is so full of gratitude, the words spill out easily. If I made a list of all the things I'm thankful for, it would go on for many pages in my new plaid notebook.

When we open our eyes, I feel history has been made—I just prayed our first prayer in the parlor now known as the Fisherman's Hat Room. We continue by drinking a toast with raspberry cream soda from plastic cups with colorful hats on them—Sheerly's find.

I look at the windows and floors as they shine under the lamps and chandeliers. I've cut back to interviewing only one business owner a month so that I could get this place in shape. As Griffins & Company fixed pipes, plaster, walls, ceilings, and other parts of the house, Minnie and I washed dishes, towels, and sheets. We dusted, shined, and polished. We hired a landscaper to cut and trim, and paid him extra to scrub away moss and algae.

One afternoon after going to three stores, I finally found a marble birdbath in the shape of a clam. As Minnie and I placed it where the old one stood, immediately the garden felt enchanted again. I think there was even a smile on the mermaid's face.

Using the Wal-Mart gift card I got for my birthday, I bought two large ivy topiaries for the front doorway.

We already have it on the community calendar that there will be an open house the week before Christmas. We will string tiny yellow and white lights all around and serve lemon cookies and raspberry cream soda as people tour the newly reopened Bailey House.

We've created brochures for people to take and circulate. The amazing thing is that we already have our first paying guests. Ropey and Beatrice Lou plan to bring the boat over, dock at the pier, and stay next Friday. They want the English Breakfast Room.

With a cry of, "Let's eat!" from Ropey, we all move into the sunroom. The official new name of this favorite room of mine is the Lawrence Room—a place for all to feel loved and welcomed, just as Lawrence made Minnie and Zane feel. A spot where everyone should feel cared for, no matter where they are on their journey. On the rectangular table, now spread with a checkered cloth from Sheerly, dishes of food stand, serving spoons beside them. There is tomato pie, macaroni and cheese, fried chicken, cornbread with bacon, steamed okra, and fried flounder. Minnie picked up a chocolate cake with fudge frosting on her way here.

As we fill our plates with food—Zane and I avoiding the fish—I catch myself looking out the window of the sunroom and smiling. Though it's dark out, I know that there are rows of honeysuckle bushes right outside. I picture Ogden in his coveralls, his straw hat tipped to one side, a pair of hedge trimmers in his hand, ready to get to work. The image is so clear, it's as though he's really there. But when I look again, he's gone. I suppose he went looking for Mrs. Bailey—walking slowly due to his bad leg—to inform her that it's time to bring out the lemon cookies and raspberry soda. We just need some of her scented napkins. Please.

After all, we have come round to celebrate.

～⌒～⌒

New Year's Eve, we decide, is a good day to move. A perfect day to put the past behind us. Minnie says she's as happy as she's been in months, and is anxious to start the new year in another location. So we load up Buck's Jeep, Minnie's car, and my truck. Before we transport the last load, Minnie, Zane, and I say good-bye to the duplex. Zane and Minnie will live in the apartment over the garage, furnished with items from the duplex, and I'll make my home in the smaller downstairs bedroom of the main house. I've already spent one night there when Ropey and Beatrice Lou became the first paying guests under our ownership.

After we get everything unloaded, we plan to enjoy New Year's Eve dancing in the parlor of the Bailey House. Zane wants to eat cottage cheese sprinkled with edible confetti. He saw the confetti on a commercial during an *Andy Griffith* rerun.

Mrs. Appleton watches us from her kitchen window, her face partially hidden by a frilly lace curtain. There was a day when I was tempted to wave at her, making her aware that she's never as inconspicuous as she thinks—but not today. There are larger things on my mind as I count the steps up to the duplex for the final time. Nostalgia covers my skin like a perfumed ointment. "This is it," I say when I reach the interior and start opening drawers and closets, making sure that nothing has been left behind. "You were a good home," I tell the bare walls, counters, and floors. Satisfied with my walk-through, I close and lock the front door.

Bo sticks his head out of his doorway. "Hey," he calls. "I'll be coming by the Bailey place real soon. Might even stay a night or two."

"That would be great."

"Don't worry. I'll leave my music at home." He winks, wishes me luck.

"Thanks, Bo."

Buck closes the hatch to his Jeep after pushing a large cardboard box of Zane's toys inside. He looks around the driveway. "Did you get everything?"

Minnie and Zane are already inside her car. Minnie rolls down her window. "Here we go!" she says with a broad smile. Zane is clapping his hands in his car seat. He has learned a new song in kindergarten: "If You're Happy and You Know It."

Buck watches as I walk toward my truck that is crammed with boxes and bags. When I get to the door, he says, "Don't forget this box."

At first I think that he's talking to Minnie. Then I realize he's speaking to me.

"What box?" I scan the driveway.

On the pavement by my Ford sits a small silver box tied with a black ribbon.

"What's this?"

Minnie and Buck smile at each other.

"It's for you," says Buck.

Tentatively, I stoop down and pick up the box. I cast a quick glance at Buck and then eagerly untie the ribbon. Inside is a black jewelry box that pops open to reveal a sparkling diamond ring. My face flushes with warmth, even though the day is chilly. "Buck!" I look into his smiling face. "Are you serious?"

And there in the driveway, Buck gets down on one knee. "Hatteras Girl," he says, looking so handsome and sweet, "even though I know jewelry isn't quite your thing, I sure hope you will agree to wear this ring and marry me."

I bend down to kiss him. "I need a good carpenter in my life." Buck does bring out the silliness in me, but my next words are serious. "I would be happy to marry you."

"And wear the ring?"

Zane's head is sticking out the car window as he bellows, "Jackie, you're supposed to say 'Yes!' "

My Hatteras relatives had a goal of seeing a ring on my finger by the end of this year. With only a few hours to spare, I slip Buck's ring onto my finger.

Doubt drifts out to sea. The realization that dreams do come true makes me smile.

I grab Buck's hand and bring him to his feet. Leaning in to kiss him, I smile and say, "Yes, I'll marry you. This is going to be wonderfully fun."

The Bailey House Lemon Cookies

1 cup of butter, softened

1½ cups of sugar

2 eggs

2 tablespoons of freshly grated lemon peel

1 tablespoon of lemon juice

2½ cups of all-purpose flour

1 teaspoon of baking soda

¼ teaspoon of salt

1½ teaspoons of cream of tartar

GLAZE:

2 ½ cups of powdered sugar

¼ cup of lemon juice

Preheat oven to 400 degrees F. In a large bowl, combine the butter and sugar together. Add the eggs. Mix lightly. Add the lemon juice and peel. In another bowl, stir together the dry ingredients. Add the dry ingredients to the batter and beat at low speed with a mixer, scraping the bowl often. Drop the dough by teaspoons onto a greased cookie sheet. Bake for 6 to 8 minutes or until the edges are lightly browned. Remove from pan and let cool.

Mix glaze ingredients and frost cookies.

Makes 5 dozen cookies.

L. J.'s Cornbread with Bacon

1¼ cups of all-purpose flour

¾ cup of white cornmeal

¼ cup of sugar

2 teaspoons of baking powder

1 teaspoon of salt

3 eggs

1 cup of sour cream

1 can of creamed corn

1 cup of crumbled bacon, fried

Mix dry ingredients in a bowl. To the dry ingredients, add the eggs, sour cream, and creamed corn. Lightly blend and then stir in bacon.

Bake in a greased 9 x 13-inch pan at 400 degrees F. for 20 minutes. Don't overcook.

Sheerly's Tomato Pie

5 plump and juicy tomatoes—homegrown, if possible

Salt and pepper to taste

1 rolled piecrust, either store-bought or homemade

3 teaspoons of fresh or dried basil

1 teaspoon of sugar

1 large Vidalia onion, sliced

6 slices of Swiss or Gruyere cheese, or a combination

1 cup of real mayonnaise (Hellmann's is best)

¼ teaspoon of Tabasco

1½ cups of sharp cheddar cheese, shredded

½ cup Parmesan cheese, grated

Peel the tomatoes and slice them. Place them in a bowl and cover with salt. Let them sit for 45 minutes. Rinse off excess salt. Form piecrust in a pie plate. Place a layer of drained tomatoes on the crust. Sprinkle with pepper, salt, 2 teaspoons of basil, and sugar. Add a layer of sliced onion. Add a layer of Swiss or Gruyere cheese. Repeat the layers. For the last layer, mix mayonnaise, Tabasco, and cheddar cheese, and spread over the top. Then sprinkle with Parmesan cheese, pepper, and the rest of the basil. Bake at 375 degrees F. for 30 to 40 minutes or until the top is browned and bubbly. Cool for 15 minutes before serving. Serves 6.

Acknowledgments

My gratitude to:

The Serious Scribes—Katharine, Martha, Jen, Catherine, and Kim.

Fellow missionary kid and Canadian Academy schoolmate Ron Theisson, for his kayaking guidance.

Colleen Baber, for telling me stories about her son Andrew so I could create a restaurant in his memory: Breakfast at Andrew's.

Marcel Hull, for the hospitality and service she offers to all who enter her international home.

Vince, my brother, for his realty help.

Tana O'Keeffe, my Outer Banks friend who lets me call her "Hatteras."

Charlene and the incredible team at Bethany House for continuing to believe in me.

My agent, Kristin Lindstrom.

My remarkable husband, Carl; his expertise in construction and ability to deal with other people's repairs-gone-wrong is truly impressive.

About the Author

Alice J. Wisler was born and raised in Japan as a missionary kid. After graduating high school, she got her BS in Social Work from Eastern Mennonite University in Virginia. She's enjoyed staying at a number of bed and breakfasts in the South, in Japan, and in England, and would secretly like to run one if it just wasn't so much work. The Outer Banks is one of her favorite vacation destinations. Currently, she lives in Durham, North Carolina, with her husband, Carl, and three children, Rachel, Benjamin, and Elizabeth. In memory of her son Daniel, she gives online grief-writing courses, designs remembrance cards, and speaks across the country on Writing the Heartache. To find out more, visit her Web site at *www.alicewisler.com.*

Questions for Conversation

1. Have you ever had a dream to do something others considered impossible? What steps did you take to make your dreams come true?

2. Jackie has to deal with her friend Minnie's grief over the deaths of significant people in her life. Have you lost anyone close to you? How do you deal with grief in your own life? How do you comfort others who are grieving?

3. Have you ever stayed at a bed and breakfast? If so, where? What would be some of the pros and cons of running a bed and breakfast?

4. For most of the story, Buck is silent about how he feels about Davis. Do you understand his silence? Have you ever kept a secret about someone to spare another person's feelings?

5. Aunt Sheerly and the other relatives plan a surprise birthday party for Jackie. Have you ever been instrumental in planning a surprise? Was it hard to keep it a secret?

6. Jackie must wait upon the Lord for her dreams to come true. Have you ever been fearful that the Lord will not answer your prayers? Has God ever answered your prayers in a different way than you expected?

7. Have you ever had a boss like Selena? How did you handle him or her?

8. What are Davis's strengths? Weaknesses? Do you think he and Vanessa will end up together?

9. Jackie and her relatives eat lunch together after church every Sunday. What traditions do you have in your family?

10. Jackie collects fishermen's hats. Do you collect anything? How did the collection start?

For additional book club resources, please visit
www.bethanyhouse.com/anopenbook.